To ana,

Thanks! Vijay

Caves of the Watchers

Book two in *The Ancient Ones* series

Lori Hines

AUTHOR'S NOTE

This is a book of fiction. Names, characters, places, and incidents are either the product of author's imagination or are used fictitiously. Any resemblance to actual persons, living or dead, business establishments, government agencies, events, or locales is entirely coincidental.

International Standard Book Number
ISBN-13: 978-1519416384
ISBN-10: 1519416385

Printed in the United States of America.

Caves of the Watchers

Chapter 1

For a brief second, Lorelei Lanier, paranormal investigator and psychic medium, saw a brilliant glimmer next to the old Ironwood tree at Vulture Mine near Wickenburg, Arizona, where fellow investigator and FBI agent Shannon Flynn stood. The sun didn't permeate through the thick, tangled branches. There were no objects to create a reflection. Yet a strange, rectangular outline appeared underneath the stiff limbs of the tree where eighteen men were hung for stealing gold.

Shannon turned her head as if realizing something was near, gazing at the spot where the portal appeared. It had vanished.

She couldn't explain it. But Lorelei knew something big was coming. This time, whatever occurred wouldn't just involve her.

Lorelei brushed a lock of her long blonde hair away from slightly parted lips as the early afternoon sun warmed her fair skin. The only sounds were the occasional high-pitched call of a quail or faint echo of traffic from Vulture Mine Road. She trudged along the dry sandy wash staring intently at the ridge of granite and stone to her right. A giant twenty-foot saguaro stood sentinel above the panel of dark rock.

She glanced at the photo she discovered a few weeks ago from their first investigation at Vulture City in Wickenburg, Arizona. Petroglyphs on a ten by five section of granite revealed a rough etching of the solar system with floating human images rising above their horizontal bodies — like the sketches found underground in Dragoon and at Wupatki, north of Flagstaff. But this particular site was different. A one-inch crack separated the two sections of rock. The second panel contained an engraving of two white lines intersecting, creating four squares. The lower right quadrant revealed a coarse image of Shiprock Peak; the remains of a forty million year old volcanic pinnacle in New Mexico.

She squeezed through two creosote bushes with yellow petals in bloom to get closer to distinguish any additional etchings. Her leg became entangled in one of its thin, stiff limbs. The branch snapped in two and scared a pale green desert hairy scorpion, six inches long, out of hiding. The arachnid scurried toward a nearby boulder. She remained still as it escaped under her legs.

"Ian, over here," she yelled.

Ian Healy, pagan, Wiccan and healer, ran over to Lorelei. Even with beads of sweat on his forehead, smears of dirt, and damp wavy locks of shoulder length hair, he still looked striking.

"Hey, beautiful," he said, kissing her on her neck. "What did you find?"

She glanced up at the long section of rock above them. "See for yourself."

He placed his arm around her waist and followed her gaze. "Amazing," he whispered. "I only wish we could tell what used to be in the other three panels. I'm guessing that map indicates the Four Corners, which means there could be underground passages all over the Southwest."

Lorelei attempted to scramble up the embankment to get a better look, but slid back down along with rocks, dirt and sticks of dead tree branches.

"Careful," Ian said. She fell into his arms and they stared into each others eyes for a few seconds.

"I wish we knew what the other three etchings were." She glanced at the section of granite. "We know the triangle is so important to the ancients because of the tunnels Brandon discovered, and the markings on the petroglyphs, pueblo and monuments in Dragoon."

Ian looked down at her and smiled, then gently lifted her emerald pendant up off her neck. "Lore, perhaps the most important indication of their existence is what happened to you."

Lorelei thought back to her encounter with Vincent Joiner, an evil dark arts magician who attempted to use another malevolent master's energy, and the energy of the ancient site, to become all powerful. Her astral abilities had taken her on a journey to the southern triangle in the night sky. There, she had combined her abilities with that of the ancient spirits to somehow create a perfect triangle surrounding the ruins and mysterious pillars. A potent reaction in between the pueblo and monuments prevented Vincent, along with Tony's spirit, from reigning over the beasts that had taken over the peaceful community of Dragoon.

Ian took a gulp of water from his bottle. "I'm curious about any tunnels. This was a mining town, so we know there are passages. But could they have been around before the mine was built? We've learned from the investigation in Dragoon how important subterranean places were to this enigmatic astral race. Such underground spots were their focus for out-of-body travel."

"The caretakers used to do tours in the mining tunnels, but they stopped allowing anyone down there years ago," Lorelei said. "It's too dangerous. But there could be another entrance unrelated to the mines. Perhaps miles from here."

"What about astral projection to spot potential underground openings?" Ian asked. "I could lay you down in one of the buildings with a blanket and keep watch over that beautiful body of yours."

"Now that sounds very tempting." Lorelei pulled him close, her lips within an inch of his. "Only I'd like to stay around for what I have in mind."

His tongue parted her lips and she slipped her hands under his shirt, rubbing his chest as they kissed.

"Come on," Shannon yelled as she walked down the hill toward them. "Don't you two ever give it a rest?"

"Hell, no," Ian said breathlessly. He quickly turned away to hide the front of his body. Then he stared up at the petroglyph.

"Well, I'll be damned," Shannon said following his gaze. "You found the rock in your picture." She winked. "And here I thought Ian was trying to hide something from me."

He rolled his eyes while walking further away from Shannon.

"Why is this particular panel of rock art above ground?" Lorelei asked. "The solar system images in southeast Arizona were in the tunnels. And where are the passages?" She sighed heavily. "Why don't I have more answers? I communicated directly with the ancient spirits in Dragoon, and spoke a language I've never heard of while helping them rid the community of evil. It still seems they don't completely trust me with all the information about their culture."

"Maybe the answers will come in time," Ian said. "You only recently discovered your ability to call upon their energy whenever and wherever needed."

Lorelei watched Shannon. She had scrambled up the embankment, tracing her fingers lightly over the stone.

"Did you find something?" Lorelei asked.

Shannon didn't respond. The panel with the etching of the solar system and prone figures had her in a trance.

"Shannon," Lorelei yelled. She exchanged a curious glance with Ian. He shrugged his shoulders.

Shannon jumped off the small hill, turning to acknowledge Lorelei. "You might have all of the answers already and don't know it yet. Could be something will happen suddenly, then," she snapped her fingers, "it will all make sense."

"Unlike what just happened with you," Lorelei mumbled. "You were pretty interested in the petroglyph."

Shannon looked confused. "What do you mean?"

Ian threw his hands. "You stood there observing the section with the picture of the universe. Are you saying you don't remember? That was seconds ago."

Lorelei could tell Shannon was embarrassed. She smacked Ian on his arm.

"I'm sorry," he said. "Maybe you subconsciously recognize this from somewhere besides the site in Dragoon."

Shannon quickly changed the subject. "Have the ancient ones tried to get in touch with you since we've been here?"

"No," Lorelei whispered. She gazed toward the direction of the dilapidated assay office with its well-weathered planks and peeling aluminum roof to see a six foot tall miner in sooty, tattered rags heading in their direction. Lorelei gasped. The man had a six inch open gash on his blackened forehead and a massive sharp-edged stone embedded in his chest. Flashes of a cave-in tiled themselves into her thoughts as he came closer, a mule walking by his side.

"Lore, honey." Ian placed his hand on her shoulder. "What are you seeing?"

"It was one of the seven workers that died at the Glory Hole while doing personal gold and silver mining. They were chipping away at the ore columns when a hundred feet of rock collapsed on top of them."

The apparition walked within ten feet of Lorelei, but he didn't seem to know she existed. He stared straight ahead, holding onto the animal's rope. The miner's transparent form stepped through a patch of cholla cactus. Plant and phantom became one for a brief instant.

Shannon and Ian stared in the same direction, but she knew they couldn't see him.

Lorelei shuddered and looked away while the ghost continued on by.

"Not a pretty sight, huh?" Ian pulled her close.

She shook her head. "No, the poor guy has a rather large rock in his stomach."

"Jesus." Shannon shivered.

Brandon Winn, co-founder of the Arizona-Irish Paranormal Research Society, came running up to Lorelei, Ian and Shannon. "Hey guys. The caretakers are waiting for us in the gift shop. I mentioned we wanted to talk to them about passages or caves that locals, tourists or prospectors might have discovered." He winked at Lorelei. "Or anything else that might prove your ancient race of friends inhabited this area."

She noticed out of the corner of her eye that the miner had stopped. He turned his wounded head in the direction of the highway. A brief breeze whispered by. Shannon unknowingly passed by the specter of the miner on her way to the caretakers' office. Then a voice uttered faintly in the dialect of the ancient ones. But Lorelei couldn't make out the words.

She couldn't take her eyes off the miner, who gazed south, staring past Shannon. He began to transform from a soot-covered, horribly disfigured entity, to a clean-cut man in his thirties or forties with medium-length brown hair and a dragon tattoo on his right arm.

His hand traveled from his once severely wounded head to his chest. He looked upward as a tear rolled down his face. He wiped it away, looking at the moisture on his forefinger. Lorelei suddenly heard the name "Jackson." Jackson's spirit turned and smiled directly at Lorelei. She couldn't tell if he was more surprised about his recent transformation or the resulting emotion. He emitted warmth, happiness and contentment where previously there had been emptiness and confusion.

She desperately wanted to ask him what had happened. Had he understood what the ancients were telling him? Did the miner get called to that spot on purpose?

Lorelei stepped toward him.

Then he and the mule faded softly away.

An abrupt thought popped into her head as if it had been planted there. One less to suffer for eternity.

Chapter 2

Rose quartz, white calcite, opal, petrified wood, and hundreds of other gems and minerals of various sizes and colors were displayed on card tables in front of the gift shop. Lorelei turned a sphere-shaped, hollowed-out purple geode over in her hand. Small, compact, sparkling crystal formations covered the interior of the amethyst.

As she turned to follow the rest of the team into the shop, she nearly tripped over three black cats. They were at her feet, purring and rubbing against her legs.

"Hey cuties." She scratched their heads and backs. "You're all getting fat from tourist food aren't you?"

"Need rescuing?" Ian laughed and grabbed her hand to help her over the animals that lived on the property. "I see your way with animals hasn't changed."

She glanced up and smiled at him. "No, I suppose not."

The inside of the building seemed to have exploded in shelves and glass-enclosed counters filled with straw hats, pottery, t-shirts and a multitude of knick knacks. Old Coca-Cola pictures adorned the dusty white-washed walls. Brochures and postcards sat atop a fifties-style ice cream cart.

A couple that looked to be in their sixties approached Lorelei and Ian. "Nice to meet you both," the man said. "My name's John Randall and this is my wife Ronnie. We're the caretakers."

Lorelei took an instant liking to the six foot tall, grey-haired man with the smiling eyes and tan cowboy hat. She wondered if the couple knew of the transformations of the Vulture City spirits, like the miner she had just encountered — a physical and soul healing change to help the phantoms move on.

Lorelei, Ian, Shannon, Brandon and Dale shook hands with John and his wife. Ronnie, who was the same height as her husband, wore jeans, a short-sleeved denim shirt with a red handkerchief, and she had facial wrinkles that belied her time in the Arizona sun.

"I understand you're here for a different sort of investigation?" Ronnie asked. She glanced at Lorelei, then at the rest of the team members.

"Yeah." Shannon looked around the store as if something would pop out and surprise her amidst all the bric-a-brac, then showed Lorelei's picture of the ancient ones' petroglyph.

"Have you seen this rock art along the wash to the ball mill and powerhouse? Lore snapped this during our paranormal investigation in November. Only she didn't know what she captured until after we left."

John and Ronnie gazed intently at the photo.

"No," John said. "Ronnie and I usually stay in the vicinity of the shop to welcome and sign-in guests, answer questions and handle sales. I'm surprised I haven't noticed this on my occasional check on the property."

John looked over at Ronnie. "What about you?"

She shook her head. "Remember, we had a stack of debris and dead creosote branches piled next to that embankment. Your brother cleared that area out only a few months ago." She observed the etchings in the image. "Though I don't know how he could have missed this while he was working."

"What about other visitors or locals?" Lorelei asked. "Have they mentioned seeing this," she tapped the picture, "or any other petroglyphs in the area? Not necessarily at Vulture Mine but maybe off of hiking trails or in the surrounding mountains?"

"Not that I'm aware of," Ronnie said. "And we've lived here for over five years and know everyone fairly well. John and I go rock hunting and prospecting with others around Vulture Peak, and have never come across art like that."

"Are you sure?" Lorelei continued to hold the picture out. "Have either of you, or any hikers or rock hounds, discovered passages or caves?" She noticed the couple glanced at each other as if she were nuts.

"Sorry," Lorelei said. "We've found evidence like this in other parts of the state — some of which are underground. Now we've discovered proof that they, these same people, might have inhabited this place."

How much should I tell people about the ancient ones? Or is it I don't want others to know about the very spirits I'm so connected with?

"We've discovered small caves above ground," John said. "I can give you the name and number of a few locals that have lived here over twenty years." He pulled out a pad of paper and a pen, and jotted down their information. "Both of these men are retired, so they spend quite a bit of time hunting for gems and know all of the trails and hidden secrets of Vulture Peak Summit, Vulture Mountains Range, Twin Peaks and Black Mountain."

"What about the mine shafts?" Shannon asked. "I know they've been closed since before you both moved here, but haven't you been down there to see where they lead or if there's anything unusual?"

"Used to lead tours to the underground chambers, but now it's too unstable," Ronnie said. "There isn't an extensive tunnel system here like there is in Bisbee. Bisbee's mines, of which the Queen Mine is just one, include more than 2,500 miles of tunnels. Vulture Mine isn't nearly that extensive. However, I've never come across rock art or any other proof of other races underground."

Lorelei stared at Shannon in desperation. She was anxious to investigate the old mining passages.

"Listen." Shannon removed her FBI badge. "This isn't an official case we're on here, but I would really appreciate it if you could let us check out those chambers. It is pretty important since sites that are associated with these glyphs tend to attract an element you don't want roaming around on your property. We'd be willing to sign a release form."

John and Ronnie stared at each other for a few seconds. Lorelei sensed fear between them.

John let out a big sigh. "I guess that would be fine since you are all professionals. Please be careful and don't touch anything. There's an entrance across from the Glory Hole pit covered in planks."

"We have three able-bodied men here who can remove the plywood." Shannon glanced at Ian, Brandon and Dale. "If you can supply us with a hammer, we'll take care of the rest and make sure it's boarded back up when we leave."

"Don't expect us to go down there with you." Ronnie gave her husband a look that told him he shouldn't even consider it. Then she passed out the release forms to the team.

John disappeared for a few minutes and came back with two hammers and five hard hats. "Watch your heads as you go in. Don't hang around in there too long."

"Thanks very much." Lorelei shook both their hands excitedly.

"Well, come on guys," Dale said. The sandy-haired ex-football player motioned for them to follow him outside. "We need to get our flashlights, water, backpacks and equipment."

"Make sure you grab the handheld GPS," Lorelei said. "I'm curious to see how these passages align with the ones in Dragoon and Flagstaff."

Shannon pulled her hair in a ponytail and put her FBI baseball cap on. "Brandon found the tunnel that headed west from the Wupatki ruin, though we still don't know how far it goes. We're assuming the passages are in a triangular pattern because of the direction they head. But there's a good chance portions of their underground realm could be caved-in."

Lorelei removed two bottles of water from a cooler and placed them in her backpack. "These mining shafts might not have anything to do with the ancient ones. We know so little about their race. As we've discovered, their language doesn't match that of any Native Americans — past or present. I'll have to see what vibes I pick up, if any."

"Wait," Brandon said. "Ian, your ex-wife and her husband were involved in a theft ring in this area, weren't they? Did anyone ever find out exactly where their operation took place since there was a suspicion that it could be associated with the astral race?"

"Unfortunately, no." Shannon slipped her audio recorder in her front jean pocket and threw her backpack on. "As you already know, Peter and Emily both vanished, like Lorelei had seen in her vision. So they can't give us any detail. And Ray, the guy that killed Alicia for hoarding some of the pottery, denied knowing anything about the additional site, or the cult that is supposed to be in this area."

Lorelei held Ian's hand when his ex-wife's name was mentioned. His ten year old son Paul still had nightmares about his mother and stepfather's disappearance, and continued to blame himself.

Lorelei, Ian, Shannon, Dale and Brandon walked in silence until they arrived at the entrance to the mine.

Ian and Brandon removed the rusted nails and yanked the two by fours from the opening. While the last of the boards fell onto the ground, Lorelei caught a cool, damp breeze from the darkness.

But that wasn't all.

Chapter 3

Wailing and moaning greeted Lorelei at the precipice to the mine, along with overwhelming suffering. She placed her hand against the cool granite wall for support and bent over to catch her breath.

Ian stood next to her, his arm around her waist.

"I heard a man's desperate scream for help."

"Dale, get the ghost box out."

He immediately removed the radio-like device from his bag, capable of helping spirits communicate with the living. He turned it on and tuned it until there was very little static. By the time he had the channel set to receive the spirit voices, the sounds had stopped.

"I don't hear them anymore," she said. "It must have been the miners that were killed during the cave-in." Lorelei stood up. "I'm fine now. Let's keep going."

The ground of the passages gradually declined and the team stopped after a few minutes of walking.

Ian glanced at his Mel-Meter to determine temperature and energy. "It's fifty-five degrees in here with an EMF, or energy reading of 1.5 milliGauss. The slightly high reading could be from the quartz in the walls."

"Lore, are you experiencing anything else?" Shannon asked.

She shook her head. She had sensed something, but it didn't pertain to any of Vulture Mine's past inhabitants. This particular vision had to do with a member of the team.

How can I tell Dale what I saw his family going through? And that he might have brought the entity home from the investigation in November?

After what her psychic senses had picked up about Dale, Lorelei couldn't concentrate on any other spirits that might be present.

"Flash," Lorelei said. She snapped two pictures in succession to see if any apparitions would show themselves. At the exact second when the blinding light from her camera illuminated the barrier of dirt and rock ahead of them, another vision rampaged through her mind. She saw Dale's wife Cindy and his son Joel being tortured by something unseen. One minute Joel was playing outside, the next he stood in front of his mother, looking like he wanted to kill her.

"Looks like this is the end of the road," Dale said. "Must be where the cave-in occurred."

"Ronnie did mention that there were a few miles of tunnels," Shannon said. "I know there's access from where the old wooden headframe still stands. I've looked right into the passages, though it could be a challenge getting down there."

Ian pulled Lorelei aside while the others were talking. He nodded toward Dale. "You know something, don't you?"

She sighed heavily.

"Lore, honey, come on. My intuition screams at me every time Dale gets near me. And it's telling me he's not being honest about things."

"Yeah, well, this vision did have something to do with Dale. His family has been having trouble, though nothing like what's about to happen."

She attempted to smile at Dale as he, Brandon and Shannon passed by on their way back out of the passage. A sick feeling began in the pit of her stomach.

"Ian," she whispered. "I don't know what to do. Should I tell him what I'm seeing?"

At that second, a low vibration echoed through the tunnel and she turned to see Dale answering his cell phone. Ten seconds later, his face paled, his jaw dropped and it seemed to Lorelei that he stopped breathing.

"I have to go," he said in shock. "Family emergency."

"Is there anything we can do?" Brandon asked. By the time he finished his sentence, Dale was halfway out of the mine shaft.

Lorelei realized it was serious. Dale's valuable equipment, including his digital camera, Tri-Field meter, GPS device and handmade ghost box remained abandoned on the ground.

Chapter 4

A fluffy brown teddy bear lay wrapped in Joel's arms. Border wallpaper with baseballs, bats and gloves and matching curtains decorated Joel's room — signs of simple boyhood innocence. But Dale knew from experience that normalcy and virtue can disappear as quickly as a cool summer breeze on a hot Arizona summer day.

He bent down to kiss his son's smooth right cheek.

What have I brought into your world?

His wife Cindy lay next to Joel. Dried pale tear streaks ran down her face, along with blotches of black mascara, and red, puffy pupils.

He kissed her gently on the lips, stirring her from a light slumber.

"I'm so glad you're home," she whispered. "I didn't want to call you, but I didn't know what else to do." Her eyes started to well up with tears again.

"Shhhh. It's okay now." Dale stroked her hair. "How are you doing?"

She quietly slipped out of Joel's bed and nodded for Dale to follow her out.

"It's been quiet the past few hours. Dale, our baby wasn't himself. He's too young to speak in a deep tone of voice like that. You should have seen the look on his face." She looked as if she would cry and placed her arms around him. "I'll never forget it. He looked at me like he didn't even know who I was."

"I feel like this might be my fault." Dale ran his hand through his hair and sat on the couch. "Maybe I brought something home with me. I mean, this crap started happening after the Vulture Mine investigation."

"Dale, is there something you're not telling me?"

He took her hand in his. "I had an encounter with something nasty at the last investigation. Something pushed me back into the storage room I was climbing out of. I didn't have far to fall, but I did catch a glimpse of it right before I fell. And we also caught it on video."

"Dale, how could you not have told me this?" Cindy's voice became louder and he could hear Joel stir. "You didn't just put yourself in danger. Now you've put me and your son in danger. You have to give this up."

"Honey, stuff like this happens to people that aren't involved in paranormal research. I've been on so many investigations and nothing has ever happened."

"Dale, you told me about the experience in that rental house when you were twenty three—with you, Bill and that Ouija board. As an investigator, you should know that stuff can make you more vulnerable." Cindy shook her head in disbelief then opened the door quietly to peek into Joel's room.

"You must be exhausted after that long drive. I know I am from dealing with something that you brought home." She walked into Joel's room and shut the door behind her.

He started to follow her, but decided it would be better to let her cool down. He went into the kitchen and pulled out a beer from the refrigerator.

The damn thing's here. I can feel its menacing presence.

Dale knew he shouldn't, but he couldn't help it.

"What do you want?" He stared around the great room. "Who the hell is here? Are you the same entity that tried to hurt me at Vulture Mine? Well, you can't hurt my wife or my son. I won't let you."

Dale glanced around nervously and slammed his bottle on the sofa table. He downed his beer quickly, then leaned back in the chair and fell asleep.

He awoke to a surreal, swirling dark cloud above him. Am I dreaming? But Cindy's shrill screams quickly brought him back to reality.

He only had himself to blame.

Cindy was right. Maybe I am attracting negative spirits because of that damn Ouija board. I should have just told Bill to kiss my ass. I had choices. I could have walked away. Instead, I chose to play with fire. Now it's not just me getting burned.

"Dale," she yelled. But he couldn't move. A horrifying face formed itself from the thick, tenebrous mass; a demonic presence with horns that protruded for a few seconds. Then they melted back into its bulging, malformed head.

"Daaadddyyyyyy!" Joel screamed.

Damn it Dale, get your butt off this fucking couch and get your family to safety.

Afraid to sit up and put his face into the evil cloud, he tried to slide out from under the entity. But it came down on him like one hundred falling bricks. And as it did, the demon transformed into one last face...Joel's. Suddenly, he couldn't breath. Cindy and Joel yelled at him to move.

Suddenly, Cindy stood above him, holding an ivory cross in her left hand. And the mass that threatened to destroy him vanished.

"Are you okay?" she asked.

Joel came over and hugged him.

"We're all getting the hell out of here. Cindy, take Joel to our room and start packing. I'm going to grab a few things from his room and we're leaving."

After taking less than ten minutes to pack, Dale drove his family to a nearby hotel.

The boy behind the registration counter fit right in with the dingy atmosphere. He had dirty blond hair, fair skin and a bad case of acne. The twenty-something clerk looked at Dale in his disheveled clothes with a haggard look on his face, to Joel and Cindy, who were still in their pajamas.

Shit. This guy probably thinks I kidnapped them.

Not the best choice, but this was the only hotel nearby with vacancies. Now he knew why.

A few hours later, Dale awoke and saw the clock on the nightstand — 4:40 a.m. Joel was not in bed with them. He ran his hand through his hair and sat up.

An oppressive atmosphere hung inside the dank, depressing room with wood-paneling and stained carpet. "Oh, please," he whispered. "Not here too."

After a minute, his eyes adjusted to the darkness. Joel stood in front of his bed, silently watching his father. "Hey, buddy, what are you doing up?" He patted the middle of the king-sized bed.

Joel didn't budge. He stood there with a glacial glare.

Cindy awoke and saw Joel. She ran over to him.

"Cindy, no! Something's taken over him." Dale tried to grab her arm, but she pulled away.

"Get away from my son. Leave him alone. He's just a child."

She attempted to pull Joel to her, but his arms hung limply. When she looked into his brown eyes, he spat in her face.

Dale jumped out of bed, but a little too late. The child pulled a light bulb from behind his back. Smashing it against the wall, Joel poked and jabbed at his mother.

"Cindy, watch out." Dale pushed her out of the way, and Joel sliced him once on his left hand. He winced in pain. Before he could get over the shock, his son ran the broken bulb across Dale's left leg, revealing muscle tissue and tendon.

Dale yelled in excruciating pain, bringing Joel back to reality.

"Oh, honey!" Cindy grabbed a towel and wrapped it around Dale's badly injured leg, while Joel stood there in shock.

A loud knock on the hotel room door startled them all.

"We have to get you to a hospital," Cindy said.

The pounding on the door became louder and angrier. "Hello in there. This is the manager. Is everything okay?"

Joel abruptly glanced at the broken bulb in his hand and the blood on his father's hand and leg. "Dad. Dad, what happened? What did I do?"

He pulled Joel close. "You didn't do anything."

Dale began to feel faint, watching the blood pour from his wounds and soak Joel's dinosaur pajamas.

Cindy answered the door, trying to hide Dale and Joel from view.

"I heard screaming in here. Is everything okay?" The balding man in his early thirties stared past Cindy and noticed the blood on Dale's leg and the carpet. He poked his head in farther when he saw Joel holding a shard of broken glass.

Dale heard the manager yell at someone to call an ambulance.

"The cut on the hand isn't that bad." Dale said. "The one on the leg is a little deeper."

He could feel a deep, open bloody trench on his upper right leg through the blood-soaked towel where tissue, tendon, muscle and bone were exposed. Head spinning, stomach roiling, he grabbed onto his wife. Then he blacked out.

Chapter 5

Eighteen years earlier

Darkness ensued with a quarter moon peeking down on a quiet, rural neighborhood while crickets serenaded unseen. Five votive candles were lined up on either side of the dining room table. The party for two involved a six-pack of ice cold beer and the remains of a large supreme pizza, box left open on the sofa table. The smell wafted throughout the twelve hundred square-foot house.

"This is kind of cool," Bill said. "Maybe we can tell our buddies at work on Monday we met some new friends over the weekend."

Dale rolled his eyes as he pulled the board from its safe haven and laid it gently on the glass table. Dale had heard frightening stories about others who had used a Ouija board, though he assumed most of them were probably made up.

"Come on, Dale," Bill said the day before, "Don't tell me you actually believe all those horror stories. Well, if you are chicken, I can always pair up with my buddy Alex. I know he has balls."

His response had been simple but direct. "Asshole."

Though Dale didn't have a tendency to do what others pressured him to, he had always been fascinated with the paranormal. As far as he and Bill knew, the rental house had no history, so it's not like they were going to come across anything anyway. Most likely, they would both take turns pushing the stupid planchette across the board to freak each other out.

"Are we ready?" Dale asked. He took a long drink from his bottle of beer. "This was your idea. You start asking the questions."

"Is anyone here with us tonight?" Bill asked.

Not a sound except for chirping in the distance.

Bill continued the questioning. "If there is anyone here, are you male or female?" He waited thirty seconds. "Man, what a bummer. Nothing but 'dead' silence."

Dale couldn't believe how totally corny Bill was at times. And he actually thought he was funny.

Dale went next. "Is there anyone here who died in this house?" Ten seconds later, the room became cooler and the planchette slowly moved to YES.

They immediately looked at each other. "You did that," they said at the same time.

"No way man," Dale said. "You must have."

"Hell, no. Come on, fess up. You're just getting back at me because I called you chicken."

"I swear I didn't move it, Bill." His voice raised a notch in surprise.

Though they both became a little frightened, they continued to probe the mysterious newcomer.

"How old are you?" Bill asked.

The planchette slowly moved to 5, then more quickly to 6. Dale shivered, rubbing his arms with his hands. His breath created a slight mist.

Something's here.

"Are you male or female?" Dale asked. Five seconds passed. The planchette spelled out MALE.

"Is there anyone else here with you?"

The candles instantly blew out. Bill and Dale suddenly found themselves sitting in complete darkness at 9:15 p.m. The leftovers flew off the sofa table and slammed into the wall next to them. Bill leapt out of the chair, knocking it to the ground, and took off like a shot. It reminded Dale of the cartoon roadrunner with the sound effects.

"Where are you going?" Dale yelled.

"I'm turning every damn light on in this house."

"Hey, Bill, where are your balls now?"

Chapter 6

Lorelei woke up gasping for air, expecting to see the Dale's son standing in front of their bed with a four inch shard of glass. Instead, she saw Ian.

"Lore, thank god." He wiped her long, damp locks away from her face. "You were yelling in your sleep."

She sat up quickly and threw her arms around his neck.

"Let me guess. You had a vision about Dale." He held her tightly. "Brandon and I both tried calling him before we went to bed, but he didn't answer our calls. Please tell me he's okay."

She grabbed a tissue from the nightstand. "We have to help his family. Ian, you can help Dale. You're Wiccan and are familiar with protection spells and cleansings."

"Honey, calm down." Ian went to the bathroom and grabbed a wet cloth to wipe her face. "Tell me about your nightmare."

"The demon, or whatever it is, took over his son and tried to kill Dale. His family has been having problems since the Vulture Mine investigation, but for some reason it got much worse recently."

"Lore, maybe it's something entirely different terrorizing his family. This might not be the entity he encountered in the assay office." His cell phone vibrated and he reached for it on the nightstand. "Hey, Brandon."

Dale's best friend spoke loudly on the other end of the phone. He sounded frantic. Lorelei leaned over so she could hear Brandon.

"I talked to Dale's wife. Something took over little Joel and he viciously attacked Dale. He's in the hospital with a deep gash in his leg. Ian, you and Lore need to help with this. Can you perform a ritual or something to help them?"

"Calm down. Of course. I'll head over to Dale's place when he returns from the hospital, but it sounds like this evil spirit isn't only attached to his home, it's attaching itself to his son. This might be much more than a simple house clearing."

Chapter 7

"Angels of protection, angels who clear, remove all spirits who don't belong." Ian held a gold chalice full of water to collect any negative energy while he stood among a circle of votive candles. Sage incense permeated Dale's living room while Cindy, Joel, Brandon and Lorelei gathered in the corner by the sliding glass doors.

Ian's forceful tone continued to chant. "Dragons blood, fern, lilac and myrrh—with this mix I sprinkle, I banish all negative spirits. You are not welcome. I ask you now go on your way. With harm to none, it shall be done."

Dale glanced at his son. Joel watched Ian with bright-eyed wonder and amazement. The pagan investigator always seemed to have an air of confidence and strength. In his royal purple cloak and robe lined by thick gold braids, he appeared indestructible. His wavy, light brown hair turned golden with energy. He looked like a living violet candle glowing warmly in the darkly lit room. Dale wondered if it had to do with the color of his cloak.

His wife's face was flushed, her breaths coming in short bursts, and she stared intently at Ian.

I can't believe this. She's turned on by him. Even when Dale put his arm around her and pulled her close, she didn't notice.

Dale wondered if Ian had any idea of the effect he had on women.

Ian glanced at Lorelei standing quietly in the corner of the living room, and Dale realized she was the only woman Ian would ever care about. As Ian continued the ritual, he continued to gaze at Lorelei as if she provided him strength.

"Negative entities hear me now—sage and lilac, dragons blood and myrrh, a concoction to keep this home safe and ensure that no more will you stir. I clean this house with light and love and pray to the waning moon above. Angels of protection, angels who clear, I ask of thee to bless thy home and hearth times three. I banish any evil to whence you came. Love be free within this place, and let the wicked leave without a trace."

Ian toured the home with the goblet held in his right hand. "Lore, can you carry the sweetgrass and pinion pine needles?" He glanced at a leaf-shaped bronze plate with a small pile of dried herbs. "These will bring in the good energy, while the spells I just did should drive the negative energy out."

Dale, Cindy and Joel followed behind Ian and Lorelei while they smudged all the spaces and rooms. The air became oppressive and Lorelei suddenly stopped. She started to say something to Ian when the heavy plate holding the incense flew from her hands and caught the side of Ian's forehead.

He bent over in agony, palm against his head.

"Ian," Lore yelled. She kneeled down and pulled his hair back to look at the wound.

After a few seconds, he stood back up and Dale saw a three-inch bright red spot above his right eyebrow.

"I'm fine. Something's not happy with me."

"That was one hell of a hit." Brandon took Ian's arm and guided him toward the couch. "I think we need to take a break."

Dale knew that Lorelei was here to help determine the purpose of the entity's presence. And he could tell by the looks she passed with Ian that they weren't going to be rid of this that easily.

Cindy handed Lorelei an ice pack.

Dale collapsed on the sofa next to Ian. "What the hell have I done? My family, my friends, I've placed everyone I care about in danger."

"You didn't ask for this." Ian winced as the cold compress was placed against his forehead. "This could have happened to any of us."

Dale glanced at Cindy, then back at Ian and Lorelei. "No. I played with a Ouija board when I was in my early twenties. I've heard that can make people more immune to this sort of stuff."

Ian sighed in frustration. "I don't remember you telling any of us this."

"I didn't. Guess I was too embarrassed. I mean, we're considered the most professional paranormal team in the state."

"Everyone makes mistakes," Lorelei said.

Dale noticed she became distracted. She started talking, though he couldn't understand what she said. He thought she was talking to Ian, but she stared at the copper-colored slate tile in the dining room.

Dale, Ian and Brandon all gasped at the same time. The ice pack dropped from Lorelei's hand. She began to whisper in the same distinct language she did in the passages under the ranch. The dialect of the ancient ones.

Ian gently placed his hand on her shoulder. She continued to talk as if in a trance.

Brandon held up his audio recorder and pointed to the red light to indicate he was taping.

Dale followed Lorelei's gaze into the dining room, but he couldn't detect any movement or sound.

"What is she saying?" Cindy whispered.

"We don't know," Dale said. "This is part of her connection to the race I mentioned. Lore did the same thing at our investigation in Dragoon."

"Could that be what's giving us trouble in our home?" Cindy asked. "One of the spirits of the extinct race?"

"I wouldn't think so. They're supposed to be peaceful." But Dale started to wonder exactly what they were dealing with. After all, the astral race was associated with Vulture Mine, Dragoon, and the Wupatki National Monument north of Flagstaff; all three sites where he had investigated.

No one moved while Lorelei conversed in an unfamiliar dialect with something, or someone, the rest of them couldn't see.

A few minutes later, Lorelei's eyes focused from Dale, Cindy, Joel, Brandon and finally Ian sitting next to her. She glanced at the cold compress in her lap, then at Ian.

"Lore, you dropped it when you started talking in that strange language from southeast, Arizona."

She made Ian hold the ice pack against his bruise, then stood up and walked toward Dale.

"What did you take?" she asked.

"I don't understand."

"Dale, you took something from Vulture Mine during our training investigation in November."

So much had happened since then. He struggled to recall if he had taken something from the ghost town.

He didn't need to answer her. Lorelei wandered over to the entertainment center. He saw her looking at five, three-inch sections of pottery displayed on a small ceramic plate.

She picked up one of the reddish-brown shards and held it tight, her eyes closed. Within a few seconds, she gasped and dropped the sharp object on the wood floor. "Dale, where did you find those?"

"I, I found the pieces of pottery down that road where the old schoolhouse is. They were a mile past the hill within a few feet of each other."

Lorelei gazed intently into Dale's eyes. The five pieces formed a shallow bowl with the outline of a black triangle inside a circle at the bottom.

"Fess up, Lore," Dale said. "Did I discover something that belonged to the ancient ones? And if they're so damn peaceful, why is my family being tortured?"

"Yes to your first question. Dale, for the spirits of the astral race to communicate with me outside of one of their sacred sites is highly unlikely."

"You're not answering my second question."

"I'm trying to," Lorelei said in frustration. "They were a harmless race—still are in fact, even as spirits. But this particular bowl represents the five sites, two of which we haven't located yet."

Dale sighed. "How the hell can you know that? There's nothing printed on the pieces."

"Come on, man," Ian dropped the ice pack and placed his hands on Lorelei's shoulders.

"Okay, I assume they told you. But those shards were out in the open and looked like other pieces I've found."

"You had a warning," Lorelei said.

Dale threw his hands up and turned away, but Cindy stopped him. "What did these spirits do to try and prevent him from taking those shards?"

Lorelei glanced at Dale.

"A huge gust of wind, only the air was very still that day," Dale said.

Lorelei threw her head back against Ian's chest and started to rub her temples. "Damn it, Dale. You know that's not all."

He glanced at his wife and son. What have I done?

"I heard distant drums. At the same time I felt strong vibrations from under the earth. When I stepped a few feet away, it stopped."

"Just like the activity under the ranch." Ian placed his arms around Lorelei's waist and held her close. "Dale might have found another of their passages."

"That's not all," Lorelei said. "He's taken an object used in ceremonies to give their underworld energy. And this is not a demon we're dealing with. Believe it or not, it's the vibrations, or the force of the Earth itself causing this horror with Dale's family. Let's say this energy understands what your worst fear is, and makes it come true."

"Of course," Dale whispered. "I've always been worried that something would follow me home, or worse yet, possess me or my family. And now," Dale collapsed on his knees on the living room floor, "it has."

Cindy grabbed Joel's hand, her purse and car keys. She left the house, slamming the door behind her.

"Honey, wait," Dale yelled. "Please don't go. I need to know you're both safe."

"They will be," Lorelei said. "You're in a holding pattern. The energy may have taken over your son, but it was to torture you. Now you have to make all this right. You have to go back and place this exactly where you found it, and as you found it."

"Wait," Ian said. "Dale, don't tell me those five sections were together when you came across them?"

Lorelei had never looked at Dale in contempt before. Not until now. One minute, one poor decision and he had lost everyone's trust and respect, including his wife's.

Chapter 8

An ancient bulldozer rested among creosote, palo verde, teddy bear cholla and four-wing saltbush. A rusted oil barrel inundated with gunshot holes lay on its side near a pale blue pickup truck, windows partially rolled down. The vehicle looked like it had been sitting there since the days when Vulture City thrived, eighty years before.

Lorelei, Dale, Ian and Shannon had come back to the ghost town to see if they could discover evidence of the ancient ones' passages. Had the series of tunnels been established during their existence so long ago? Did they inhabit the Southwest before the first inhabitants made their way to America by way of the Bering Land Bridge? Or did they live through the infamous drought from 1276 to 1299 A.D.? Though they occasionally reached out to her, there was still so much she didn't know.

Lorelei had walked a quarter mile past where Dale had found the pottery. A tall, flat rock two feet across and ten feet tall with an arrow-shaped point at the top leaned precariously to the right against a massive, round boulder. For some reason, she felt compelled to place her hand on the smooth black surface.

Ian ran up to her. "Hey, Dale's about to put the ancient ones pottery back together. I think it's a good idea for you to be there in case they attempt to communicate. He's rather anxious to know if they are going to let him off the hook."

She smiled. "Of course I'll be there."

Ian stared at the rock intently.

"Honey, what's the matter?" she asked.

"I take it you realize this is no ordinary rock." Ian ran his hand lightly over the surface.

"Yes, no." She sighed. "I don't know. I felt strangely drawn toward it."

"Lore, I'm seeing two very prominent auras involved with this structure. Gold, which represents enlightenment and divine protection, and pure white for spiritual, etheric qualities."

Lorelei turned to Ian. "This has to be a sign from them. Those are all aspects of an astral race." She glanced toward the bottom of the unique rock. "I wonder what this mysterious monument represents. There aren't any drawings on it."

Ian drew her to him and kissed her gently on the lips. She kept her mouth close to his, teasing him with her warm breath. She slid her tongue inside his mouth slowly and placed her hand on his back. Lorelei didn't realize it, but her hand was still against the rock as he lifted her off the ground in ecstasy. He dropped her suddenly and stepped away.

"Ian," she said breathlessly. "What's the matter?" He glanced at the stone, and then her hand, which still rested against it.

"Lore, Ian," Shannon yelled. "Are you both coming? Dale wants to get his little ceremony over with and I'm anxious to see if we can find another passage, or any other evidence."

"Come on," Ian said. He took her hand and guided her away from the stone. He nearly tripped while he continued to look back at it.

* * *

Ian watched as Dale carefully pieced the five shards together to form the shallow bowl he had taken from a section of desert right by the hill. At first, nothing happened. A few seconds later, the desert floor began to vibrate. Ian didn't see anything special or sacrificial about the site where the bowl had been found. So he didn't understand why the Earth would react like this when the pieces were taken or placed back.

"Shannon, are you feeling anything over there?" Ian asked. She had placed herself five feet away from where the pieces were taken.

"No." Then she stepped a few feet forward and her mouth dropped.

Lorelei moved closer to him as the trembling increased, then suddenly stopped.

Dale immediately looked over at Lorelei. "Is that it?" he asked. "The nightmare my family's been going through. Is it over?"

His heart sank when she glanced at Dale in frustration.

"I, I don't know." She played with the pewter pendant around her neck. "From my communications with them during Ian's ritual, yes. Now, I can't tell." Lorelei stared at the ground.

"This isn't her fault," Ian said. "You're the one who selfishly took something that didn't belong to you just because it was lying in the open. That's obviously some sort of altar. They gave you some pretty huge clues, Dale."

"Well, if we can find a way underground, then maybe there's evidence directly underneath this spot. I've got it marked on my GPS." Shannon glanced up at Ian and Lorelei. "And I also pinpointed the rock neither of you were going to tell me about."

"Shannon, we didn't get a chance," Lorelei said.

"That's okay. I'll forgive you." Shannon winked at Lorelei. "This time. Anyways, the rock glowed bright red on the thermal imager while you stood next to it. The EMF reading spiked all the way to twenty five."

Lorelei glanced at the pottery and toward the direction of the arrow-like monument. "All we can do is follow the GPS's coordinates based on our energy readings and the markers we're finding. Hopefully, I'll get a sense for where an underground access point might be. That is, if there's one nearby at all."

Shannon and Dale walked ahead, leaving Ian and Lorelei behind. Ian wanted to tell her what he experienced, but he didn't have the nerve. The vision he had while holding her scared him.

Is it possible that I'm going to turn to the dark arts?

It was the one fear Ian had never been able to rid himself of. After all, Ian looked almost exactly like Annie O'Shea's husband Jeff, the original owners of the Texas Canyon Ranch where Lorelei discovered her tie to the amazing ancient race. Ian also had the same skills and powers as Jeff—and Jeff had turned to black magic. The thought of turning against Lorelei jarred him so badly that he had to stop and catch his breath.

"Ian, what's going on?" Lorelei placed her hand on his arm. "Something happened back there at that mystical stone."

He started to tell her, but couldn't. Another vision flashed through his thoughts right before they stopped kissing, and he didn't want to admit to himself the arrow-shaped monument might not only be a reminder of one's worst fears. It could predict the future. A future that involved a life without Lorelei.

Since he couldn't talk to her about his experience, Ian did the only thing he never expected to. He walked away from her.

Chapter 9

Lorelei wandered around the playground next to the decrepit one room schoolhouse. The two-person swing set sat long abandoned, but not forgotten. Lorelei sensed two children sitting on the canvas seats, gently swinging back and forth.

An overgrown palo verde reached its stiff green branches through a weathered window frame while a delicate breeze refreshed her senses. She glanced down at her watch. It read 6:00 p.m. Lorelei, Shannon, Ian and Dale had been walking through the desert brush and down the jeep trail for two hours to try and find any evidence of underground passages.

Dale and Ian decided to follow the energy line further west. Ian still hadn't said a word to her about what he experienced at the mystical leaning stone, but she couldn't understand why he wouldn't talk about it. He had never kept anything from her in the past four months since they had been dating. And Ian had never walked away from her.

She stared toward the hill where Dale had found the invisible altar and the pottery shards. An unusual sound startled her. She glanced behind to see one of the two swings moving; not just back and forth, but the chains were being twisted together.

A transparent eight year old little girl gazed at her with bright blue eyes. Her curious smile drew Lorelei forward. She slowly picked up her digital camera from around her neck and snapped a photo.

"Hi sweetie," she said. "Can I sit next to you?" Lorelei held onto the chains and slowly sat in the swing next to the child apparition. The brown-haired ghost with the pale blue dress and matching hair ribbon in her braids reached out to her. She shivered as the girl's arm went through her upper body.

"So your name's Jenny?"

The child giggled then let go of the chains she had completely twisted together.

"My name is Lorelei. But my friends call me Lore."

Jenny seemed not to hear as the swing rapidly unwound itself. The apparition watched, transfixed. While the u-shaped seat settled back into position, the little girl vanished.

"We all know you." The little girl's whisper surrounded her. "You're one of them."

"That was fricking awesome," Dale said.

"Where did you come from?" Lorelei quickly stood up from the swing.

"Shannon and I watched from back there." Dale pointed to a straight line of stately saguaros that bordered a dry arroyo. A Harris Hawk with its brown body and white-striped tail stood on the top of the closest cactus.

"Hey, Lore." Shannon touched her on the shoulder. "Are you still communicating with whatever played with the swing?"

"No. But I think the little girl knows about them."

"You mean the ancients?"

"Yes. Her exact words were, "We all know you. You're one of them."

"Maybe she meant that you were a living being," Dale said.

"What the hell?" Shannon stared intently toward the old schoolhouse.

Lorelei turned her head to see a long blue ribbon attach itself to a limb on the palo verde tree that grew into the building. The material untangled and drifted into the back of the antiquated structure.

"That's what she wore in her hair," Lorelei whispered. She glanced at Shannon and Dale. All three of them went running through the back door of the schoolhouse.

"Careful," Dale said. "There are planks missing."

"Do you see the ribbon?" Lorelei glanced around anxiously, looking around in the small room with the protruding branches.

"Here, I found her ribbon," Dale said. "Perhaps she was referring to the ancient ones."

Lorelei pushed Shannon gently aside and looked down to see pale blue among the dirt and broken boards that had fallen onto the desert floor a foot below. Underneath the rotting planks they stood on was a section of partially collapsed earth.

"How do we know that's an entrance to an underground passage or cave?" Lorelei asked.

"Only one way to find out." Dale reached down to grab a long piece of plywood.

"Be careful," Shannon said. "God knows what's waiting under there." She shuddered and stepped back as he poked at the ground with the plank.

The board fell through and into the foot-wide opening. Dale and Lorelei bumped heads as they bent down toward the aperture.

"Ouch." Lorelei straightened up and rubbed her head. "Did you hear it drop?"

"Yeah," he said. "A definite clinking sound. Hard to say how far down this hole goes."

"I'd rather not tear up this building," Lorelei said. "Is there a way we can widen the hole without breaking up a piece of history?"

"There's already a sizeable portion of the floor missing here," Shannon said. "All we'd have to do is take out two more boards."

Dale used his heavy duty flashlight to peer into the darkness. "It's kind of hard to tell how far down it is, especially since it's getting dark."

"This has to be a sign," Lorelei said. "First I encounter a little girl spirit who makes reference to the ancient ones, and then her hair ribbon happens to end up by this opening we've all been looking for."

"Lore, we can't prove she was talking about the ancients," Shannon said. "And for all we know, this could be a regular hole in the ground."

"Let me get my special underground camera and GPS device to see what we've got," Dale said, smiling broadly. "Another handy piece of equipment to help in these investigations."

"I think you're on this team just to play with stuff." Shannon laughed and punched him playfully on the arm.

"Dale, did you call your wife to find out if she's had any problems with strange activity in your home?" Lorelei asked.

"Yeah, right after our little ceremony. Cindy said the house is as peaceful as it has ever been. She and Joel haven't sensed anything."

"I'm so glad," Lorelei said. "You shouldn't have any more issues. Well, hopefully not."

Dale started to leave the old schoolhouse to get more equipment.

"Where's Ian?" Lorelei asked. "Wasn't he with you?"

"I thought he was right behind me. Don't worry, I'll probably find him on my way to the car." He winked at her then ran off.

Is Ian trying to avoid me?

Lorelei paced up and down the dusty wooden planks, watching Dale hurriedly walk toward his car. His flashlight beam bounced across the dirt road and briefly spotlighted three small shadow figures darting in front of him. He continued onward. He hadn't seen them.

Lorelei smiled. They ran into the desert, playing among the creosote bushes then jumped back out behind Dale. He stopped for a few seconds and looked around as if he sensed something. That's when the three spirits circled him and played Ring Around the Rosy. The tallest girl's ponytail bobbed up and down with every excited jump. Dale nervously glanced around and quickened his pace to the parking lot.

"So what's going on with you and Ian?" Shannon placed her audio recorder on a window sill. "I haven't heard him tell you he loves you," she glanced at her watch, "in, oh, I'd say forty-five minutes now."

"Something happened at that odd-shaped rock. The one that you mentioned showed red on the thermal. We were kissing and he pulled away all of a sudden."

"Boy, the fun never ends with you and Ian around." Shannon grinned.

Lorelei rolled her eyes. "Shannon, seriously, he walked away from me. Ian's never done that before. He's always told me how he feels. I think he had some sort of disturbing vision that included me."

"Honey, don't worry. He'll open up. The two of you are more in love, and have more of a bond than any other couple I've known."

Shannon stared at Lorelei in a contemplative manner. "Lore, what if that damn stone drew out Ian's worst fears? Consider what happened to Dale and his family."

"Ian didn't have anything to do with messing with their sacrificial altar."

"I know. But maybe there's something about this place. I don't know if Ian's mentioned this to you, but he's absolutely terrified that he's going to turn to the dark arts like Jeff O'Shea, since Jeff was into witchcraft also. And because the both of you were the spitting image of Jeff and Annie."

"I guess we do have secrets in our relationship." Lorelei ran her hand through her hair. The planks squeaked in frustration as she angrily threw her backpack on the ground. "Damn it, I've opened up about my ex-husband, my frustrations with my talents, my own worst fears, and he can't even be honest with me about something that I thought brought us closer together."

"Lore, it's not like he's cheated on you. If that's really what he saw back there, he's afraid to tell you because he thinks you're going to reject him. You know first-hand what Jeff was capable of, and if there's a chance that Ian will end up like that. . . ."

"You can't honestly think that." Lorelei stood within an inch of Shannon's face.

"No, I don't." Shannon placed her hand on Lorelei's shoulder. "But he does. And if Ian would turn to the dark arts, he would risk losing you."

Chapter 10

Ian crossed the desolate two-lane highway leading to Vulture City; his flashlight the only guide toward an unknown destination. He found a narrow trail overgrown with creosote and prickly pear and pointed his beam into the distance to see two greenish-gold orbs hanging in mid-air. Taking a few steps forward, he noticed the outline of a wary coyote, head bent low, watching him intently.

"Hey there, buddy," he whispered. "I'm not going to hurt you."

The coyote continued to observe him for ten seconds. Then the animal leapt into the darkness.

The path narrowed until Ian had to step over large rocks and through patches of cholla. He didn't know why, but he had to keep going. After twenty minutes of hiking, he encountered a graveyard with five rows of weathered crosses. Ian gazed upon the small unmarked graves with hand-sized stones below the wooden crosses.

He slowly walked down the first row of shrines and noticed the majority of the mounds were five feet in height or under. At the end of the cemetery was a venerable, twenty-foot-tall saguaro with five arms, two of which hung lifelessly.

He knew he should get back to the group, and to Lorelei, but he couldn't face her yet. He couldn't tell her what the aberrant arrow-shaped stone had made him see.

Ian turned away from the saguaro to face the wooden crosses. Shadows darted everywhere, crossing through the beam of light, revealing human shapes of all sizes.

"What the hell?" he whispered. "We haven't seen activity like this at Vulture Mine. If this is the graveyard of the ancients, could this be attracting more entities? Or are these spirits the ancients?"

Glancing back across the road toward the ghost town, Ian realized the cemetery could be in direct alignment with the hill and the bizarre rock that gave him his vision.

He pulled out his night vision camera and started to film while he walked back to the entrance through the long rows of dated crosses. Unintelligible whispers and brief breezes inundated him. But he didn't feel threatened.

"Are you all part of the race of people that are involved in astral travel?" Ian spun around rapidly as soft, invisible tendrils wrapped itself around his waist and then vanished.

Ian held tightly on to the camera, even while he remained surrounded by spirits. He shivered uncontrollably. February evenings became cool — but not this early. He removed his temperature probe from his back pocket. It had suddenly dropped to forty degrees. His brown leather jacket didn't do much to manage the cold.

"Do you know of Annie O'Shea, the original owner of Texas Canyon Ranch?"

For a split second, the whispers and shadow movement stopped. Then the dark mists raced around the white crosses. Some shot up into the atmosphere and others merged together and separated again. Their ghostly breezes were so strong that Ian's hair blew in every direction, forcing him to keep pushing his wavy locks away from his face.

Holy crap. Were tales of Annie's bravery told among all of the ancients? Should I mention Lorelei's name?

Ian arrived at the entrance to the cemetery and everything stopped. No unusual breezes or shadowy specters remained. At least that he could see. No insects buzzed or chirped.

He jumped when a lone coyote howled.

"What caused all that spirit activity?" Ian whispered while continuing to film. He looked around and didn't see any more movement or hear the whispers. He suddenly realized there was something else missing — the five rows of crosses.

Chapter 11

Lorelei stood in front of the old caretaker's house on the hill, scanning the parking lot. She looked toward the visitor and gift shop, the assay office and the dirt path leading to the power mill. She could not find Ian.

The long abandoned, one story house must have been rather charming in its day with pale yellow trim and matching shutters, bay window and a porch running along the length of the home. Now the cracked dirt-caked windows, peeling paint, ripped screen door hanging off the hinges and overgrown weeds in the yard reflected its age and lack of care.

Lorelei, Shannon and Dale had been looking for Ian for an hour. For some reason, Lorelei's psychic senses weren't providing an indication of his condition or location. She was worried sick.

"Lore, he's fine. I just know it." Shannon gave her a hug and glanced toward the entrance to the ghost town. "Did you try him on his cell phone?"

"Yes, but there's no answer. Maybe he's avoiding me on purpose."

"I seriously doubt that. He probably found something interesting."

Suddenly, the splendor of the full moon vanished and Lorelei and Shannon were swathed in pitch darkness.

They glanced up to see a dance of dark figures.

"What the hell is that?" Shannon said.

"Ian. He had something to do with this. I just know." She nearly slid down the hill in an effort to get to the bottom.

"Lore, wait up," Shannon yelled. "Where are you going?"

Lorelei heard someone running directly behind her, which she assumed was Shannon or Dale. Out of the corner of her eye, she noticed Dale's flashlight near the assay office where he had last seen Ian. Shannon still struggled to get down the hill.

She ran as fast as she could past the dilapidated row of storefronts and toward the main road.

That's when she saw Ian heading in her direction from a narrow path, his backpack slung over his shoulder.

"Ian, thank god."

She started to cross the road to greet him.

"Lore, no," he screamed. She glanced in the direction of his terror-filled eyes. A car came straight at her. It came closer; its bright lights blinding her. Ian ran toward her, but he was too far to help. She stood frozen in place, staring at the vehicle's eyes bearing down on her.

Please, not like this.

Someone pushed her so hard she ended up in the next lane. The automobile kept going. Whoever had been driving hadn't seen her.

Lorelei lay face down on the blacktop trying to catch her breath.

"Jesus." Ian ran over and helped her sit up, then helped her across the road to Vulture Mine. "Honey, are you okay?" Ian held her so tightly she had to push him away.

She nodded her head. "I'm fine now." Lorelei turned to glance back. Dale and Shannon were running hurriedly toward her.

"What the hell?" Dale asked. "Lore, why were you running like that?"

"I, I don't know. After I saw that weird display in the sky, I had a vision of Ian. I wanted to make sure he was all right."

"Ian, you jackass!" Shannon ran up to him and hit him on his shoulder. "You could have gotten her killed. What's wrong with you? You know better than to go off on your own out here."

He sighed. "I know. I'm sorry." He kissed Lorelei's head. "I was drawn to that side of the highway and I found a graveyard. Well, I think I did. Only it's not there now."

Ian held her face in his hands. "Wait. What display are you talking about?"

Lorelei gazed into his bluish-grey eyes. "It was you, wasn't it? We all saw shadows flitting back and forth across the moon. At one point, they blocked out the light."

"There was a period of extreme activity when I was in the cemetery. But then the shadows vanished."

"I need to see what you found," Lorelei said.

"Lore, you've had enough excitement," Shannon said.

But she couldn't wait. She wanted to see if the cemetery was related to the ancient ones.

Ian was right behind her. He grabbed her as a six foot rattlesnake lie coiled in the middle of the pathway.

"That's enough," he said. "You aren't meant to go any further."

"Damn it Ian, I want answers." Lorelei pounded her fist against his chest in frustration. "Why did they lead you over here and not me? I was the one that helped them keep their dimension peaceful. I was the one that risked my life in Dragoon. And I'm the one they choose to communicate with."

"I think Dale and I will head back over to the old schoolhouse," Shannon said. "We've got that hole to investigate."

"Baby, I'm so sorry. I feel like this is my fault. I should have told you what happened at that rock."

"Yes, it is your fault." She placed her arms around his waist. "Ian, you're nothing like Jeff. Hell, we don't even know what he was like. You come from a very close family and are so caring about everybody. I'm psychic, and I'm not seeing you transform into some dark arts master."

"You can't see that far into the future."

"Ian, you look a lot like Jeff. Maybe that vision involved his past and not your future."

She took both his hands in hers. "All I know is that as afraid as you are of losing me, I'm more terrified of losing you. This has been a fairy tale for both of us. I can't even think about...." Lorelei closed her eyes and a tear rolled down her cheek.

"I love you so much," Ian said. Then he kissed her on the lips, holding her head in his hands. "I'm so sorry." He looked at her skinned hands. "You were hurt. We're going back to the hotel tonight and get you patched up."

Ian stared at the winding lane she ended up in. "Wait. Lore, I saw you get pushed. Shannon and Dale were nowhere near at the time."

"Yeah. Someone, or something, saved me." She stared back at the road in astonishment. "I heard someone running behind me, but I was only concerned with finding you. She glanced up at him. "Did you see anything?"

"No. Just the car as it headed right for you."

"Ian, I don't want to go right now. I'll get the medical kit and get cleaned up, but you need to see the hole that we found."

"Looks like all of us were busy for the last hour." He placed his hand in hers while they walked toward the dirt parking lot. "So what's the deal with this hole? Is it a tunnel?"

"Yes. It's under some planks at the back of the old schoolhouse. And you're not going to believe how we found it."

"Your psychic abilities?"

"No." Lorelei pulled out a blue ribbon from her jacket. "I connected with a little girl spirit playing by the swings. After she vanished, this blew into the schoolhouse and we found it by the opening. Dale poked a piece of plywood in and it fell through, but he's using his remote night vision camera to see if it's a genuine passageway."

"Did Dale mention we smelled steak by the old mess hall? That is, before I decided to roam on my own. He setup a tripod and camera to see if we can catch the mess hall in action." Ian gave her a sexy smirk.

"No, he didn't. And you're just looking at me that way so I forgive you for scaring me to death."

"Don't worry. You got me back." His brows furrowed and he gazed at the ground. He cleared his throat and she could tell he tried to control his emotion.

Lorelei gently pushed him against his car, ran her hands through his hair and kissed his neck.

"Baby, this isn't fair," Ian said. She brushed her lips against his and Ian moaned. Then she slipped her tongue into his slightly parted lips and licked her way lengthwise.

"I want you, Ian Healy. Now and forever," she whispered in his ear.

He placed his hands on either side of her face. "Please, Lore. Let me take you back to the hotel. I want to show you how much I love you. I want to make you feel like you've never felt before." He pulled her close. She thought she would go insane from desire.

"Lore, Ian," Shannon yelled.

"Shit," Ian said. "She always has such good timing." He took a deep breath as Lorelei pulled away.

She kissed him lightly. "We'll continue this later, I promise. I love you, Ian."

"Go ahead, sexy" he said breathlessly. "I need a minute here.

I'll get the first aid kit and bring it over."

Shannon's beam of light came closer. "Guys, hurry up. You need to see this."

Lorelei didn't say anything to Shannon, frustrated that they had been interrupted. Shannon did have an uncanny ability to interrupt many of their romantic moments, which included her urgent pages or phone calls while at home with Ian.

Shannon put her arm around Lorelei and pulled her close as they were walking. "I'm so glad you're all right. Dale and I saw the car coming. We thought you were a goner."

Lorelei glanced at Shannon and smiled.

"I did it again, didn't I?" Shannon asked, staring ahead.

"What do you mean?"

"You know. I interrupted another moment with Ian. I'm not stupid, Lore. I don't know why it keeps happening, but it's always me that walks in on you guys during your most intense moments. Ian got mad at me a few times when I called your home. Joe thinks it's rather funny. How come Dale or Brandon never encounter your little sessions of passion?"

Lorelei laughed and hugged Shannon in return. "I don't know. I was a little upset, which is why I was so quiet. It's not like you plan it on purpose. Heck, if you didn't have Joe, I would say you had it planned out of jealousy."

"I am slightly jealous. Joe's in Utah for the next week. And he sent me a really hot half-naked picture over my cell with a message that said, BE READY BABY, I MISS YOU."

"Did you send him one back?"

"Not yet. I'm going to wait until I pick him up from the airport. Then I'm going to drive him home wearing a lacy teddy underneath a sexy, low cut top. I'll undress a little at a time and take the long way home. I'm going to make the bastard suffer just like he's doing with me."

"Yeah, right. You actually think you're going to make it back? Knowing the both of you, you'll be pulled over by the side of the road in no time."

They entered the threshold of the musty, eighty year old schoolhouse.

"Lore, take a look." Dale showed her the video screen from the underground footage.

Ian ran in the schoolhouse and stood behind Lorelei to see

what Dale had found.

"Guys, this is the bottom. You can see the piece of wood I dropped. That's twenty feet down and I didn't see any tunnels. But when I pulled the camera up, I noticed this."

Another opening, horizontal to the first, was five feet below the schoolhouse.

"It's big enough for someone to crawl through. I stretched down there and looked in with the flashlight. The tunnel seems to open up further in."

"Did you get any unusual energy readings?" Ian asked.

"Yes." Dale glanced at the glowing green display on his Mel Meter. "This jumped to ten milligaus as I brought the camera back up."

"We should wait until tomorrow morning to investigate," Shannon said. "It's going to be very tricky getting in there let alone in the dark."

Lorelei kneeled down and shined her light toward the newly discovered tunnel. "Looks like it only heads toward the hill," Lorelei said. She stood up, suddenly feeling light headed. Leaning over, Lorelei watched the floorboards spin, so she grabbed onto the doorframe.

"Lore," Ian held her by the shoulders. "Honey, what happened?"

"Feeling a little dizzy. Tired I guess."

"That's enough. Ian, get her home," Shannon said.

"No," Lorelei yelled. "I just need to rest at the hotel." She didn't have a vision, but an overwhelming sensation of dread had accompanied the vertigo.

"Stay here," Ian said. He guided her to the front steps and pulled out a towel for her to sit on. "I'll bring the car over." He glanced up at Dale and Shannon. "Make sure she doesn't move."

"Did you see or sense something?" Shannon asked.

Lorelei shook her head. "That's weird. I never get dizzy spells."

"You've been through a lot tonight. You were really worried about Ian, and then you almost were killed by a car. That's quite a bit of stress."

Lorelei slowly stood up as Ian pulled his Lexus in front of the dilapidated structure. Ian threw the drivers side door open and he ran over to help her into the car.

"Ian, I'm fine now."

"Let me take care of you." He helped her into the passenger side.

But she forced her way out of his grip and took the towel that she had been sitting on. Something told her things were about to change — or perhaps already had.

"Honey, I'm sorry. I have to try something." She ran toward the hill and the mystical stone.

She quickly laid the towel on a sandy spot between the altar and the arrow-shaped rock. Then she lay down with her hands next to her side and started to deep breathe.

Come on. Prove to yourself you can still do this.

The more she concentrated, the less connected she felt to the ancient ones. Lorelei didn't know when it happened, but she had lost her ability for instantaneous astral travel.

Chapter 12

Ian threw his hands up in frustration and watched as Lorelei raced down the old jeep trail, her beam spotlighting desert brush and a few moths fluttering frantically in front of her. After her spell in the schoolhouse, he needed to make sure she would be okay.

"Lore, wait," he yelled. She didn't seem to hear.

He stopped and watched while she placed the towel down.

She's attempting astral travel. But why now?

Not wanting to interrupt her, Ian stood quietly. Her beautiful, silky blonde hair splayed out and her flawless fair skin glowed under the moonlight. The scene looked so surreal, he thought he might be dreaming. Next to her, he could have sworn he saw a shadow figure, about six feet tall. When Lorelei stirred restlessly, it disappeared into the stillness of the night.

Suddenly, she sat up and slammed her fist onto the ground. "Damn it." Lorelei yanked the towel from the ground and glanced over at Ian.

"It's over," she said. He could see a tear running down her face as she approached him.

He pulled her close. "What's going on?"

"When I stood up back there in the schoolhouse, I had the worst feeling. Not of anything spiritual, a feeling of apprehension. I knew. I guess I had to prove it to myself. Ian, I can't perform out-of-body anymore. Could I be losing my bond with ancient ones?"

"It's probably stress." Ian placed his arm around her waist and they walked back to the car. "You had a near death experience after all."

"I'll give astral travel another try tomorrow when we come back out."

"Lore, did you feel a presence when you were trying to project?"

"No. I was too focused." She stopped him in mid-stride.

"What did you see?"

He sighed. "It might have been nothing. I thought a saw a six foot dark figure standing within a few feet looking down at you."

"I didn't feel threatened during that brief period. I wonder if the same apparition saved my life."

"Possibly," Ian opened the car door for her. "I'm curious as to where this thing came from." He slid behind the wheel of the vehicle. "Maybe something has taken a liking to you. Or might be trying to give you a message."

They drove down the dirt road and waved goodbye to Shannon and Dale who were loading equipment into their cars.

"What if the thing you saw came from that arrow-shaped rock where you had your vision?" Lorelei reached behind and placed her bag in the back seat. "I mean, what if it has something to do with the ancient ones?"

Ian knew she wanted all the answers, especially since she had connected so well with the astral race during their investigation in Dragoon. Why would they communicate with her about Dale's mistake, yet prevent her from getting to what could be a very sacred place? And he still couldn't bring himself to reveal the last part of the oracle's message. He didn't want to scare her—or perhaps he didn't want to face the future.

He smiled and stroked her face. "There's still so much we don't know about these primitive people, and I doubt we ever will. Well, maybe they'll let you in on all their secrets someday."

She took his hand and kissed it. "I'm keeping my promise you know."

A few minutes later, she leaned over and seductively leaned up against him, blowing on his neck. She placed her right hand under his shirt and rubbed her hand over his stomach and nipples.

No woman had ever made him this crazy with desire. He knew no one ever would again. Lorelei's touch somehow brought peace and ecstasy at the same time.

He quickly pulled over at a bend in the road, which had the space of a scenic pull off. He had barely slid the seat back when she threw herself on top of him. She ground against him until he thought he would explode, then unzipped his jeans and reached inside.

Her gentle strokes teased him, burned him. "You are one hell of a woman. I will never stop wanting you."

She pushed him back so hard the seat reclined all the way

down. Then she undid her own jeans.

He surprised her by reaching inside her underwear. He didn't know if it was the silky, sensuous red lace, or her pure desire, but Ian ripped them off and placed his hand inside her.

She gasped and threw her head back so hard he thought she might hurt herself. Her wetness slowly surrounded his hand and he slowly, sensuously painted her inner thighs. Then he placed both hands inside her sweatshirt, lifting it off over her head. Her perfect round breasts taunted him in her matching red bra, so he took a hold of the clasps and yanked until they snapped off.

He pulled her toward him, licking the circumference of her nipple. She entangled her hands in his hair and stretched the strands until his eyes watered. But he couldn't stop. He not only loved the feel of her, he loved her reactions to his arduous teasing. He placed his mouth over her breast and bit, then nibbled and sucked until her legs wrapped around him.

Rolling her over, he entered her quickly, holding her tight. He did something he had never been able to do with any other woman. He held her buttocks while deep inside her. Then without moving, his manhood bent slightly up and down.

She gasped repeatedly and grabbed his bottom, attempting to push him further inside.

They exploded inside each other. Ian kissed her long and hard until they had to come up for air.

They wiped each others tears away. "Are you okay?" Ian asked.

"Absolutely," she whispered. "Just thinking about what you can do to me drives me insane."

"Looking at you drives me crazy." Ian kissed her on both sides of her face. "Sorry about the sexy lingerie."

"No problem. I had hoped for that reaction. I figured I'd be able to wait until the hotel."

She slid back into the passenger seat and they both got dressed. Then he took her scraped hands and kissed them softly. Ian placed his hands on either side of her face, gazing intently into her hazel eyes. "I love you so much. I loved you before I knew about your astral abilities, before we found out about our likeness to Annie and Jeff, and before you put your own life in jeopardy to stop Melissa's ex. And that will never change, no matter what happens."

But when she stared back at him, Ian thought he detected a shadow of worry swimming inside the reflections of her bluish-green eyes.

Chapter 13

Shannon sat at the two person table in the Horseshoe Café in Wickenburg, waiting for Dennis London to arrive. Sizzling emanated from the kitchen. The smell of bacon and eggs wafted throughout the restaurant. Cowboy chaps, a cow-spotted hide, gun holsters, horse saddles and a massive steer horn adorned beige walls; the perfect western atmosphere for the ideal western town.

A thirty-something man glanced around nervously at the locals after he walked in. Black hair, sideburns and spiky hair made him a standout in a crowd of retired city escapees and ranchers. The look on his face said it all. 'What the hell am I doing in a place like this?'

He seemed relieved when Shannon waved him over.

"Hey, you must be Dennis."

"Yeah."

"Hi, I'm Shannon Flynn." She shook his hand and noticed he had a very firm grip. "My boss, Adam Frasier, mentioned you came across a cave while hiking yesterday. Shannon showed him her ID. "I'm working with a group of researchers. We're trying to determine a tie-in to some passages in the area, as well as a possible art theft."

"Wow. I'll help anyway I can."

"For starters, tell me about this cave. How did you find it?"

The waitress approached their table. "Would you like a menu?" she asked.

Dennis glanced around at the humble décor and simple plates of food. "Uh, no, thanks." He said it as if she were crazy for asking.

Afraid you're going to get poisoned?

"I was out hiking early in the morning and noticed this cool hill with large rocks placed in circular patterns. I thought it might be evidence of Indian ruins, so I climbed up to check it out."

"Was this a popular trail you were on?"

"No, I stay away from those. I found a very narrow pathway

overgrown with brush and cactus. I had walked for a few miles to the back of this butte. That's when I saw the piles of stones. I marked the location on my GPS unit so I can provide that information."

"That would be a huge help. We really appreciate it."

Dennis tapped his spoon onto the paper placemat and his knees made the table tremble.

"Did you go into the cave?"

"Heck yes. It was too tempting not to. I almost didn't notice the opening because it is lower to the ground and partially covered by rocks."

"You said 'almost.' How did you find it?"

"This is going to sound strange."

I'm dating a shaman, my best friend's a psychic in tune with an ancient astral race, and my hobby is the paranormal.

"Try me."

"I heard voices. So I knelt down and saw a light inside. I yelled 'hello.' I got excited and pulled a few more rocks out of the way. It's tricky because the entrance is the top of the cave. I had to scramble down some armchair-sized boulders."

"But you didn't see anyone else?"

"No, and I roamed around in there for a few minutes."

"Were you able to decipher what was said, or if the voices were male or female?"

He shook his head. "Sounded like multiple voices speaking at once. I couldn't tell what they were saying."

"Did you hear those noises while you were in the cave?"

"I would hear whispers coming from one corner, then when I'd walk over to investigate, those sounds would emanate from the center of the chamber. That's when I decided I'd had enough and I climbed back out."

"Did you experience any earthly vibrations or humming?"

Dennis shook his right leg rapidly up and down, making the table quake even harder, garnering attention from nearby patrons.

"No." But he didn't look her in the eye.

"Adam told me you saw some interesting drawings inside. Tell me about them."

"They weren't like any petroglyphs I've seen, and I've explored many parts of the Southwest seeking ruins and rock art." Dennis glanced down at the spoon, sliding the end back and forth between his fingers. "These images were way at the top, scrawled onto the wall. I couldn't make all the etchings out, but I did see a large pictograph of a pair of eyes. They seemed to be staring at a depiction of a starfield on the ceiling."

"How large were these eyes?"

"At least two feet in height. Maybe I was being paranoid after hearing the whispers, but I could have sworn they were watching me. For some reason, I decided to look back at the rock art. I'm really good with detail, and the pupils weren't in the original position, which were focused intently toward the stars etched on the ceiling. They stared in my direction. That's when I hauled my ass out of there real quick."

"What about pottery or shards?"

"I didn't notice anything like that. My attention was focused on the rock art."

Shannon wondered if this man had found relics, and felt guilty for taking some with him. Maybe that's why he was so nervous. Or could he be affiliated with Peter and Emily's pottery theft ring?

Chapter 14

A strong wind pelted Lorelei sideways. She grabbed onto a six foot tall boulder shaped somewhat like a Hershey's kiss, only narrower. She had climbed up a steep hill among large black stones that seemed to be lined in terraces down the hill. Interspersed throughout were piles of similar boulders in circular patterns.

Boulders along the side of the butte were covered with petroglyphs of spirals, deer, stick figures and lizards. Haunting whispers echoed from within a chamber below the rock face—a section she originally thought was a hiding spot for snakes and other desert wildlife.

She gazed upon the Weaver Mountains to the north, hearing the bizarre voices again.

"Who's there?"

It became silent. The breeze itself seemed to stop in anticipation of what would come from below.

She had to know who, or what, might be down there. Flattening a pile of rocks in her way, Lorelei found herself staring into a dry cave. The floor was fifteen feet below. Glancing to her left, she noticed a layer of massive boulders leading down. She couldn't see anyone and the whispers had stopped, yet she felt she weren't alone.

"Hello?" A hawk's scream made her jump and her head nearly hit the section of rock above her.

A shaft of light pierced the top of the chamber and descended directly in between two boulders, landing in the middle of the cave. Black soot covered the ceiling and highlighted the hundreds of stars painted in white and yellow.

They appear to be twinkling.

She stared, mesmerized by the beauty of the lifelike illustration of the heavens; until the feeling of being watched began again. She cautiously climbed down a few massive boulders until she got to the bottom of the antechamber. Glancing upward and to her left, a massive pair of painted eyes observed the petroglyph stars. Each of the eyes were at least two feet tall by two feet wide, a foot apart, and as realistic as any photograph she had seen.

She stepped closer. The iris and pupils, which seemed to be gazing toward the stars, morphed and changed color. For a brief second, they turned orange-red.

Is that a trick of light?

Then the eyes moved in her direction.

Lorelei abruptly sat up as the morning light filtered in through the dark blue curtains in the motel room.

"Morning sunshine," Ian said. "Another interesting dream?"

"Yeah, you could say that." He handed her a cup of coffee and sat next to her. She took a sip. "Has Shannon called yet?"

"No, was she supposed to? I thought we were going to meet her at Vulture Mine."

"Plans have changed." Lorelei climbed out of bed and started to undress for the shower. "I was a man named Dennis in this vision. Shannon is interviewing him this morning."

"So now you're taking the part in dreams of people you don't know?"

"Yes," Lorelei dressed quickly in jeans and a sweater. "We have to get out to a place near Vulture City. There is a rather large set of pictograph eyes in a cave. Eyes capable of gazing back at those who find them."

Chapter 15

A cool, steady wind refreshed Lorelei's senses as she headed along the narrow trail toward the dry cave Dennis saw the day before; the same day the team found the tunnel at Vulture Mine.

"We've got a problem with investigating the passage under the old schoolhouse," Shannon said. "The caretakers are afraid we'll get hurt and they'll be liable. And the structure might be at risk when we start making our way through there, especially since the passage is only five feet down."

"That leaves us where we started," Dale said. "Unless they let us dig down outside of the schoolhouse."

"That's a no go also." Shannon stopped to inspect a section of stones, all of which were approximately a foot tall by a foot wide. "They're anxious to let visitors back in to the ghost town, including another paranormal group that wanted to come for a training investigation."

"It's not like the place is losing money," Ian said. "The FBI is paying them their weekend traffic."

"And more," Shannon said. "Maybe they're concerned what others in the community might think."

"Or Ronnie and John might have something to hide." Lorelei snapped a picture of a spiral, mountain goat and mask petroglyphs on the side of a mammoth tan and grey square-like rock.

Everyone became quiet, even Dale and Brandon who were having their own conversation ten feet away.

"I didn't get that impression when I first talked with them," Shannon said.

"What?" Lorelei looked confused. "What are you talking about? Why are you all staring at me that way?"

"Honey." Ian came over and put his arm around her. "Don't you remember? You just implied that the caretakers of Vulture Mine had something to hide."

Lorelei suddenly noticed a look of concern from Ian. She sensed it had to do with something more than the memory lapse.

"I don't know why I said that. I definitely didn't get bad vibes from either John or Ronnie."

Ian stood in front of her and lifted her chin up so she gazed into his amazing purple-specked irises. As confused as she was right now, he still took her breath away. The morning light filtered through his blond highlights and his five o'clock shadow made him look like he had walked out of the pages of GQ.

"Are you okay?" he asked.

"Uh, I think I'm all right. I swear, I don't remember making that statement. They both seemed so nice. Not sure why I would say such a thing."

"What did your intuition tell you about them when we all first interviewed them?" Shannon asked.

"That's just it. Nothing negative at all. I haven't had any visions about them either."

Brandon walked up to Lorelei, standing so close that Shannon and Dale's mouths dropped. Ian stared at him in shock.

Brandon glanced back at the rest of the group. "We all know that for her to make such a comment isn't in vain, even if she doesn't remember what she said. Perhaps there's more on their property, or in this area, than they're admitting."

"No one said she was nuts." Ian moved between Brandon and Lorelei. "She isn't only my girlfriend, she's the love of my life. I believe whatever she tells me."

Lorelei placed her hand on Ian's arm, calming him down. He backed away and took her hand as they continued climbing toward the cave.

What the hell's going on with Brandon? He's never the type to get into anyone's physical space.

She heard Brandon and Dale whispering together while they hiked up behind Shannon. She stopped at the Hershey's kiss rock. "We're here." A cool breeze greeted her as she stared at the cragged peaks, desert vegetation and red-tailed hawks floating on the currents above them. She could see five hikers on a main trail in the distance.

Ian held her closer as Brandon approached. His arm muscles tensed.

The friction between Ian and Brandon was forgotten when she recognized the opening from her dream. She leaned down on her knees and stared into a hollow section, five feet across by two feet tall, under a massive rock face.

"Let me go first." Ian pulled out his flashlight and crawled in next to her.

"We won't need that." Lorelei sidled next to him and pointed down.

He gasped as an intense shaft of light penetrated the ceiling. "How can there be light?" he whispered. "There's a butte that lies above this whole hill."

She placed her arm across his back. "There must be a crack at the top of this hill. But it's strange how it seems to head straight down into the center of the cave."

"What are you two up to?" Shannon asked. "There are three very anxious explorers waiting outside. Is this the right place?"

"Yes," Ian said. "A dry cave with natural lighting. There is a series of boulders leading down, but they are rather large, so it could be treacherous."

"You and Lore go first and yell when you're both at the bottom," Shannon said.

"Déjà vu, huh?" Ian asked.

She watched as he scooted across the dirt and smaller rocks and onto the first boulder.

"Do you mean this morning's vision of Dennis, or our first underground excursion at Dragoon?"

"The latter, of course."

Lorelei smiled nervously. "Yeah. I think I fell in love with you when you helped me down into the passages at the ranch. You knew how afraid I was and were so patient."

"Nope. It was definitely before that. I saw the way you looked at me during our first investigation at Vulture Mine—when Dale, Brandon and I were walking toward the assay office." He winked at her then slid out of sight onto the next step. "Dale's exact words were, "She wants you bad, man.""

"Oh did he?" Lorelei laughed.

"Come on," he said. "I'm going to wait for you here."

She threw her leg over and onto the stone three feet below. Glancing down, she grabbed tightly onto the rock.

"Baby, you're going to be fine. You know what to do. Look at me only. I'll catch you."

She stared into his eyes for a few seconds, but that was all it took. She quickly sat on the boulder and scooted herself over the side and onto the next one, where Ian waited, taking her into his arms.

"Great job. Two more to go, but this next step's a bigger one."

"After you," she said. Lorelei sat patiently on the boulder as Ian jumped down to the next. She slid off and leapt into his arms. For some reason, she couldn't let him go.

"Lore, you're fine. We're there," he whispered.

"I know." She pulled away. "My senses are telling me to be close to you right now."

Ian turned away and stared at his feet.

"Damn it! You're still hiding something from me." She grabbed his arm and made him face her. "What else happened at that stone near the schoolhouse?"

Lorelei was shocked when he pulled her to him. He held her so close she could feel his heart beating rapidly. "I saw a man taking you by force, though I couldn't tell where it happened. What if that arrow-like rock doesn't just reveal your worst nightmares? What if it predicts…?"

"The future," Lorelei whispered. She wondered if her unfounded sense to be close to Ian was based on what he had seen at the extraordinary stone.

"What's the status?" Dale yelled. "Shannon's about to pace this damn hill into another dimension."

"Sorry. Ian and I are down."

Ian took her hands tightly in his. "I'm sure it was nothing. I'll make sure you're safe." Lorelei could feel him shaking. He turned and gazed up into the source of the brightness. "This butte has to be at least a hundred feet tall. There must be a crack or hole originating from the top.

Lorelei watched Shannon, Brandon and Dale descend into the cave.

Ian stared at the middle of the ground where the sun's ray reflected. "I wonder if this has anything to do with archaeoastronomy. In other words, maybe there's something in the starfield on the ceiling or even in this cave revealed by sunset or sunrise. Perhaps another pictograph or petroglyph which might indicate the equinoxes and solstices, or the times for planting."

Brandon, Shannon and Dale gazed from the heavenly display on the ceiling to the imposing eyes on the cave wall.

"We're still a few weeks away from the vernal or spring

equinox," Shannon said. "That's not until March 20th."

"How would whatever tribe inhabited this area be able to push themselves through a hundred feet of solid rock in order to create a small crevice of light that happens to land in the middle of this cave?" Lorelei asked.

Shannon observed the bold painting of eyes at the top of the cave wall. "There could have been a natural crack in the butte when they moved into the area. We haven't climbed to the top. There might be an opening up there that cuts through the whole hill."

The rest of the group followed Shannon's stare to the lifelike eyes.

"Pretty creepy," Ian said. "That could be why Dennis felt as if he weren't alone." He looked over at Lorelei. "And you saw all this," he did a 360 turn, "through Dennis's eyes?"

"Yes. While he described his adventure in this place to Shannon."

"Wait," Dale said. "Isn't that telepathy?"

"Sort of," Ian said. "But telepathy is mind reading, not visually seeing what someone else is talking about. Perhaps Lore is developing a new talent."

Shannon had lost focus on the conversation. Instead, she observed the celestial display surrounding the natural skylight. Her body was completely still and her hands had formed a prayer position in front of her chest.

Lorelei approached her cautiously and snapped her fingers in front of her friend's face. Shannon didn't flinch.

Chapter 16

The false celestial images above called to Shannon. The white and gold stars twinkled enticingly. The drawing of the planets beckoned; perfect circles shaded in with white.

Shannon gasped as Lorelei waved a hand in front of her face. Ian, Brandon and Dale also gawked at her in astonishment.

"Uh, sorry about that." Shannon glanced around the cave. "There's something special about this place."

She had forgotten her friends were with her.

What the hell is happening to me?

"Is there something we should know?" Lorelei asked.

"I, I don't think so." Confused and embarrassed, Shannon couldn't look at Lorelei or anyone else. "Perhaps whatever voices Dennis heard might be communicating to me."

"Is anyone else here feeling anything unusual?" Lorelei glanced from Ian to Dale and Brandon.

They all shook their heads and continued to stare at Shannon.

Shannon noticed the irises on the painting of the eyes didn't seem to have any particular hue. They were reddish-orange one second, black another, and finally changed to dark blue.

She wanted to change the subject. "Are you guys witnessing the same thing with this creepy picture?"

"The color changes constantly," Lorelei said. "I noticed the same thing when I picked up on Dennis' vision. These change with every move you make."

"Has anyone seen these eyes shift in a different direction?" Shannon asked. "Dennis said that they watched him as he left the cave."

"No." Ian glared at Brandon who stared at Lorelei.

Shannon wanted to get Brandon's attention to avoid an incident with Ian. "Brandon, are we getting any unusual readings?"

Brandon finally broke his gaze away from Lorelei. "Uh, yeah, actually there is. My Mel-Meter is showing spikes of three point two and up to five milliGauss, but the temperature is normal for underground."

"Let's all see what we can find, whether that's evidence of passages, rock art that might be associated with this unique race, or objects such as pottery," Shannon said.

Shannon became uncomfortable, though not from the environment. She remained confused about her actions a few minutes ago. She had looked like a fool in front of the team. She had also gone into a brief trance in front of the petroglyph panel at Vulture Mine.

The cave wall formed a convex ceiling. Ian kneeled down to inspect the ground where the daylight penetrated.

"Did you find something?" Lorelei leaned over Ian.

"Unfortunately, no. I hoped a symbol would be illuminated."

Lorelei sighed. "Well, this could just be a regular hole." She looked from Shannon, up to the colorful star arrangement, and back to Shannon. "It's not the sun at all. Maybe the moonlight reveals something."

"Hey guys." Dale looked down at the GPS unit Brandon was holding. This cave is in alignment with the hill where the weird rock is—the one that showed red hot on the thermal."

"The cemetery I found last night." Ian removed two granola bars from his backpack and handed one to Lorelei. "It was off the same side of the trail as this butte we're under. I didn't get any GPS readings, but seems like those graves were between this cave and the oracle stone."

Brandon shuddered as he watched the painted eyes. "Does the FBI have any idea what happened to Peter and Emily since the kidnapping and pottery theft ring mystery? Could they still be in this area since there was evidence that Peter arrived in Wickenburg during that investigation?"

Ian sighed heavily and sat down on a nearby boulder, his hands on his forehead. Lorelei sat down next to him, rubbing his back gently.

Brandon stared down at the ground in guilt.

"Local law enforcement states Peter and Emily haven't been spotted in the area. This sidekick of Peter's, Ray—the one who killed Alicia Atwell—turned informant, so the feds are keeping in close contact to see if there are any other theft operations. Ray had mentioned there was a cave in the Vulture Mountains where they were hiding some artifacts, but this couldn't be it because he said it was more like a small hole than an open chamber like this. Plus Ray mentioned the small cave they were using wasn't that close to Vulture Mine. Adam's got a local prospector and a few agents to help him find the spot again. Ray claims Peter's in hiding, but doesn't know where. It's obvious Peter had some major connections. Maybe him and Emily have taken on new identities and moved on to another location."

Shannon sat on the other side of Ian and placed her arm around his shoulder. "I'm sorry. I know your ex-wife abandoning her son is still a shock."

"Unfortunately, Peter and Emily's theft operation is all part of the mystery." Ian said. "It's so frustrating. Paul still cries in his sleep."

Lorelei placed her hand against the wall with the painted eyes. "I'm not getting the feeling they're associated with this place. Actually, I'm not sensing anything negative at all in here."

"We need to come back for a night investigation to follow up on Lorelei's suggestion about the moonlight's impact," Shannon said.

"I'll leave a camera set up on a tripod in here and an audio recorder," Brandon said. "So we can see what goes on while we're away."

"Make sure it faces both the painting of the eyes and the ceiling," Lorelei said. Then she bent down to remove her own digital camera from her backpack, and Brandon checked out her behind.

"That's enough," Ian yelled. "I've watched you stare at Lorelei all fucking day, Brandon. What the hell is up with you? We used to be friends. This explains why you've been pulling away from me. You want my girlfriend."

Brandon wouldn't, or couldn't look back at Ian. Lorelei gazed at Brandon in disbelief.

Brandon's own eyes reflected anger, frustration and pain. He picked up his bag and quickly scrambled up the boulders and out the cave.

Dale started setting up the tripod Brandon had left.

Lorelei walked up to Dale. "Fess up. We all noticed you and Brandon whispering together before the group came down here. Why is Brandon acting this way?"

"He's had feelings for you for a while, but they've been getting stronger. Brandon's had some bad experiences with women and has been keeping himself occupied with his software company and developing equipment for the Arizona-Irish. You're one of the only women he's been around lately, so considering how lonely he is." Dale finished mounting the camera. "I didn't expect such a blowup from Ian."

"It's my fault," Ian said. "I should have pulled him aside instead of embarrassing him like that."

"Yes, that would have been more appropriate," Lorelei said. "I can't believe you reacted that way. You know Brandon would never act on his emotions."

Ian threw up his hands. "I'll go talk to him." He passed by Lorelei on his way out. "Be careful coming back up."

"Of course. I'll see you in a few." Lorelei gave him a weak smile, then turned back to Dale. "How long have you known?"

"I found out about it a few days ago. I didn't want to say anything because I knew it would create tension. I thought Brandon would be able to handle himself better."

"How long has he felt this way?" Lorelei took a few pictures of the cave and pictographs and placed her camera back in her bag.

"His feelings for you have been growing the past few months. Listen, he knows there's no chance. Brandon sees the way you and Ian look at each other. He admitted to me that you and Ian belong together. And hell, that guy doesn't have the confidence to hit up on a damn flea, let alone a woman."

Dale helped Lorelei up the largest of the boulders, and then they waited for Shannon.

"Do I dare to look and see if those eyes are watching us?" Lorelei glanced back and noticed they were still focused on the opening in the roof.

"Brandon," Ian yelled. "Brandon, where are you?"

"What's going on up there?" Shannon asked. She crawled out behind Lorelei through the three-foot-high opening with Dale right behind her.

"How could he have disappeared from view so quickly?" Ian asked.

Lorelei wandered around the sloping hill. "Brandon," she yelled.

"Ssshhhh." Shannon threw her hand up to get their attention. "I thought I heard something." She cautiously approached one of the rooms surrounded by darkened stones.

"In here. Shannon, I'm down here."

Brandon stood inside a collapsed section of ground seven feet down. Pebbles and dirt covered his black hair and he attempted to clean his wireframe glasses with his dusty shirt.

"Over here," Shannon yelled. "I found Brandon." She turned her attention to the hole he had fallen through. "Are you hurt?"

"My ankle hurts a little but I can walk." He glanced around inside his underground prison.

Ian, Lorelei and Dale ran up to Shannon and peeked into the hole.

"Thank god," Ian said. "I've been looking all over. I knew you couldn't have gone anywhere that quickly."

Lorelei smacked him on the arm.

"I'm so sorry," Ian said. "I shouldn't have yelled at you like that in front of everyone."

"I'm starting to believe that everything happens for a reason," Brandon said.

"What do you mean?" Dale asked. "Is there a hot chic down there with you?"

Everyone laughed.

Leave it to Dale to lighten the mood.

"No." Brandon smiled. "I'm standing in a passage that leads to another dry cave and in the opposite direction of the chamber we were just in."

Brandon was quiet for a few seconds, his eyes darting from one side of the tunnel to the other. "There are whispering voices coming from somewhere down here. I can't pinpoint where—sounds like it's from all around."

"Any vibrations or humming?" Shannon asked.

"No. But my Tri-Field spiked up to twenty."

"Awesome," Dale said. "Make way, I'm coming down." Then he took a flying leap, landing next to Brandon.

"You're insane," Shannon said. "You could have broken a leg. We don't need two injured people."

"It's not that far down," Dale said.

Brandon rolled his eyes and laughed. "No, but it would have been much safer using those." He pointed to a descending series of indentations the size of footholds.

"Oh wow." Lorelei peeked underground. "So this must have been a regular entrance."

"It's obvious Dale's up for this last minute investigation." Shannon looked up at Lorelei and Ian.

"Let's do this," Lorelei said. She glanced at Ian.

"What? I do whatever you tell me to." Ian laughed.

Dale unzipped the front compartment of his backpack and removed a handheld thermal imaging camera. "You mean like pulling off the side of the road at night and having passionate sex in your car?"

Shannon went into hysterical laughter, tears coming down the side of her face. "Dale and I both saw your steamed up car windows last night."

Ian glanced at Lorelei.

Her face was bright red and she stamped her foot in frustration. "Never mind." She gritted her teeth. "Let's check this out, okay?" She threw her legs over the edge, planted her feet in the manmade rungs and descended to the bottom.

Shannon laughed so hard, she missed the last foothold and slipped onto the ground. She turned to see Lorelei staring at her and smiling in revenge.

Shannon put her hands on her hips. "Hey, I didn't say it. Dale did."

Ian climbed down last.

"Brandon and Dale are already at the other chamber," Lorelei said. "I've got my audio recorder going to see if we can catch those voices Brandon mentioned. I wonder if they're the same as Dennis heard. Maybe the ancient ones."

"Hey," Brandon yelled. "You guys need to see this."

Shannon raced down the passage first, heading in the same direction as the cave under the butte. Her flashlight revealed dark pink, white and black splotches of quartz along the side of the tunnel. She ran into a smaller chamber than the first with piles of collapsed stone everywhere. Gray stone walls showed red petroglyphs of deer, snakes and a picture of a ladder.

Dale and Brandon were bent over examining reddish-brown ceramic bowls and vases sticking up out of the rubble.

"Don't touch anything," Shannon yelled. "This might be evidence."

"This chamber is next to the one we were just in," Brandon said. "The GPS reading is virtually the same."

"There was no collapsed wall in the first cave we were in," Shannon said. She glanced back to see Lorelei staring down into a clay water pitcher.

"I think these objects might be indicative of the ancients residing in this area," Lorelei said.

"How do you know?"

Lorelei moved aside so Shannon could get a better look into the jar. It was the same color and had the same exact black triangle inside a circle as the bowl Dale had found.

Chapter 17

Lorelei gazed into a ceramic bowl on top of the collapsed rubble. All of a sudden, a stark vision implanted itself into her thoughts so vehemently that she fell back onto a pile of sharp rocks.

"Ouch!" She carefully lifted herself off the pile of crumbled stone.

Ian ran over to her. "Are you all right?"

Lorelei hurriedly opened her backpack and pulled out a notepad and pen. She began to sketch the map she had seen in her vision.

"What are you up to?"

"It's a very rough drawing of this cave system. As soon as I looked into that bowl, I saw a blueprint in my head."

"Where are we now? Is this particular chamber on that drawing?"

"We're in this room." She indicated a roughly drawn circle. "This antechamber we're in represents north, but it's divided into two sections. The smaller cave is the one we're in now, and the one with the painted eyes is right next to this." Lorelei glanced back at the wall separating the two. "There's another sanctum to the south, on the other side of the tunnel where Brandon fell—that same spot also represents the exact center of the structure. However, I also saw a passage with east and west caves."

Shannon, Brandon and Dale bent over her, observing the roughly drawn diagram.

"This is strange," Dale said. "You've illustrated the four caves with two intersecting tunnels, one dividing the north and south chambers, and the other separating the east and west, but I didn't notice another corridor crossing the one we came in on, which would lead to the east and west caves."

Lorelei realized he was right, but couldn't explain the anomaly.

Shannon stared down at her feet and closed her eyes for a few seconds.

"You're really scaring me," Lorelei said. "You're not going into another trance, are you?"

"Another level under," Shannon whispered. She looked at Lorelei and Ian. "What if the east and west chambers are further below the earth?"

"I guess it's possible," Lorelei said.

Shannon looked out into the passage. "The south cave should be a mile straight that way."

"Only one way to find out if there is another connecting route." Brandon grabbed his bag and headed toward the passage. "Dale and I could check it out and see if there's a way into the east/west caves. And perhaps check out the south cave."

Lorelei had already packed her camera and voice recorder and walked out the cave. "I'd like to go." She glanced at Ian. "You don't mind, do you?"

"No. Guess I'll stay here with Shannon and take some pictures. See if we get any audio or thermal hits."

Before she left, Lorelei heard Shannon on the phone with Special Agent in Charge, Adam Frasier. She was talking to him about sending an evidence response team and an archaeologist to their location.

She kissed Ian on the cheek. "I'll see you soon. We'll let you and Shannon know what we find."

Ten minutes later they passed by the spot where they had entered the tunnel. Brandon suddenly stopped, causing Lorelei to bump into him.

"S, sorry," he stuttered. "I got a large spike on my Tri-Field meter. It went up to fifteen."

"My EMF detector read the same," Dale said.

They stood in silence for a minute to see if anything causing the high energy fluctuations would reveal itself. Through the opening, three turkey vultures floated on the thermals, dark brown and white wings stretched wide, scanning the desert below for leftovers.

"The soul," Lorelei whispered, staring into the sky.

Brandon and Dale glanced back at her, then at each other.

"This is the direct center of the cave system — the conscience of this subterranean labyrinth."

"A portal of some sort?" Dale asked.

Lorelei didn't answer. This particular spot was very powerful, possibly because it was the meeting point for all of the chambers.

"Damn." Brandon continued to stare at his EMF meter. "This device is still reading fifteen." He glanced at Dale's dimly lit Mel-Meter. "And so is his."

"Let's keep going," Lorelei said.

Ten minutes later they arrived at the southernmost cave.

"Were either of you able to verify that the distance between the north and south chambers was a mile?" Lorelei asked.

"Yes." Dale looked at his GPS device. "The entrance, or possibly the portal, is in the exact center."

Dripping echoed throughout the room. "Over there." Lorelei pointed to a shallow pool of dark green water in the center of the cave. A beam of light penetrated the brackish pond.

"The light isn't the only thing that's the same." Brandon stared at the ceiling with the ethereal stars to a pair of eyes.

Lorelei gazed upward at a rock face streaked with white. "This is an exact copy of the other image."

"If there are two other caves below us, I wonder if they have the same features," Dale said.

Brandon got on the radio. "Shannon or Ian. Are you there?"

"Ian, over."

"We found another chamber. It's exactly a mile from the one you're in."

"Shannon and I have been looking, but can't find evidence of any other aperture. There has to be a way the ancients, or whoever else inhabited these caves, traveled between levels. That is, if the east and west chambers are further below the earth."

"We'll see what we can find," Brandon said.

Lorelei walked slowly around the chamber, running her hand along the cool stone surface to see if she could pick up any vibrations or images. Her flashlight cut through the darkness of a one inch crevice that ran from the top of the chamber to the ground. Broken bits of stone and rubble rested in the crack.

"No indication or visions as to where these passages start?" Dale asked.

Dale nervously watched the unsettling eyes while he walked slowly by. It didn't appear they were watching him back. As with the other painting, these eyes were focused on the effigy of the heavens.

An abrupt vision interrupted Lorelei's thoughts. She shook

her head adamantly.

"Tell me, Brandon." She pulled her hair back into a ponytail and took a sip of water. "Do you know any women with long, straight black hair, green eyes, tall and athletic?"

He glanced at Dale.

"No, why?"

"I see you with someone fitting that description. She's rather exotic looking and stunning." Lorelei walked up to within a few feet of him. "I had a profound flash of the two of you together."

"Details," Dale said. "What were they doing?"

Lorelei smacked Dale on the arm and turned to look at Brandon, who had stopped taking pictures.

"Not that. But she is going to be the love of your life. I just witnessed you with your future wife."

Brandon stared at Lorelei as if she had gone nuts. "If it were anyone else but you, I'd laugh. Are you sure?"

"I know you've had problems with relationships in the past," Lorelei said. "But that's about to change. And very soon."

"How will we meet?"

"I think some things are better off as a surprise." She removed her EMF detector and started taking readings.

"What a tease." Dale smirked at her. "Isn't that like a woman to get a man going and then walk away."

"He won't have long to wait."

"Do you see anything pertaining to me?"

Lorelei walked up to him. She looked Dale in the eyes. "Only that you'll die at the hands of a particular blonde psychic if you ever reveal her intimate moments in front of the group ever again."

"Hey, there was nothing secret about what you and Ian were doing in his car."

Brandon and Dale laughed as she chased Dale around the cave.

"Guys, stop," Brandon said. He stared up at the menacing orbs. "Not sure, but I think I observed those things moving in your direction. Take a look at the thermal imager."

A red heat signature showed against a backdrop of damp rock.

The eyes transformed from black to brown to grey. The expression changed from placid to a cool stare. Then the chamber began to tremble.

We've pissed something off.

"Brandon, Dale, can you hear me?" Shannon asked over the radio.

"Yeah, we've got a problem," Dale yelled.

"Get out, repeat, get out now!" Shannon shouted. "Ian and I will meet you above ground."

Lorelei ran out of the south chamber with Brandon and Dale following her. Fluttering and chirping noises came from behind, followed by a slight breeze. Tiny black bodies surrounded Lorelei, Brandon and Dale. The three investigators ducked down as the bats chased after them, scraping the top of their heads with their tiny claws. The popping and squeaking from their echolocation temporarily drowned out the anger of the realm they had invaded. After the bats disappeared into the passage, Lorelei could hear the rumbling of the earth.

Her senses screamed at her. She had to stop and look back.

The painted eyes were looking at her. They were glowing orange-red.

Chapter 18

Ian grabbed onto protruding stone as the ground shook underneath his feet. He tried to run, but the tremors made his body sway from side to side.

Shannon used the rocks on the passage wall to guide her along. She looked back to make sure Ian was behind her.

Glancing up, he noticed a very fine crack began to form on the ceiling.

Please let us all get out of here safely.

A rattlesnake, shaken out of its hiding place, slithered rapidly under Shannon's foot. She nearly stepped on it, but Ian pushed her forward and out of the reptile's way.

"What the hell?" she screamed. "I'm moving as fast as I can."

He pointed behind him to the retreating snake.

Shannon glanced back for a second then pushed her way along the wall at a quicker pace.

Dale and Brandon headed toward them. He didn't see Lorelei.

"Where's Lore?" Ian yelled above the noise of the earth moving.

"She was right behind us," Dale said. "I heard her back there."

"Are you fucking kidding me? You should have kept a watch on her." Ian ran toward the opposite cave. "Go ahead and get out."

The tremors started to subside so he ran faster. "Lore!" he screamed. She stood completely still in the middle of the passage, staring straight ahead into the chamber.

"Damn it, Lore." Ian leapt toward her. He reached to grab her, but a cracking sound came from above. A deafening, thunderous roar overtook the tunnel as the ceiling caved in between her and Ian. Large stones, dirt and debris rained down and clouded the tunnel.

"No." Ian coughed uncontrollably from the dust.

Shannon, Brandon and Dale ran up to him, out of breath and in shock. "Lore's inside." Ian frantically looked for a way in. "Lore, can you hear me?"

Her muffled voice emanated from the other side of the collapsed roof. "Yes. Are you okay?"

"Baby, I'm fine. We all are."

"Please get me out of here." She hardly ever panicked. Something about her voice told him Lore was terrified.

Is there something in there with her?

"Shit." Shannon glanced at her BlackBerry. "This thing isn't getting any reception down here now. I'm going back out for a minute to get some help."

Ian tried pushing some of the rocks, but they wouldn't budge. He slammed his fists into the sharp edges of the rubble, tearing up both hands. He grabbed Brandon and Dale's shirts, pushing them up against the wall. "Why weren't you watching her?"

"She started out ahead of us," Dale said. "She must have stopped. Ian, I'm sorry."

"It wasn't just your fault," Brandon said. "Ian, we'll both stay down here and do everything we can until she's out of there."

"She'll be fine. You know what a survivor she is." Dale placed a hand on Ian's shoulder cautiously. Ian released his grip on them.

"We know there's air and light in there because of the hole in the ceiling," Brandon said. He pushed against different sections of the rock to see if he could break through.

Ian noticed a fist-sized area of rock shake then drop at his feet.

"Ian." Lorelei reached her hand through and grabbed for his.

He took her trembling fingers in his bloodied hands and kissed them, then held them tight. "Baby, I'm here. I'm not leaving until we get you out."

"Ian, you can't. No one can."

"Lore, stop it."

"No, listen to me. I was freaking out for a minute. I need to be here. Those painted eyes somehow held me in a trance. They wanted me here. I know how strange that sounds. But I don't think I'm in any further danger. Right after I became trapped, they went back to watching the stars."

"Lore, what if this is punishment for us fooling around in there?" Dale asked. "Shit, this should have happened to me."

"Dale, no. I'm not feeling threatened. Maybe I'll find the entrance to the next level of passages."

Ian slumped against the wall of the tunnel. "If you're sure."

He gripped her hand tightly in both of his. "I'm still staying until you figure out what it is you need to do. Or until we get you out of there."

"I would hope so," she said. "Please don't blame anyone."

Shannon ran up to Ian, Brandon and Dale. "You found a way through." She glanced at Ian holding Lorelei's hand. "Sort of. I'm trying to get help to get you out."

"I think I have to figure that out myself."

"Lore says this happened for a reason," Ian said tiredly. "She's supposed to discover a clue among this mishap."

"We have to at least try and get her out of there," Shannon said.

"That wall's not budging without more help," Brandon said. "If we try, this whole damn place might collapse."

"Then Dale, Brandon and I can go back to the other chamber while Ian keeps Lore company," Shannon said. "We can try and get to her through one of the other passages she saw in her vision."

"If you can find it." Ian slumped against the pile of rock. "We both scoured that place and didn't find anything that looked like an entrance."

"We'll have to try harder." Shannon handed him a walkie-talkie. "Hang on to this and let me know if either of you need help." She leaned down and whispered to Ian. "If those tremors start again, get the hell out of here."

"No."

"You're not going to help her if you get killed yourself."

"I can hear you both," Lorelei said. "Ian, she's right. I'll be fine in here. Get to safety if it happens again."

He didn't want to think about abandoning her and prayed he wouldn't have to.

"Ian, please," she begged, squeezing his hand tightly. "Tell me you'll get to safety if you need to. I don't want to make it out of here to find out you've been seriously hurt. Or worse."

He sighed. "Okay. Damn it."

Chapter 19

Ronnie had always considered herself to be a non-believer when it came to the paranormal. That changed when she and John moved to Vulture Mine.

The smell of steaks grilling and cakes baking from the deserted dining hall, a tall, thin man in his fifties standing on the black widow-infested porch of the bunkhouse, children's voices and giggles at the old schoolhouse, and shadow people darting between the antiquated buildings. Ronnie and John had encountered many bizarre phenomena.

None of the activity made her feel as uneasy as she did inside the original caretakers' house on the hill overlooking the parking lot and gift shop. Ronnie carefully pulled open the squeaky screen door, partially hanging off its hinges, and entered the empty, dust and insect-infested living area where she had discovered the first diary. Mattie Olson's secrets were no longer hidden among the floors of the modest 1,400 square foot home. They were being held tightly in Ronnie's right hand. She hoped she could find additional clues regarding the ancient race in the home.

Mattie had taken care of the property from 1952 until 1980, and rumor had it that the seventy-eight year old went insane from living on her own for so long. Or perhaps she went crazy from the apparitions that inundated the area; not only spirits of the inhabitants of Vulture City, but the phantoms whose enigmas were alluded to with pencil scribbles on the yellowed pages of Mattie's journal.

The pinging of a shovel hitting against hard desert ground reverberated up to Ronnie as John attempted to dig the hole under the old schoolhouse. The Arizona-Irish had found what Ronnie and John hoped would lead to the CAVES OF THE WATCHERS—chambers that supposedly held Native American artifacts and other secrets—including those of the 'ancient' race.

"Come on, old lady," Ronnie whispered. "Give me a hint

regarding those treasures." Mexican free tailed bats, with their distinct long tails, velvety dark brown fur and narrow pointed wings, hung from the rafters. The beige carpet was stained and the walls were plastered thick with desert dust. A few bark scorpions scampered up the wall, creating a trail as they searched for an easy meal.

The living creatures weren't a threat to Ronnie. The unseen, particularly Mattie's ghost, scared her more than any wild animal. Every time Ronnie walked in, she could feel the woman in the house. Since she had discovered the diary a few weeks ago, Mattie's presence had turned angry.

Ronnie roamed around looking for any cracks in the foundation or sides of the house. A cold breeze passed behind her, causing her hair to move. She jumped and turned around to see a shadow a few inches taller than her staring from the kitchen.

Lips parted, breathing in short spurts, and trembling from head to toe, Ronnie slowly backed toward the door, watching the entity the whole time.

"Mattie?"

The dark figure came at her and Ronnie could briefly make out what looked like hair to the mid-back.

"Get out." The ragged remnants of the long beige curtains responded to a strong, sudden breeze.

Ronnie burst through the door and into the afternoon sun.

I'm missing something.

She glanced down and noticed the diary was no longer in her hands. She turned her head. Mattie stood inside the doorway watching her.

Mattie's ghost held the journal to her chest. A content smile spread across her face.

Chapter 20

Twilight descended from the foot-wide aperture in the ceiling of the cave. Lorelei had fallen asleep with a folded up towel for a pillow, and she could barely move due to the stiffness in her neck and back. She stood up to stretch while soft orange and pink hues illuminated the chamber.

Ian moved on the other side of the collapsed barrier. His muffled, drowsy voice broke the silence. "Lore?"

"Honey, I'm here. I had to get up off the hard ground for a few minutes." The closer darkness came, the more excited she became.

"Has anything unusual happened in there?"

Lorelei gazed up at the black-sooted roof with its hundreds of stars etched in white and yellow. The temperature began to drop. She walked around restlessly, rubbing her arms with her hands.

"Baby, come here," Ian said.

Lorelei kneeled in front of the fist-sized hole and gazed into the only part of him she could clearly see — his fierce blue-grey eyes. His purplish specks started to swim and she could feel warmth coursing through her. She wanted nothing more than to be in his arms."

"How much longer do I have to wait to hold you?"

"Not long now," she whispered. "I think Shannon was right. The moonlight will reveal something."

She could hear Ian walking around. "I wonder what's going on with Shannon. That was a pretty intense trance this morning."

"She was also praying." Shannon had never come across as a spiritual person, so to see her react that way came as a shock. To the whole team."

"What if something's attached itself to her? Maybe one of the ancients."

"But why?" Lorelei asked. "They've been communicating to a certain extent through me."

"I don't know. But Shannon's changing somehow. It all started happening after she saw the petroglyph panel at Vulture Mine."

I can't look over there. If those eyes are watching me, I might not have the courage to go through with this.

She couldn't help it. For a split second, the eyes were focused directly on her. A few seconds later they turned toward the moonlight that started to filter through the ceiling.

Ian was talking to her, but Lorelei stayed engrossed in the scene unfolding before her. The full moon's rays pierced the opening, slicing the center of the chamber and illuminating a distinct shape below the surface of the shallow water—a circle with a triangle inside.

Lorelei placed her hand in the cool water, feeling for anything out of the ordinary.

She looked up to see the light gradually sliding across the ground and into a nook with two boulders leaning together to the left, both ten feet high and a foot thick with a two-inch gap in between.

This is what I've been waiting for.

The moonlight illuminated a hole in the ground between the boulders, but the space was too small to squeeze through.

"I take it you found something."

She turned in response to Ian's voice. "Yes. There is access underground between two rocks, but how the hell can I get into it?"

Lorelei glanced at the small pool. "Could this actually work?" Lorelei ran over and stood on the symbol of the triangle inside the circle.

She couldn't believe what happened next. Judging by the gasp from the other side of the rubble, neither could Ian.

No sound and no movement. The two boulders had vanished into thin air.

Lorelei looked back at the fist sized opening where she had been holding hands with Ian. "Did you see that? Ian, those rocks felt like any other. They were real."

"This is some weird shit," he said. "Maybe they're just invisible."

She ran over to the underground entrance and carefully felt where the stones had been. She excitedly swiped her hands back and forth. Nothing but air.

"Oh wow! Honey, I can't feel the rocks. And I'll bet the other chamber has a hidden entrance also."

She dipped her flashlight into the darkness to see the ground only five feet below.

"I'm heading over to the north chamber now," Brandon said. "Hopefully, we'll find a way to meet up with you."

"Wait," Lorelei yelled. "There's a circle with a triangle inside. It's a marking in the direct middle of the cave. Maybe the dirt is hiding that very same symbol in the first cave we found."

"Lore, we don't know what's further down," Ian said. "I don't know if I want you taking the risk."

She walked over to the pile of rubble between her and the rest of the team and reached her hand through the small hole. Ian took her hand and kissed it.

Shannon's voice echoed loudly. "She'll be fine. Ian, let's go. You're coming with us."

"I love you," she said.

"I love you too, baby."

Shannon shoved a walkie-talkie through the aperture. "Take this and keep in touch. Hopefully, we'll soon you soon."

Lorelei walked over and descended into the tunnel. As she stepped off the last rung, she heard a cat meowing. She removed her flashlight from her back pocket, turned it on, and pointed it in either direction.

A black cat sat in the darkness a few feet in front of her. Its yellow eye shine reflected back from murky shadows. The animal meowed again and swished its tail.

"No way," she whispered, walking closer. Lorelei saw the one-inch scar on its right ear. "You're one of the three cats that roam the ghost town. How did you get here?"

The feline rubbed against her leg, purring repeatedly. Every time she tried to move, it would step in front of her.

Her compass read north. She headed in the direction of the first cave with the cat following her. She gasped. On either side of the catacomb were recessed openings, five feet long by three feet wide and two feet above the ground. The unusual chambers lined both sides of the tunnel as far as she could see.

The cat, which had been circling her, stopped in the middle of the passage. It stood stiffly, the hairs on its back on end and its tail straight in the air. Its eyes were focused on the hollowed out, bed-like depression of quartz in front of her.

"What's the matter?" Lorelei leaned down to pet the feline, but it hissed and darted off. She knew animals were sensitive to spirit activity, so she removed her Mel-Meter. The glowing green display indicated an energy reading of twenty. After a few seconds, the device shut off.

These were fresh batteries. What the hell is lying inside that chamber?

She extended a shaky hand into the opening. Then something grabbed onto her wrist, pulling her forward.

Her pentagram necklace hovered in the air. She quickly pulled away and the chain broke. The emerald in the middle of the pentacle irradiated brilliantly, and then dropped onto the stone surface.

She stared into the carved out portion of the wall. Her EMF detector came back on. She inserted the device into the chamber of the wall where the mysterious apparition had appeared. It read zero. Whatever was there seconds before seemed to have vanished.

Snatching the necklace from the table, Lorelei gazed at the emerald. Only the ancients can cause the pendant to do that. Was this spirit reliving an out of body experience?

Lorelei jumped when a small dark shape caressed her ankles. The cat stared up at her and meowed. "Sure, now you come back." She smiled and pointed her flashlight on either side of the passageway.

The EMF meter did not detect any further energy as she walked along the wall and held the device up against each of the recessed openings.

"If you were one of the ancient ones," she yelled, "why won't you communicate with me? What is this place?"

Lorelei placed her hand on the cool, horizontal stone surface. She lay down on the hard stone bed and closed her eyes. Breathing deeply and slowly, she hoped to get a vision or sense of what might be around her.

Fifteen minutes later she opened her eyes. Nothing had happened. Lorelei slammed her fists against the rock beneath her. She began to cry, though she wasn't sure if it was from the pain that shot up her arms, or the frustration of her lack of visions regarding the ancient ones.

The walkie-talkie she had placed on the ground crackled with static. After a few seconds a voice came through. "Lore, this is Ian." He sounded breathless.

The disappointment she felt subsided. "Ian, you aren't going to believe what I've found. This passage is lined with recessed bed chambers of some sort. I was grabbed by something lying in one of them. It had to be one of the astral travelers because it held my necklace and the emerald lit up like it did in Dragoon."

"Did the entity communicate with you?"

She sighed. "No. Where are you?"

Light pierced the tunnel and illuminated her. "Right here, baby." Rapid footsteps echoed throughout the tunnel. She saw Ian running toward her.

She ran into his arms and he lifted her off the ground and whirled her around. Then he placed her back down and kissed her passionately.

Lorelei placed her hands on the side of his face. "I missed you so much," she whispered into his ear.

"Uh hum." Shannon cleared her throat.

"So there was another entry?" Lorelei said.

Dale, Brandon and Ian looked over at Shannon.

"Yeah," Ian said. "The symbol you used to gain access to this tunnel, the triangle inside a circle, was buried under a few inches of dirt in the north cave with the painted eyes. Shannon was the only one who could gain access. She stepped on the sign and a massive boulder disappeared."

Lorelei stared at Shannon. *What the hell is she not telling us?*

"The camera happened to be focused in the direction the action occurred," Brandon said. "We caught the moonlight slowly working its way toward the hidden opening."

Shannon attempted to change the subject. "Lore, did you notice the position of the painted eyes when the moonlight was moving around the cave?" Shannon took the camera from Brandon and rewound the video.

"Take a look." Shannon pointed to the LCD screen.

Lorelei, Shannon, Ian, Brandon and Dale watched the beam of light as it crossed the ground in the north cave with the painted eyes.

"The time stamp on this footage reflects the same moments you experienced the phenomena in the south cave," Dale said. "If there are other chambers on this deeper level of tunnels, then I'll bet that same thing was happening. The significance of all this is still unknown."

Ian threw his backpack over his shoulder. "Let's see if we can find the east/west tunnel and the other two caves. I didn't notice anything, but then I was so intent on meeting up with Lore."

Lorelei placed her arm around his waist. "These bed-like insets, probably used for astral travel, seem to be all the way down the tunnel. But we're heading north. So where would the east/west corridor be? Maybe I wasn't so accurate in my replication of the map."

They walked for another ten minutes. Brandon used an EMF meter and Dale had the thermal imager going. Neither piece of equipment showed anything anomalous.

Shannon and Dale started to spotlight the ground with their flashlights.

"What are you up to?" Lorelei asked.

"Looking for that circle and triangle marking. We might have to access the missing passage the same way we found the entrance to this place. Where we're standing now is the central point according to my GPS, since this spot is exactly a half mile from where Ian, Dale, Brandon, Ian and I started. This should be directly under the hole leading outside."

"Good thinking," Ian said.

"Holy shit." Dale stared at the rock wall inside one of the horizontal stone berths.

Lorelei followed his gaze and saw a triangle inside a circle.

Brandon glanced at Lorelei and Shannon. "So which of you is going to give this a try?"

Lorelei reached in to touch the symbol.

"That's not going to work," Shannon said. "Think about it. You said yourself those are out of body chambers."

"They want to guarantee only those with their abilities can gain access." Lorelei laid down on the cool stone surface.

Ian kissed her lightly on her lips. "Have a safe journey. Make this a short one."

His beautiful blue-grey eyes sparkled and his irises began to change. Lorelei was lulled into a peace of mind as his purple specks danced, separated, and grouped together again.

Ian whispered, "I love you." His words escorted Lorelei as her soul left her body. Her silver cord, a long, bright elastic cable an inch wide that emanated from her upper spine, sparkled like tinsel on a Christmas tree.

The second she abandoned her physical form, the astral compartment vanished, and the east/west passage was revealed.

Brandon and Dale stared at the east and west tunnels in awe, waving their hands repeatedly across the spot where the astral chamber had been.

"Unbelievable," Dale whispered. "Invisible rocks are one

thing, but disappearing passages? What, and who, were these people?"

Ian observed the ceiling where her soul awaited. He was the only one who could see her astral self. "Baby, you did it. Come back to us."

She was conscious within seconds; her physical form on the floor directly below where the astral chamber had been. Ian helped her up.

"If the out of body chamber vanished, how can your body still be here?" Brandon asked.

Lorelei looked at Ian and Shannon, then Brandon. "I, I don't know."

Shannon zipped up her leather jacket. "Brandon, Dale, you both can head east. Lore, Ian and I will go to the west passage."

Lorelei wondered if the circle surrounding the triangle in this cave system had something to do with the seven chakra points and their relationship to healing. After all, humans carry energy that drives and maintains the life functions; energy that flows not only throughout living beings, but into the very fabric of the universe.

Ian stopped suddenly, staring at Lorelei. He was always able to read her mind after an astral session. "Of course. The word "chakra" means a wheel or circle."

"Okay, I think you two are up to your telepathy tricks again." Shannon shined her flashlight into the darkness. "Energy does tend to swirl in a circular motion as it moves within the chakras, so maybe that's where the circle comes into play. Though, I'm not so sure about the triangle".

Lorelei and Ian glanced at her in surprise.

"What? You don't date a shaman without learning some of this stuff."

Is that why Shannon's been having these strange experiences? Is her relationship with Joe opening her up to higher spiritual encounters?

Ian observed the stone walls intently. "A triangle has three points. The "Way of Heavenly Transformation," as part of the Heavenly Code, states the seven chakras consist of three gates and three palaces, giving rise to the third birth in human life. Maybe the triangle, with its three points, is somehow tied into the Heavenly Code. I mean, we're talking about an extremely spiritual race."

"Could the points of the triangle also relate to Heaven, Earth and human?" Shannon asked.

"Makes sense," Ian replied. "According to the scripture of

Chun-Bu-Kyung, mankind exists as a 'bridge' between Heaven and Earth. Considering how important astral travel was to them, that could be a possibility."

The cat reappeared from out of nowhere, rubbing up against Lorelei's legs.

"Hey sweetie, where have you been?"

She glanced up to see Ian and Shannon gaping at her.

"Uh, honey." Ian looked down at her ankles where Lorelei had petted the feline. "Do you want to fill us in on something?"

"What? Neither of you see the cat?"

Ian shook his head slowly back and forth.

"They don't see it. So that explains how it got here. This damn cat is a spirit."

A few seconds later, Lorelei sensed something behind her. Shannon and Ian stood completely still, their mouths wide open. She turned to see a lithe shadow figure with long hair. The entity smiled at her and bent to pick up the black cat as it ran into her arms.

"Her pet," Lorelei whispered.

Ian placed his arm around her shoulders.

The solitary darkness of Vulture Mine Road, the brightness of the car headlights and Ian's terrified face all came back to her.

"She's the one who saved me last night."

Ian slowly lifted his camcorder while Shannon used the thermal imaging camera to catch proof of the spirit's existence.

Lorelei walked cautiously toward the woman presence. Tall and stately, the arcane apparition began to vanish in a swirl of mist with the feline still in her arms. They both gazed intently at her as she and the cat became nothing but vapor.

Lorelei rubbed her arms from the chill in the air. The brisk cold cut through her green ski jacket.

An object lay at her feet. She didn't notice the spirit holding it. Nor did she hear it drop in front of her. She bent down to pick up the hardbound book, wiping the dust from the cover. It read DIARY.

Shannon and Ian stood on either side of her.

Lorelei flipped to the back cover to a name scrawled in blue ink — MATTIE OLSON.

She nearly dropped the book when the pages flung themselves in the opposite direction.

Shannon and Ian jumped back a step.

The journal had opened itself to an entry from October 17th,

1955:

They are the Caves of the Watchers – I suppose because of the massive sets of eyes that sometimes seem to follow me. Though I have only discovered two antechambers, I know there are two others. I've seen them in my dreams. No one knows of this place, except for me. What else does the race of people who used to inhabit this underground dwelling have in store for me?

As she was about to flip through the following pages for further entries, Dale's voice crackled through the walkie-talkie.

"Dale, here. We're at the east cave. It is similar to the north and south caves, but there isn't a set of eyes or a source of light. Brandon and I will take some pictures, video and voice recordings — the usual investigative techniques to see if there's anything here and find out what this place might have been used for and why it's this far underground."

"Sounds good," Shannon said. "Lore, Ian and I haven't made it to our destination yet. We had an interesting interruption a few minutes ago."

"You're going to make us wait to find out the details, aren't you?" Dale asked.

"Shannon, over and out." She glanced at Lorelei and Ian. "Let's keep going."

Lorelei's flashlight flickered and went out. "Damn."

Ian removed extra batteries from his bag. "If there isn't anything special about the caves at this level, why would they hide them so well?"

Shannon's light went out, then Ian's.

Lorelei couldn't see Ian or Shannon. Or her hand in front of her face.

A loud burst of static erupted from the walkie-talkie.

"Must be Dale or Brandon trying to get through," Ian said. "Wonder if they've had the same problem. My camcorder stopped running also."

Lorelei noticed her audio recorder and digital camera were powered down.

The tunnel walls began to transform from the brown and tans of the earth to golden. Then they collapsed in on themselves.

She closed her eyes tightly and reopened them. The corridor was now a circular funhouse; sides spinning with the most brilliant, enticing light at the end.

"Lore, where are you?" Ian yelled.

She could hear the panic in his voice. She attempted to reach for him, or anything solid.

"Ian, what's happening?"

"It's not just you."

"Shannon!" Lorelei yelled. There was no response.

A hand grabbed at her in desperation. A sensuous, musky scent surrounded her as he placed his arms around her waist.

"Ian, thank god." The tunnel was ablaze. She nestled her face in Ian's chest to shield her eyes from the dizzying array of light and shapes.

"It's so beautiful," Ian said.

Lorelei turned her head to see a figure standing in the center of the light. Tranquility and nirvana were the only words she could think of. The last time she had felt such peace was during her near death experience on Interstate 51 in Phoenix. Her car spun out across five lanes of traffic. About to hit the cement barrier at seventy miles per hour, her vehicle suddenly veered away. She had felt as if she had been enveloped in an angel's arms.

The radiance retreated. The tunnel walls solidified again and changed back to their normal earth tones. Lorelei's flashlight and equipment turned on. Ian looked down at her, kissing her on her head.

Lorelei's beam slid across the sides of the rock surface and into the darkness.

"Shannon," Ian yelled.

Shannon's backpack lay on the ground, but she was nowhere around. Lorelei wondered if she had been drawn further into the tunnel, and into the light.

* * *

One minute, Shannon, Lore and Ian had been walking through a dark tunnel. The next, they were blinded by resplendent white light.

Shannon attempted to grab onto the walls, but she couldn't get a hold of a moving target. The sides of the passage were a swirling shaft. Unable to see straight or connect with anything solid, Shannon fell to the ground on her knees.

Ian yelled for Lorelei as the light crept through the subterranean realm. Shannon started to scream out, but suddenly felt a calmness she had never experienced. She stood up and headed toward the welcoming radiance.

Five figures waited.

Shannon couldn't determine whether they were male or female. Whether they were happy or unhappy.

Yet somehow, it all felt familiar.

Chapter 21

Ronnie had heard about Richard Warburton. What she had heard about the man of the occult was not good, especially when he was crossed. And Ronnie did not have the best news for him. She had lost the damn diary to a ghost. One second it was tightly in her hand, the next Mattie's spirit was holding it to her chest.

John had not supported her. "You lost the fucking thing, so you're responsible for telling Richard. You've been creeped out about that old house since we moved here. You probably got so scared you dropped the journal."

She knew it hadn't slipped from her hands. So how could the old caretaker have gotten it back?

Ronnie had heard that Richard and his wife Liza specialized in Native American artifact theft in Arizona; or at least it began that way. Now the couple was extending their operation to Utah, New Mexico and Colorado. Supposedly, an area off of Vulture Mine Road also held some precious secrets. Keys to a race of ancient people that involved much more than archaeological artifacts.

The journal she discovered talked about the mysterious four caves that Richard and Liza suspected were a primary clue, though Ronnie didn't find a reference mentioning where the chambers were.

Richard demanded to pick the diary up himself. She also knew the black arts master would be coming to get a feel for their property to see if this special place they were seeking might be part of old Vulture City, especially since the Arizona-Irish investigators had just found evidence of petroglyphs.

She trembled in fear as she picked up the broom to sweep the gift shop. It was 9:00 p.m. He would arrive any minute. And Ronnie couldn't lie — not to someone capable of telepathy and mind control.

A car pulled into the dirt parking lot. Stepping out onto the patio, she noticed a black luxury car. The person that got out of the vehicle was over six feet in height, lean with short dark hair; a strikingly good looking man in his fifties.

Ronnie glanced around for John as the intimidating looking stranger approached, but he was nowhere in sight.

Figures. The chicken shit bastard.

She extended a shaky hand. "Richard, I assume. Nice to meet you. I'm Ronnie."

"Likewise."

His deep voice captivated her. His piercing blue eyes stared right through her. She saw herself reflected in anger.

He already knows.

John ran toward her and Richard from the jeep trail leading to the old schoolhouse. Instead of turning to glance in the direction of her husband, Richard continued to gaze into Ronnie's eyes while holding firmly onto her right hand.

"Here, here's my husband John," Ronnie stuttered.

Richard gradually released her from his focus and his grip.

John's jeans and sweatshirt were dusty. He had been trying to find last minute evidence under the schoolhouse.

"John Randall. I see you met my wife."

"Yes." Richard glanced back at Ronnie. Terrified she would never be able to escape from his gaze again, she stared down at the ground.

"Where did you find it?" Richard asked.

Ronnie glimpsed at her husband. "You mean the diary?"

"Of course. You've lost it haven't you? If this particular entity somehow managed to get it back from you, shouldn't we seek the journal where it was last seen?"

Ronnie let out a sigh of relief. Maybe she was off the hook. "Sure. It happened up there." She pointed to the old house surrounded by saguaros on the gently sloping hill.

Ronnie, John and Richard walked in silence. Ronnie and John's lanterns showed them the way along the footpath. She wondered what would happen if Richard couldn't determine the location of Mattie's diary.

Richard stepped ahead of Ronnie and John, and took one long stride into the home. He walked into the middle of the living room with his back to them. Eyes closed, he breathed deeply.

A minute later, without moving, Richard said, "It's not here. Nor is the spirit who took it." He quickly turned to face Ronnie and John. "I'm sensing she's passed it on to a woman who has been on your property recently. This person is more than a visitor."

"We have a team of paranormal investigators," John said. "A psychic medium, an FBI agent and a few others."

Richard approached the couple, towering over them. For a second, Ronnie thought he would walk right through them.

"What does the medium look like?" Richard asked.

"Long blonde hair, five foot six," John said. "Her boyfriend's name is Ian."

Richard put his hand up to stop John from talking. "I know exactly who they both are."

Ronnie could have sworn she saw Richard's eyes turn dark.

"Why did you allow this group to come out here?" Richard asked, glancing from John to Ronnie.

Ronnie couldn't breathe. She suddenly wished for the presence of Mattie Olson. She had come across some fairly mean spirits since living in a ghost town. Nothing that felt as malevolent as this particular man.

What have we gotten ourselves into?

"I, we, figured they could help us find what we were looking for," Ronnie said. "They discovered a tunnel here and we've both been digging to see if . . ."

"Your property, though intriguing, is not part of the mystery." Richard brushed past Ronnie and kicked the screen door off its hinges. "You've made a terrible mistake by losing that journal, and you're both going to help find it." He gazed up at the stars and smiled. But it wasn't a warm expression. "I want the girl named Lorelei. I don't care how you do it. Get her to me." He turned and stood within inches of Ronnie's face. "Alone."

Ronnie wondered how he knew Lorelei, and how she would be able to get Lorelei to Vulture City without Ian or the rest of the team.

"I can give you their information," Ronnie said.

"No." He responded in a sharp tone. "Get her here. I'll do the rest." He walked back down the rock covered hill quickly and effortlessly in the pitch darkness.

"I think we'd better do this" John said. "Because I don't want to see what will happen if we fail again."

Chapter 22

Twenty-foot-tall desert fan palms graciously bent over a lake in the Hassayampa River Preserve outside of Wickenburg, Arizona. Two ring-necked ducks, black with a brown ring around the neck, floated by within twenty feet of Lorelei. They occasionally dipped their heads below the surface. Blue sky and white clouds were reflected in the placid water and a couple of red-eared sliders sunned themselves on a log nearby.

Amid all this tranquility, she hoped to find some answers inside the diary Mattie had left at her feet. Did the caretaker herself have a connection with the ancient ones? Did they lead Mattie to the Caves of the Watchers through her dreams?

A slight breeze blew the book open to an entry dated November 30, 1955:

My visions have not stopped. In fact, they have increased in frequency. I believe they are trying to tell me there is so much more here.

Since I've been going to the Caves of the Watchers, spirit activity at old Vulture City has increased ten-fold. I'm encountering shadows, mists, sounds and smells on a daily basis, and so are the visitors. Some of these experiences aren't so welcoming. One unfortunate young woman found herself being dragged into the bunkhouse. Then she heard what sounded like doors slamming, though there are no doors on the structure.

Is there something about my visits to the caverns? Or are the entities on my property anxious in anticipation of something to come?

Many of the following entries entered in pencil were illegible. Until another one scribbled in blue ink toward the end of the journal caught her attention.

I am terrified for my safety. The more of the mystery being uncovered, the more strange things are happening. I haven't told anyone of my discoveries. I don't think they want me to.

John and Ronnie hadn't mentioned the Caves of the Watchers or the passages near Vulture Mine. Did they know about Mattie Olson? Lorelei wanted to talk to the caretakers before she and Ian headed back to Cottonwood in a few hours.

She dialed John and Ronnie's cell phone number.

"Vulture Mine, this is Ronnie."

"Hi, this is Lorelei with the Arizona-Irish."

"Oh, hi," Ronnie said excitedly.

"Can I stop by before I leave town? I wanted to talk with you about one of the other caretakers that used to live there."

"Of course. We'll be here all day. Are you on your way now?"

"Sure. I should be there in half an hour."

"Can you give us until three o'clock?"

Lorelei heard what sounded like tapping on the other end of the line.

She glanced at her watch. It was 1:30 p.m. "Um, okay. See you then."

As she hung up, she realized Ronnie had sounded nervous. If they were supposed to be there all afternoon, why did she have to wait over an hour?

Driving through the old western town toward Vulture Mine Road an hour later, she felt apprehensive, though she wasn't sure why. She drove the last mile to the ghost town, pulled the car over and sat there. Her hands gripped the steering wheel tightly and her breath came in shallow gasps.

She jumped when her phone rang. Ian's number showed in the display.

"Hey, beautiful."

"Hi, honey." Lorelei instantly felt better hearing his voice.

"Is everything all right?"

Ian always knew when something wasn't right. "Yes. I'm almost to Vulture Mine to talk with Ronnie about Mattie's diary. I should be back to the hotel by four thirty so we can all have dinner together before we head home."

She pulled back onto the highway.

Ian didn't respond. He sighed. "Lore, you know how in tune we are to each others emotions. What's going on?"

"Have you talked with Paul?"

"Yes. And you're ignoring what you know I was about to ask. Please. Come back to the hotel and get me. We'll talk to them together."

"That's not necessary. I've got to go. See you shortly and I love you." She hung up.

She pulled into the dirt driveway and passed the row of dilapidated saloons and hotels. As she parked in the main lot by the gift shop, a black Mercedes peeled around the corner and sat directly behind her car. She glanced in the rearview mirror and saw a short, stout man in the drivers side and a taller gentleman in the passenger seat.

Grabbing her cell, she started to dial Ian's number. He had already texted her. I KNOW SOMETHING'S WRONG! PLS CALL!

Shit. Ian's vision at the arrow rock! This is what he saw.

A massive, burly man in his thirties with a receding hairline and prominent unibrow pounded on her window and motioned with his finger for her to climb out.

Ian called her. When she went to pick up, Mr. Unibrow pointed a gun at her while trying to open her locked door.

Why didn't I listen to my intuition back there? God, please don't let me die like this.

Ian texted her again. ON MY WAY TO VM! PLEASE BE OK.

Glass shards sliced her face as his pistol broke through her window. She jumped into the passenger seat to get away, but he had thrown open her door and grabbed her shirt from behind.

"No!" She screamed, kicking at him as she was dragged from the car. "Leave me alone." Lorelei tried desperately to pull away, but he picked her up effortlessly and shoved her into the back of the waiting black vehicle.

She turned her head to look through the rear window. John and Ronnie stood there watching while the car pulled away. Neither of them moved. The car she was in drove out of sight. The couple slowly turned and headed back into the gift shop.

Lorelei frantically looked for her cell phone, then realized it had been left in Ian's car along with her purse.

A voice boomed from the tall, dark-haired man in the passenger seat. "Hello again, Lorelei." Then he turned his head to face her with a nefarious smirk.

The second his dark eyes gazed into hers, fear and dread overwhelmed her.

"Come now. Don't look so shocked. You didn't think I'd let you get away with stripping my astral abilities and ruining my business?"

"Peter," she whispered. Nothing about the striking man before her resembled the person she had last seen at Peter and Emily's place in Flagstaff. His new look entailed black hair, dark eyes, more youthful looks and a malevolent personality.

"Pretty amazing transition, isn't it?" he asked. "Name's Richard now."

The journal lay in Peter's lap. The man who yanked her from the car must have grabbed it at the same time.

"The physical change isn't the only thing I've been working on," he continued. Peter turned back around to face the windshield and slid his sunglasses back on. "It's also interesting what a master of mind control can achieve. I know about your connection to the ancient ones. I have since the afternoon you and Ian came by to take Paul. But you don't deserve that bond with such a powerful race."

Peter did not speak. Yet his voice resounded loudly in her mind. "You are losing your link with them because you are weak-minded."

"Son of a bitch! You're the weak one." Lorelei kicked his seat in anger and frustration. "Abandoning Paul, having Alicia kidnapped and killed, and torturing me through your telepathy and astral abilities. Those are the actions of a coward!"

He sat completely still in the passenger seat with his eyes closed, staring straight ahead.

A sudden, excruciating pain ripped through her head. It felt like a knife had stabbed her and was being twisted inside her brain. She screamed out loud and threw herself down sideways on the back seat. Writhing in agony, she pressed in on both sides of her head with her hands.

The torture subsided after a minute. She slowly sat up.

For the first time, Mr. Unibrow spoke. It was a very deep voice that sent chills down her spine. "If you think that was bad, you don't want to know what he can really do."

Lorelei noticed they were heading south. No traffic came from the other direction. No one she could flag down.

Ian, please hear me. I need you.

"He can't hear you." Peter's tone taunted her.

She glared at him through his leather seat. He had picked up the diary and started to flip through.

Whether from the searing pain Peter had deliberately caused, or from another mind spell, Lorelei became exhausted. She struggled to keep her eyes open but couldn't.

As her head fell against the window, she thought she saw a woman with long grey hair sitting next to her. And she was stroking a cat.

Chapter 23

The headache hit with a vehemence Ian had never experienced. He yelled aloud and bent his head to his lap with the palms of his hands against his forehead. The pain was more than he could handle.

"Ian." Shannon placed her hand on his shoulder. She started to pull her jeep off the side of the road.

"No." He gritted his teeth in agony. "We need to find Lorelei." Ian could only see bright flashes of light when he opened his eyes. He threw his head back against the car seat, but it didn't alleviate the agony. "This is something she's going through."

Shannon continued to watch him closely as they raced toward Vulture Mine. "Does she have migraines?"

"No." Ian sighed in relief as the pain subsided. "Oh god, Shannon, I think she's being tortured." His voiced started to crack. "I could tell something was off when I talked to her last. Her intuition screamed at her to not go back there, yet she did anyway. I saw her being abducted through my vision at that strange rock. I still let her go off alone."

"Don't blame yourself. You know how she is. She has so much vested in this mystery with the ancient ones and now with Mattie Olson. I don't think she wanted to leave without discovering more about Mattie's connection to their race and the Caves of the Watchers."

Shannon pulled up to the dirt road leading to the ghost town. The iron gates were closed. She placed a gentle hand on his shoulder. "We'll find her. I promise. You know the ancients wouldn't let anything happen to her."

Ian jumped out of the car, squeezed his body under the iron gate and ran full force toward the parking lot.

Shannon ran behind him. "Ian, wait!"

He didn't want to wait. He wanted to see if he could save Lorelei. Ian came to a sudden stop as he arrived at the dirt parking lot.

Bending over to catch his breath, he noticed there were no cars.

"When you talked to Lore on the phone," Shannon took a few seconds to catch her breath, "did she mention if she was here?"

Ian shook his head. "She said she was almost here. I assumed within a few minutes." He walked quickly toward the gift shop.

"I didn't see your Lexus off the road," Shannon said. "Maybe it's on the property somewhere."

The CLOSED sign hung on the door to the visitor center and gift shop.

Ian peered inside. "I don't see anyone. Damn it." He pounded his fist hard against the wood.

Shannon approached the trailer cautiously, fifty feet away, where John and Ronnie lived. She removed her Glock from the holster and knocked loudly on the door. No one answered.

"FBI, this is Shannon." She kicked the door in, extending her arms and holding the gun tightly in her hands.

"John and Ronnie are in on it. I just know it," Ian said. "And I doubt either one of them are here right now." He ran into the trailer and didn't see Lorelei. Two empty coffee mugs sat next to the kitchen sink.

"I think you're right." Shannon indicated the master bedroom with clothes pulled out from drawers and strewn over the bed. Extra suitcases were on the floor.

Ian went outside, glanced around anxiously and headed to the dirt road leading to the assay office, bunkhouse and mess hall.

"We need to stay together," Shannon said. "You aren't armed and I don't need you to go off and get injured, or worse. If someone was waiting for Lore, they could still be here."

Ian noticed an object glinting in the parking lot. "Over here." He pulled Shannon's arm, almost dragging her ten feet to the spot.

Shattered glass was everywhere. He collapsed on the ground, his knees on the shards. He picked up the object and held it tightly in his right hand.

His voice choked. "Baby, what happened to you?"

"Ian, what did you find?"

He opened his palm to reveal Lorelei's emerald pendant. "She had this on this morning. She always has this on."

Shannon's eyes closed for a second. Then she made a call on her BlackBerry. "Adam, Shannon. We've got a possible kidnapping at Vulture Mine."

Shannon's voice cracked while she talked to the special agent in charge. "Looks like something happened to Lorelei. I need a team of investigators out here pronto."

Ian stood up slowly and did a three sixty turn. Is she here? Could they be hiding her in the mining tunnels? Or has she been taken somewhere else?

Shannon placed her hands on his shoulders. "I don't know about you, but my intuition's telling me we'll find her. She's the strongest woman I've ever met. That includes any person I work with in law enforcement."

Tears began to roll down his face and he threw his arms around her. He sobbed uncontrollably, and could feel Shannon quaking as he held onto her.

"I can't lose her."

Shannon pulled away. "Don't think like that. When we do find her, promise me you'll take her out of this state and away from all of this madness. You both need to forget about the ancient ones, about her abilities, about everything she's been through."

She wiped his tears away with her fingers. "Now let's go find your car."

"What do you mean?" he asked.

"Consider the broken glass in this spot, her necklace." Shannon pointed to a pattern on the ground. "And these tracks, which pattern happens to look like the tires on your Lexus, head down that jeep road toward the old schoolhouse. There are tracks of a different vehicle parked right behind yours." Shannon observed the tread impression on the ground. "However, that particular car turned north to exit Vulture Mine."

"Shit, she was ambushed," Ian said. "I wonder if the caretakers took her."

"Not sure what their motive would be. They're probably working with someone."

Ian and Shannon followed the tire prints along the Jeep trail and past the schoolhouse, swing set and slide.

Memories came flooding back of the time Ian had worked alone with Lorelei at the old schoolhouse. Her beautiful face and porcelain skin were reflected in the moonlight, and her smile made him realize how much he needed her.

He couldn't think of that for too long, or he would miss her so much he wouldn't be able to focus. He pushed thoughts of what she might be going through out of his mind. He wouldn't make it through this if he let his emotions overcome him. She might not either.

The tracks of his Lexus went for almost a mile and then veered off into an area with little vegetation. Shannon stood on the edge of a deep arroyo where the pattern ended. Ian's car rested front-end down on top of a clump of creosote.

Rage overwhelmed him. Lorelei had been abducted and his car carelessly dumped in a dry wash.

"Shannon, what if she's still in the car?" Evidence suggested she had been taken, but he had to make sure she wasn't lying there injured. He slid down the steep incline. Tripping over a large rock, Ian grabbed onto a mesquite tree to get his balance and jumped to the bottom. He ran to the car and looked inside. Lorelei's cell phone was next to the drivers seat. Her purse was in the passenger side. Items had spilled out as if it had fallen over, or knocked over in a struggle.

Shannon gently tugged on his arm to get him away from the vehicle. "Ian, maybe I should take you back to the hotel. Dale said he would give you a ride to Phoenix."

Spots of blood on the passenger seat put him in a state of panic. "I'm not going anywhere." Ian turned to face Shannon. He shook her arms vehemently. "She's been hurt. I have to stay here and help. I need to do what I can to get her back."

"Ian, this is a crime scene. You can't touch anything and it's getting dark. I'm taking you back to town. Maybe Brandon or Dale can stay in town and keep you company." Shannon turned Ian to face her. "I promise I'll let you know if we find anything out."

He let out a heavy sigh. She was right. He wouldn't be able to help.

Shannon placed her arm inside his and they walked back to her car. Her phone rang and she glanced at Ian. "Hey, Joe. Can you get back to Arizona anytime soon? Lore's been kidnapped and I'm dealing with a crime scene. Ian can use your support."

Ian could hear Joe's reaction on the other end of the phone. She started to hand the phone to him, but he didn't want to talk about it. "I, I can't. Tell him I'll see him when he gets back." He walked quickly ahead to her Jeep.

He placed his forehead on the top of her vehicle. Dear God, please let her be all right. Let me feel her in my arms again.

A peculiar vibration passed through his fist. He had forgotten he still held her pentagram pendant.

Opening his hand slowly, Ian saw the emerald glowing; first brightly, then ebbing in power. Warmth flooded throughout his body as the necklace took on a life of its own.

Shannon got into her Jeep with Ian.

"They came through for her." Ian stared intently at the pewter pendant. A slight smile crossed his face.

"What are you talking about?" Shannon started the car and drove onto the highway.

He didn't hear her question. "Lore thought they abandoned her. But they've never left her side."

Chapter 24

Lorelei woke up to coyotes howling. They sounded close. The building creaked and moaned as the wind whipped through. The biting cold made her shiver uncontrollably. She tried to rub her arms but couldn't. Her hands had been bound together. She pulled her knees up to her chest for warmth and comfort, and realized they had cuffed those also.

"You bastard!" she yelled.

Another coyote howled in response.

After a few minutes her eyes adjusted to the pitch blackness. There were rakes, shovels, an old tractor, and hay, which lay sparsely across the floor of an old barn. Moonlight peered into primitive boards and the whole structure leaned precariously to the right.

Lorelei recalled feeling exhausted as she rode in the back seat of her captor's vehicle.

Where the hell am I now? And where is Peter?

She looked around for a way out and saw the twenty-foot tall double doors. Pulling her feet in and sliding her back against the wall to stand up, she jumped across the dusty floorboards, grabbed onto the push bar of a lawnmower, and shoved it against the wood. The doors wouldn't move.

Another strong wind blew and she looked for something to keep her warm. She glanced over to the other side of the barn and noticed a blanket. She hopped toward it and reached down to grab it with both bound hands. She didn't know how she could throw it over her shoulders.

She shook the blanket to make sure no scorpions or other insects were inside. Then gasped as bones and bone fragments spilled out.

Lorelei started to yell as loud as she could. "Hellooooo! Is anyone out there?" She peered through a gap in the wall, but couldn't see anything, or anyone, around.

"Hello. Please, I need help." After a few seconds of silence, she started to cry. She had no idea where she was. Even if she could communicate with Ian telepathically, she wouldn't know how to tell him to find her.

She used the old lawnmower to guide her to the other side of the structure and looked through a two-inch crack. There was nothing but desert brush and a great horned owl that perched atop a twenty foot tall saguaro.

She supported herself on the wall and slid back down on the ground. Lorelei wondered what Peter was after. Could this be revenge?

No, this is more than that. He must be seeking something. Perhaps the Caves of the Watchers. He mentioned the ancient ones in the car. Is it possible that he and Emily have a bond with them as well?

She sat on a pile of hay and slid the blanket over her legs. She forced herself to slow her breathing. Closing her eyes, she went to touch her pendant as a tool to communicate with Ian. It wasn't on her neck.

She used the next best thing; the matching ring Ian had given her at the Wupatki ruin.

Ian, I hope you can hear me. I'm all right, but I don't know where I am. Peter has taken me south of Vulture Mine. He used mind control to put me to sleep. All I know is I'm still in the desert in an old barn. At least for now. I'm sorry I didn't listen. I miss you so much.

Lorelei sat up suddenly when something big hit the other side of the structure.

She could make out movement through the cracks. The shape didn't appear human-like. Glancing over at the shovels and rakes, she realized she wouldn't be able to use them as a weapon if needed. She was helpless.

Her heart racing, Lorelei stared at the spot she had seen the thing. She screamed as another hard thump hit against the barn. This time, only five feet away.

She quickly scooted on her butt away from the wall. "Peter, is that you?" she yelled. "Is this your way of getting back at me?"

Snarling, growling and heavy breathing emanated from the other side. She couldn't stop trembling, from fear and from the cold night air. She wondered if this could be another mind control trap. Was Peter making her think there was something out there? Or did he have the ability to shapeshift?

Footsteps circled the structure. She was being stalked.

"I know it's you Peter! Showing off your talents?"

The terrifying animal noises didn't stop. A four foot tall shadow prowled next to the barn, occasionally blocking out the moonlight coming through the slats.

"How long are they going to leave me in here?" she whispered, pulling the blanket up with her cuffed hands.

She imagined Ian's arms around her, his mystical blue-grey eyes gazing into hers to ease her emotional turmoil and headaches. She smiled thinking of his embrace and soft kisses on her face and lips.

A few minutes later, the threatening sounds ceased.

Glancing over at the pile of bones, Lorelei noticed splinters that could be used to possibly release her from the handcuffs. If Peter was still reading her mind, he would know what she was up to. She had to work fast.

Using her legs as leverage, she slid over on her butt and found a three-inch sliver of bone. She hoped the makeshift pick wouldn't break.

Her fingers and hands trembled from the cold. She couldn't maneuver the shard with her bound wrists. "Damn it!"

She glanced up at the gaps between the panels of wood and considered body slamming her way out. If she could escape, she wouldn't get far.

Tears rolled down her face. She bent her knees up to her chest and threw her head down.

"Mom, if you're listening, please give me the strength to get through this."

Within seconds, Lorelei detected the scent of lavender. Her mother's favorite perfume.

She glimpsed around the barn and felt a presence directly behind her.

"Mom, is it really you?" Lorelei sniffled and wiped her tears away with the back of her hand. The spirit gently stroked her hair and face.

"She can't help you," the voice responded. The female whisper transformed into low grumbling that echoed throughout the room. "No one can."

"Peter, you bastard! Leave me alone."

Intuition told her he wanted to wear her down by making her

insane with fear, exhaustion and uncertainty.

"Still afraid of me, aren't you? Is that why you can't face me? It's not going to work. You won't break me."

Lorelei lay down on the hay, dust and debris. She realized she had no other choice than to try out of body travel. She had to figure out her location.

She thought of Ian's soft wavy hair, handsome face, striking eyes and amazing arms, and smiled. Forcing herself to breathe deeply, she imagined her soul separating from her body. This time it did.

As she rose into the night sky, she noticed the barn sat at least five miles in on a winding dirt road. Shotgun shells, beer cans and other trash littered the clearing in front of the structure. There was no sign of whatever had been lurking around the barn. She didn't see a place nearby where Peter could be hiding out.

They had left her in the middle of nowhere.

Straying north, Lorelei looked for a familiar landmark and saw the splayed-out, dilapidated buildings of Vulture Mine. But the ghost town wasn't deserted. Law enforcement looked for something, or someone, all over the property, guns drawn as they peeked cautiously into building after building. They were looking for her.

Shannon stood by a deep wash, staring down at a vehicle. She seemed to be wiping tears from her eyes.

Ian's car. The caretakers tried to get rid of it after I was taken.

From her vantage point one hundred feet above the desert, many people roamed Vulture City. She didn't see Ian. Lorelei floated down toward Shannon.

"I'm all right," Lorelei whispered. "For now."

Shannon turned her head quickly in response. "Lore?"

"It's my astral self. Peter abducted me from here. The caretakers are in on it."

"Can you tell me where you are?"

"I'm in a very old barn off of Vulture Mine Road. A winding dirt trail heading west goes way back, and I'm guessing it's about ten miles from here. They threw me into a black Mercedes."

"Have you visited Ian? Lore, he's miserable."

"Tell him I'm sorry and I love him so much. Find me, Shannon. Because I'm not sure what Peter has planned. I need to get back to my physical form. I don't want to leave my body unprotected with the games he's playing. And Peter has changed his looks."

Lorelei sensed something was happening at the barn. She

couldn't stay to reveal further details. "I've got to go now."

"Lore, wait."

When she arrived back at the barn, two men were hurriedly removing the steel bar she had seen across the two massive doors.

He knows.

She descended into her body just in time for Peter's henchmen to burst into her prison.

Chapter 25

"Agent Harris," Shannon yelled. "You're with me." She watched the young, five foot nine agent climb up from the dry wash where Ian's car had been disposed of. The temperature in the desert at night was fifty-five degrees and dropping. The chilling breeze made it feel much colder.

Shannon was concerned about Lorelei. Peter was keeping her in a barn, subject to extreme winter temperatures without the proper attire.

"I received a tip about the victim," Shannon said. "She could be in a barn on a winding dirt road off of Vulture Mine Road."

"There are all sorts of dirt roads in this area." Agent Harris looked at Shannon as if she were asking to pinpoint a needle in a haystack. But that's exactly what they needed to do.

"She might be within a ten mile perimeter south of here. The dirt road is to the west."

She didn't want to reveal how she got the tip, especially to a young rookie.

Shannon and Agent Harris got into her Jeep and she pulled out from the parking lot.

She was nearly to the exit when she saw something emerge among the brush and cactus. Shannon gasped and slammed on the brakes. A man riding a horse materialized out of nowhere within thirty feet of the entrance to Vulture City. The animal trotted in front her vehicle, and then the rider pulled back on the reigns to stop.

Harris gripped the dashboard and Shannon held onto the steering wheel tightly. The apparition, highlighted by her headlights, sat atop his translucent horse and gazed at them intently; an intimidating character in a long black coat and matching vest, red scarf and black cowboy hat. After thirty seconds, he removed his gun from his holster. Then a loud cracking sound cut through the air and a bullet breezed between Shannon and Agent Harris.

Harris' eyes were wide with fright and his jaw had nearly dropped to the floor.

The rider and horse stopped in front of the archaic two-story saloon. The cowboy jumped off his stallion and hitched the animal to a rotting post. The man sauntered through the swinging doors into the ramshackle bar. Then the equine faded from sight.

Bent forward, Agent Harris gazed at something no longer there.

"Are you all right?" Shannon asked. "I need your full attention to help find my friend."

"Y, yes," he stuttered. "Sorry. That was unbelievable. I've always been a skeptic. Yet I can't explain what happened."

"I always had an explanation for everything," she said. "Until I became a paranormal investigator and started handling supernatural cases." Shannon drove down the highway at seventy miles per hour. "This woman we're trying to save is more important than most of us can imagine because of her abilities."

"Isn't she special to you? I know you've been through a lot together."

Shannon swallowed her tears. She couldn't discuss it without breaking down.

Her BlackBerry buzzed and she glanced down to see a text from Joe.

I'M HERE, BABE.

She hit the button for Joe's cell number. He picked up immediately, but she didn't give him a chance to respond. "What does 'I'm here' mean? In Wickenburg, at Vulture Mine, at the hotel with Ian? Why do you have to be so damn vague?"

She meant to tell him she missed him.

Harris fidgeted in his seat and tried to ignore her outburst by staring out the window.

Great, Shannon. Let your co-workers think you're an emotional wreck.

"We're going to find her," Joe said. "I'll see you at Vulture Mine when you return."

Shannon placed her cell phone in the cup holder next to her. "We're coming up on eight miles." She slowed her speed to thirty miles per hour. "Watch for any dirt roads heading west."

Intuition told her it would be too late. Peter's telepathic abilities surpassed anyone Joe and Ian had heard of. He would know what Lorelei had done and move her. Or worse.

She had come upon mile eleven and still no dirt road.

"Are you sure we're in the right vicinity?" Harris asked.

"Yes. Lore, I mean my tip, might be off by a few miles."

The agent had caught her verbal misstep. He stared at her in confusion.

"Right there." She yelled and made a hard right turn onto a narrow dirt road. "There's supposed to be a barn, if this is the right trail."

The Jeep hit a bump in the road. Shannon and Agent Harris went airborne and their heads hit the roof. It didn't slow her down. Wheels crunched against dirt and rocks pinged the underside and outside of the jeep while she attempted to find Lorelei's hiding place. The thick cloud of dust in front of the windshield settled and her headlights spotlighted two coyotes walking across their path. She quickly turned the steering wheel to the right, placing the vehicle in a clearing.

"The barn," Harris said.

She glanced over to see a structure with large painted red doors leaning to the right.

They jumped out of her car and ran twenty feet toward the building.

Positioning herself at the far door with her gun drawn, Shannon opened the door inward, hearing it creak in the wind.

Shannon entered first, both arms outstretched with the gun held tightly in her hands. Brooms, rakes and shovels rested against decrepit boards. A thin layer of hay covered the ground and pallets ten feet high were stacked in the corner.

She waited for ten seconds then nodded to Harris to enter.

Shannon smelled honeysuckle. Lorelei's scent. She followed the smell to a blanket lying on the ground. Long blonde hairs had stuck to the fabric.

Agent Harris stared at the Southwestern blanket with white fringes. "Uh, you might want to move a few feet in the other direction."

"What? I found evidence."

"It's also proof Lore wasn't the only one in here." Harris used his flashlight to reveal a large tarantula.

Shannon stood up quickly and jumped a few feet back. "Jesus. I hate those damn things. I swear, they follow me wherever I go."

Harris placed his hand over his mouth, trying not to laugh.

"So the rumor is true."

Shannon ignored his comment and walked toward a pile of bones. She placed a glove on and gently picked up what looked like a finger bone. "What, or who, has been in here?" She placed some residue and other fragments inside a small plastic bag.

"Agent, contact a few investigators from the evidence response team stationed at Vulture City."

While he walked out to her car to access the radio, Shannon noticed drag marks.

"Stop," she yelled to Agent Harris. He was about to step into the section of dirt and hay where her eyes were focused.

Harris glanced up at Shannon. "Those look like..."

"I know exactly what they are," she snapped. She sighed. "I'm sorry." She knelt down and stared at the two lines running parallel."

"Heel marks," he said. "I wonder why she was moved. It's like whoever abducted her knew we were tipped off."

She could feel Harris watching her.

Peter, you bastard. When I find you, I can guarantee you won't get away again.

"That's not all." Shannon gazed at a set of footprints heading backward toward the doors. "We might have proof of our suspect. Or one of them at least."

"I did see a fresh set of tire tracks going back to the highway," Harris said. "I'll have evidence response evaluate those as well."

"There could be people living in the immediate vicinity." Shannon looked up at him. "I did see a private property sign on the opposite side of the road only a mile back."

"No worries," Harris said. "I'll see if I can locate a residence around here. Maybe there is a potential hideaway or a neighbor that might have seen something."

Harris got on his cell phone to contact one of the evidence response team members while Shannon walked around the barn. She stopped when she saw fresh markings on the ground—four parallel lines, five inches long.

"What the hell is capable of leaving claw marks like that." She shuddered, wondering what else Lorelei had encountered while being held captive here.

"There's another crime scene tech heading out here," Harris said. He stared over Shannon's shoulder. "Jesus, I didn't think Arizona had animals capable of leaving such tracks."

"Wolves and bears maybe," Shannon said. "But there aren't any in this part of the state."

Shannon followed Harris' gaze. The same scratches were on the side of the building. Shannon ran her finger over the claw marks, which went all the way through the wood. She could clearly see inside the antiquated structure.

"Jesus," Harris whispered. "Those damn scratches are a quarter inch across."

Shannon turned her head away so he couldn't see her eyes welling up. "Do what you can to help find her." She stood up, walked to her vehicle and drove away from the barn.

When Shannon returned to Vulture Mine, Joe's truck was parked in front of the saloon where she had seen the apparition of the cowboy.

Joe Luna, Native American healer and shaman, stepped out of his truck. His lean, six foot frame, long braided hair, and dark, sexy good looks made her realize just how much she missed him.

She drove past the gate and parked behind him. He approached her Jeep and waited for her to get out.

Quickly putting the car in park, Shannon removed the keys and threw open the door. Joe gently pulled her out of the seat and into his arms. "I missed you," he whispered in her ear.

Her emotions had been pent up all day because she was with Ian, Agent Harris, or other investigators. Joe's arms encouraged her to release her feelings.

She let out a deep sob and the tears started to fall. She quaked within his strong hold, crying until she couldn't breathe.

"Ssshhhh. Calm down." He held her tighter. Then he pulled away and kissed her gently on the lips.

"They dragged her from the barn. They knew she contacted me by astral travel. Lore had been handcuffed. I could tell by drag marks on the ground." She gazed into his eyes. "Peter's torturing her with excruciating headaches and extreme elements. Not to mention the horrible claw marks we found that went right through the side of the barn." She rubbed her arms with her hands, gazing at the hitching post where the spirit horse had been tied.

"I don't think they are going to let anything happen to her." Joe stroked her face.

"What are you talking about?" Shannon yelled. "Didn't you hear what I just said?"

"No." Joe held her hands in his. "Not her abductors, babe. I meant the ancient ones."

"Then why did they let her get kidnapped?"

"Because she's seeking the same answers Peter is. I'm pretty sure he knew about the ancient ones from the second he met Lore, possibly before. He obviously feels she can provide insight into their culture and their treasures. Maybe this is how Lore is supposed to find out more about not only this mysterious race, but herself."

"What about revenge?" Shannon asked. "I mean, she did strip his astral abilities."

"I'm sure that's part of it." Joe held her hand while they walked over to join the crime scene investigators and FBI agents. "I'm surprised he's still in the area considering he was last seen in Wickenburg. There are known cults specializing in black magic here, so maybe he's been sharpening his abilities."

"Lore mentioned he's changed his looks and identity, which is why he's gone undetected. I still think it's a rather stupid move on Peter's part to stick around and then kidnap Lore. He knows how strong her talents are."

Joe waved to the group of investigators. "That's why he's trying to weaken her defenses by playing mind games. Giving her physical pain through mind control, leaving her alone out in the middle of nowhere, and who knows what else."

"I don't understand why he hasn't made his move earlier," Shannon said.

"You all walked into Peter's territory by coming back to the ghost town. He simply took the opportunity."

Shannon stopped and looked at Joe. "Maybe she couldn't listen to her intuition about coming back here to interview John and Ronnie." Shannon shivered as a cold wind blew by. "Because Peter made it impossible to."

Chapter 26

"Peter." Ian whispered to Shannon and Joe. "How could I not have known?" It was 1:00 a.m. Ian stared at Lorelei's short-sleeved nightshirt lying on the king-sized bed, and opened suitcase in their hotel room.

"I think you should get out of here for awhile," Joe said. "Have you eaten anything?"

Ian nodded his head. "I can't. Can't eat or sleep." He got up and paced the small room with the mauve carpet, warm beige walls and matching modern block-style comforters.

He looked at Shannon. "Shouldn't you be out looking for her? After all, Peter and Emily have abandoned Paul, murdered Alicia Atwell, have somehow managed to escape the watch of the FBI, and now have my fucking girlfriend!"

He stood glowering at Shannon. Ian felt physically ill thinking of Lorelei suffering in the cold, alone in an old barn and being tortured by Emily's vindictive husband. Blind fury raced through his veins. He picked up a vase of fake flowers and threw them into the wall above the bed.

Shannon flinched.

When he looked in her eyes, Ian saw sadness, shock and frustration. Tears rolled down her cheeks.

Joe came and placed his arm around her shoulder.

Clenching his fists, Ian said, "You'd better find that monster first, because if I do, he'll be dead."

Thirty seconds later, a muffled voice emanated through the thin walls. "What the hell was that?"

"Sorry," Joe yelled. "We have an emergency situation over here. It won't happen again."

Brandon had gradually stepped backwards and stood up against the door.

Ian huffed and sat down on the edge of the bed, placing his

hands on the back of his head with his elbows on his knees. He had never felt so helpless.

"My babysitter said she would keep Paul until Tuesday, but if we can't find Lore by then." His voice cracked as he glanced up at Shannon and Joe. "I can't handle the idea of leaving here without her. Intuition's telling me I won't have a choice."

Joe sat next to Ian. "Even if that does happen, Shannon, I, and a whole team of agents and investigators are out there searching for Lore. Think about everything that's occurred in the past year between the first case in Dragoon, Arizona, and now. The universe pulling the two of you together and Lore's connection to this amazing race of individuals. Trust me man, she's on this earth for a reason. And she's not going to be destroyed that easily."

"I wish I could have been at Vulture Mine when Lore showed up in her astral form," Ian said. "To hear her voice, feel her presence around me again."

"I'm sure she looked for you. It's a good thing you weren't there. It would have made all this much harder," Joe said.

"What about the Caves of the Watchers?" Brandon asked.

"There were artifacts down there." Shannon looked at Joe. "In one of the four chambers. Adam sent a special team to the caves to see if Peter or his minions have been down there."

Ian grabbed his wallet. "Let's go check it out." He slipped his jacket on. "I'm not going to stay here and do nothing. Maybe they took her back there."

No one moved.

"Damn it, Shannon," he yelled. "I've been in worse situations. I can handle myself. This is my future wife we're talking about."

"Oh, Ian." Shannon wrapped her arms around his shoulders and gave him a big hug. "You proposed."

"No." A tear rolled down Ian's right cheek. "I had planned on asking her to marry me tonight after we returned to Cottonwood." He pulled a small jewelry box from his jacket. He couldn't open it, fearing he would break down. Or prevent her return.

"Brandon, can you hang around to keep Ian company?" Joe asked.

"Sure."

Shannon's BlackBerry rang. "Hey, Harris."

Her face transformed from tired to shocked. "Great job finding them. I'll be right there." Shannon was halfway out the door.

"One of the agents found the caretakers. They never left the property. Apparently, they gathered some camping equipment and supplies and staked out underground. They were in the mining tunnels where the blacksmith shop is."

Ian ran out the door after her. "I'm coming with you."

Shannon sighed. "I know you're anxious to find Lorelei. We all are. But Ronnie and John probably won't talk with you glaring and threatening them. Not to mention you'll be interfering in an official investigation. I need you to stay here with Brandon."

"Babe, I'll stay here," Joe said. "I'll talk with you as soon as you find something out." He kissed her on the lips. "See you later."

"Make sure he gets something to eat and tries to get some sleep," she whispered, shutting the door behind her.

Brandon sat next to Ian. "There is a twenty-four hour café outside town."

Ian lifted the chain of Lorelei's pewter pendant away from his neck, holding it tightly.

Ian pleaded with Joe. "Isn't there something we can do? I can't sit in a fucking restaurant, or do anything else for that matter, while my girlfriend's in the company of a lunatic. Joe, that brief, yet torturous headache I experienced is probably just a hint of what he's putting her through."

Joe sighed, threw up his hands and removed his car keys from his back pocket. "We could drive back down Vulture Mine Road past the ghost town. The investigators aren't going to want us around at the barn where Peter hid Lorelei, but we can check things out on the main highway."

Ian hurriedly threw his flashlight, a first aid kit, a few bottles of water and a GPS device and his gun into his backpack. "We need to check out those chambers again. Maybe that's where he took her."

He saw Joe and Brandon exchange a cautious glance.

"Whoa there, my friend," Joe said. "I mentioned checking out the road. Besides, Shannon just mentioned those caves are FBI territory right now."

Joe approached Ian and placed both hands on his shoulders. "You're not going to help Lorelei by getting injured out in the middle of nowhere, especially considering the state you're in. I know she wouldn't want you to risk your life."

Ian sighed. A grievous respiration of defeat. "Okay. You win. Maybe I'll be able to get a sense of where she's at when we drive around out there." He glanced up to see a woman with auburn hair to her mid-back walk by the window. Then she stopped and stared through the closed curtains.

He recognized her high cheekbones and cat-like eyes.

"Emily," he yelled. "He made it across the room in three large strides and flung the hotel room door open, but she had already started down the corridor. Ian chased her past more rooms, an ice machine and the office. "Where is Lorelei? What are you going to do with her?"

Emily didn't look back. She jumped into the passenger seat of a black car, which peeled out of the parking lot.

Three of the guests peeked out their doors to see what happened. The manager of the hotel ran out of the office, glaring at Ian.

"That woman," Ian said breathlessly. "The one who got into the Mercedes. "Is she staying here?"

"What woman?" The tall, thin man stood in a navy robe. "And I want you all," he glanced back at Joe and Brandon, "to get the hell off of my property now. You've caused enough trouble. I've got other guests complaining."

"Come on," Joe yelled from his truck. "We're going to follow her."

Ian jumped in next to Joe, and Brandon got in the back seat. "I know that was Emily. I'd recognize her anywhere. But she changed her hair."

"Seems like they've both made some serious changes to their appearance," Joe said. "In order to avoid being detected by the law."

"Weird," Brandon said. "She gazed through the closed curtains as if she knew Ian was in the room."

Ian shivered remembering her steel gaze.

"The manager acted as if he hadn't seen her," Joe said. "Mind trick maybe, though we had no problem seeing her. I wonder if she was visiting someone, or if her and Peter are staying there. If so, that would be rather ironic." Joe sped up as the black vehicle accelerated along Highway 93. "Were you able to see who was driving?"

"No. Try to get closer." Ian held onto the dashboard. "Lore could be in there. We already know she was abducted in a vehicle like that."

Joe hit a single button on his phone. "Shannon, we're pursuing Emily in a black car heading south along Highway 93. She walked right by Ian's room and took off when he went after her. Then she jumped into a black Mercedes. You need to check with the guests to see if any of them knew her or Peter, and check with the hotel to see if she was a paying guest."

Ian squinted to determine movement inside the car or to see if he could spot Lorelei. His pulse raced and veins popped in response to the pressure he placed on his hands and arms while holding onto the dashboard.

While Joe pursued the vehicle, a yellow Hummer cut his truck off, blocking the view of the Mercedes. "Damn."

Joe swerved quickly into the left lane to pass.

The driver of the Hummer slammed on his brakes.

Ian and Brandon gasped. The Mercedes had vanished.

"Where the fuck did it go?" Ian yelled.

The vehicle Joe pursued had disappeared from view.

Ian noticed the Hummer still sat in the right lane, the driver's hands frozen to the steering wheel with his eyes wide open.

Chapter 27

Messy, dirty grey hair, dark circles under the eyes and an unkempt appearance added an air of desperation to Ronnie and John. They no longer seemed warm and caring. Shannon sensed something else other than guilt with the caretakers of Vulture Mine. Terror. The same level of emotion she had experienced while interviewing Peter's counterpart, Ray, regarding Alicia Atwell's murder. They all knew what the sorcerer was capable of and were terrified Peter would use his abilities on them to keep them from talking.

These two definitely knew who they were dealing with. It pissed Shannon off all the more that they would hand over Lorelei so willingly.

Shannon and Harris escorted the handcuffed caretakers down a gently sloping hill in the darkness from the dilapidated wooden headframe towering over the main shaft, where Ronnie and John had entered the mining passages. A six foot shadow leapt out in front of them and toward the blacksmith shop.

She could feel Ronnie tense while she held her by the arm. The woman's breath came in short bursts.

"I would think you'd be used to this sort of stuff by now," Shannon said nervously. Her flashlight darted among the desert brush and prickly pear. The light revealed stiff branches of a creosote. A rattlesnake lay underneath coiled around a rusty tin can. When the bush began to shake back and forth aggressively, the reptile's heart-shaped head lifted off the ground and it rattled its tail.

Ronnie and John glanced at each other, then at Shannon and Harris.

"P, probably an animal," Harris muttered. He seemed to tighten his grip on John's arm.

Another dark amoeba-like form, three feet wide and four feet tall glided out into the open, two inches above the ground. Stopping in the middle of the path, the enigmatic entity observed them while it morphed into a human; a figure with wavy red hair, wearing navy slacks, a white shirt and FBI jacket.

Jesus. What kind of ghost is this?

Ronnie stepped back quickly, pulling Shannon with her. Shannon didn't seem to notice. She was transfixed as the viscous blob that mimicked her changed back to its original shape.

"Have either of you seen this thing before?" Shannon whispered. Part of her feared speaking loudly might encourage it to attack. Whatever that might entail, she didn't want to know.

Neither answered her question. Ronnie's trembling added to Shannon's own trepidation. After living on the property for five years, these people had to have witnessed a lot of mysterious activity. So for this adventurous couple to be afraid made her wonder what they were dealing with.

Whether it was the intimidating thing in front of her, or Lorelei's abduction by a black arts magician, Shannon suddenly felt as if they were surrounded. Had Peter somehow stirred up ghostly activity? Or could the spirits of Vulture Mine be retaliating for what happened to Lorelei?

The miniature blob-like mass darkened, folding in on itself numerous times and rotating as it hovered. Thirty seconds later, the bizarre figure bounced off the ground and up into the night air where it vanished.

Harris grabbed John's arm and guided him quickly around the spot where the bizarre phantom that had mocked Shannon put on the morbid show.

"Something's very wrong here," Ronnie whispered, glancing around nervously. She dragged Shannon along in an effort to escape the ghostly activity.

"Damn right, something's wrong." Shannon shot her a dirty look. "You handed my best friend over to a very dangerous man. Maybe the spirits you've been living with for the past five years don't take a liking to traitors."

Harris' eyes caught Shannon's with a look that said, "What the hell have you gotten me into?"

She wondered if any of the other agents or crime scene investigators had experienced such phenomena. Vulture City hadn't seemed so threatening during their first investigation. So what the hell was stirring up all of this activity?

Shannon could see intermittent shadows and orbs following

them, darting between buildings and vanishing into arroyos while they walked back to the parking lot.

Twenty minutes later, Shannon and Harris sat them down in the gift shop.

Shannon knelt down in front of Ronnie. She knew the woman was weaker emotionally, whether from guilt, exhaustion or the recent ghostly activity, Shannon couldn't tell.

"You realize you're an accomplice to kidnapping."

Ronnie glanced away. Her hazel eyes focused on the glass counter. "Lorelei called me and said she wanted to come and talk to us. We didn't have anything to do with her abduction. We weren't even around when it happened."

Shannon looked from Ronnie to John. He stared at the rock and gem display outside the dusty window.

Shannon placed her face within inches of Ronnie's. "Then why were you hiding out underground?" She pointed to the two bedrolls and pillows the agents had found. "I'd say you were trying to get away."

Ronnie wouldn't look at Shannon. Instead, she gazed toward the front of the shop.

"We discovered Ian Healy's car. The Lexus Lorelei drove here before she disappeared."

Shannon stood up and moved over to face Ronnie again. "Come now, you're not going to blame this on one of your feisty ghost town spirits are you?" She grabbed onto both arms of the chair, boxing in her suspect. She closed in on her until she could feel Ronnie's breath; a sour smell that made her back away a foot. "We've found latent prints on the inside and outside of that vehicle. And this." Shannon held up a small plastic bag with two strands of long grey hairs. "Also called trace evidence, this sample will be run through mitochondrial DNA testing to verify who else was in the car besides Lorelei."

Ronnie's gaze detracted from Shannon to the see-through bag. Her eyes widened. John also stared at the strands Shannon held in her hand. He passed his wife a look that said, "I can't rely on you to do anything right."

Ronnie didn't notice. Her breathing increased the longer she looked at the evidence.

Come on, fess up woman.

"The Feds will go easier on you if you admit you both helped trap Lorelei Lanier so that Peter Taylor could take her." Shannon held up the plastic bag within inches of Ronnie. "Before we prove you drove their car into that arroyo."

Shannon saw the brief look of surprise between the couple. They only knew Peter as his alias, Richard Warburton. The same fear that flashed through Ray, Peter's accomplice in the kidnapping of Alicia Atwell, unmasked itself in Ronnie's expression. John and Ronnie knew what Peter was capable of. And they didn't want to find out what he might do to them if they confessed.

"Agent Harris, take Agent Jennings with you and transport these two to the Phoenix FBI office," Shannon said. "Along with this evidence." She handed him the hair sample.

After Harris left with the caretakers, Shannon received a call from Joe.

"You're not going to believe this," Joe said.

"Did you catch up with that black car Emily got into?"

"Not quite. The car was right in front of us until a Hummer got in between. I went to pass immediately, and the vehicle Emily got into disappeared."

"What? It must have sped ahead."

"No, babe. The car is gone. The driver of the Hummer was so shaken after it happened, he had to pull off the side of the road. He witnessed the same thing."

"Peter's a master at mind games. Maybe the car was still there, but no one could see it."

"If he could manage that trick, then that also explains how he and Emily have managed to stay hidden from the FBI for so long. I did continue driving down the highway to see if it would reappear, but it didn't."

"Were you able to tell if Lore was in the vehicle?"

"No, but the guy driving the Hummer thought he only saw the driver and the person in the back, which we know was Emily. But those windows were tinted very dark, not to mention this occurred at night."

"What about a license plate number?"

"DMV says the car's registered to a Steve Coleman. I wonder if that's who Emily met with at the hotel."

Shannon sighed and ran her hand through her thick, wavy hair. "Why isn't Lore drawing on the power of the ancient ones? We all witnessed that energy field surrounding her in Cottonwood."

"None of us have all the answers. Not even Lorelei. I've told

Ian, this was meant to happen. Whether Peter and Emily realize it or not, I think they've started in motion a series of events the universe intends to finish. I doubt it's going to work out in their favor."

"Does this 'series of events' you're referring to have anything to do with the spirit world going crazy? Because the situation at Vulture Mine has intensified ten-fold compared to our first investigation. Something really scary looking transformed into an exact image of me. Then Harris and I experienced threatening shadows and bizarre light shows while we were walking John and Ronnie back in cuffs. Not to mention that cowboy we saw riding a horse. He stopped right in front of my Jeep then fired his gun. Only I have no idea at what."

"Yeah, the members of the evidence response team seemed rather jumpy. I'm sure they encountered activity also." Joe became quiet for a few seconds. "Wait. You just said some sort of entity mutated into you?"

"Yeah, down to the last detail. Ronnie and John seemed pretty terrified. And they're used to spirit activity, though I guess nothing quite this extreme." Shannon stepped outside the gift shop. "I wonder if all this activity is because of Lore. Maybe the ghosts sense what she's going through."

"That might be part of it," Joe said. "However, I believe there's something much larger occurring."

Chapter 28

A brisk breeze and dark, threatening skies greeted Brandon at 7:00 a.m. as he went to check on Ian. He shivered, pulling his jacket tighter. Two similar sized, oval cloud formations right next to each other looked like eyes peering down.

"This is rather apropos considering the situation," he muttered.

He had trouble comprehending what he had seen the night before. The car Joe had been pursuing vanished. Brandon wondered if the Mercedes really did drop out of sight. Or if the people inside the car make them think it did.

He glanced five doors down toward the end of the hotel to see an exotic looking woman, 5'8 with long jet-black hair, walk out of her room. Brandon noticed her eyes immediately. Deep emerald irises caught his attention from twenty feet away. He stood, transfixed. His leather coat suddenly became heavy. The menacing sky no longer felt depressing. For a brief period, perhaps thirty seconds, Brandon couldn't remember where he was.

"Hi," the woman said as she approached him. "I heard a knock on my door a minute ago. I was on the phone."

He could only stand there in disbelief, staring helplessly at the unique beauty. Her green eyes gazed back with a sparkling intensity he had never seen.

Hard pounding distracted Brandon. He looked over his shoulder at Shannon and Joe who had knocked on a guest's door. No one answered.

Brandon waved and caught Shannon's attention. "It must have been my friends over there. They're with the FBI and are talking with anyone who might have seen suspicious activity last night."

Shannon came over, and glanced from the woman to Brandon. A slight smirk escaped her lips.

"Shannon Flynn."

"Nice to meet you. My name's Jacenda." She shook hands with Shannon, but kept glancing over at Brandon.

"Oh, s, sorry. I'm Brandon." He took her hand. When he went to release it, Jacenda held on. She licked her slightly parted lips then twisted strands of her hair nervously.

Shannon showed her badge to Jacenda. Brandon noticed her gaze diverted from Jacenda to Brandon and back to Jacenda in curiosity. "I'm with the FBI and I'm trying to find out if anyone staying at this hotel might have witnessed any unusual activity either last night or within the past few days."

"As a matter of fact, I heard strong knocking last night about 10:00 p.m. I looked out to see a petite woman with auburn hair." Jacenda pointed at Shannon. "Slightly darker than yours. Very well dressed with a fur-lined jacket, nice black boots."

Shannon showed Jacenda an 8 ½ by 11 photo of Emily. "Did she look anything like this?"

"Her hair was much darker, but that's definitely her."

"Did you see the other person or hear what they said?" Shannon asked.

"No. Whoever she talked to was in the room. Then she stepped inside and I couldn't hear anything other than occasional mumbling."

Shannon glanced down at a small notebook. "According to the manager, there wasn't a guest staying next to you." She looked up at Jacenda. "Are you sure it was right next door?"

She nodded her head.

Brandon wondered if the beautiful, sensuous woman before him could be involved. Her verdant eyes captured his, and in them he saw hurt and surprise.

"Did you happen to see a tall, striking gentleman with salt and pepper hair around here?"

"No. But I just checked in yesterday morning and I haven't been here that much. He could have been the person she visited next door."

"Have you seen a black Mercedes parked here?" Shannon pointed to the parking spaces in front of Jacenda's room.

She shook her head. "I've seen different vehicles coming and going, but none with that description."

Shannon handed a business card to the exotic beauty. "If you can think of anything else or see that woman again, please let us know right away."

Jacenda went to her room for a few seconds. She returned with her purse and pulled a card out. "Here's my information in case you need it. I'm from Phoenix but I'm passing through here on vacation."

Shannon glanced at her card, then over at Brandon.

"I think the two of you might have a lot in common. Brandon here is into computers also."

His hand shook as he took the card from Shannon. Jacenda was a network engineer with a large client of his.

"Joe and I can watch over Ian. Brandon, why don't you take Jacenda out to breakfast? I'm sure she'd like an idea of places to visit around here."

"That would be fantastic. I haven't had a chance to tour downtown Wickenburg yet." She looked at Brandon excitedly. "If you don't mind."

"Not at all." He thought his heart would explode from the intense beating.

"I just love historic places like Wickenburg," Jacenda said. "I guess that goes along with my hobby as a paranormal investigator."

Shannon gasped out loud, her mouth wide open.

Brandon had to grab onto the cement wall.

Did Lorelei have any idea how much I had in common with the woman from her vision? Or the circumstances under which we would meet?

Chapter 29

Lorelei woke up nauseous and groggy, lying on a couch in a smoke-filled room. The thumping in her head became a pounding explosion when she inhaled the smothering scent.

She remembered being dragged from the barn near Vulture Mine. Mr. Unibrow and another of Peter's minion's had been there when she returned to her physical form. Peter knew she had traveled out of body, and he didn't like it.

They had to have been hiding out close by in order to get to her that fast. Her astral experience lasted less than ten minutes.

After a few moments her eyes adjusted to her environment. The smoke emanated from a twenty-something man staring at her from the corner of the room. She struggled to sit up with her handcuffed wrists and ankles and went into a coughing fit from the swirling white cloud hanging in the air.

She caught her breath and then noticed a single windowpane had been pushed up six inches, but the huge cracks from the top to the bottom of the glass made her wonder if it was functional.

Is he a captive as well? Or is he here to guard me?

The right side of the young man's head had been shaved. His thick, dark mane hung to the left and the top had been tinted in royal blue.

Suddenly, the pane of glass shot up of its own accord, making her jump, but releasing much of the smoke. Her mysterious roommate didn't react in shock. He merely sat completely still underneath the window, looking at her.

The intensity of the sun's early morning rays poured through.

Lorelei stared at him, then at the open window above him. Is this person another of Peter's watchdogs? Could he be using such powers to intimidate me?

He glanced over at her. The side of his mouth erupted into a half grin and he shook his head from side to side.

She realized he had heard her thoughts.

The young man, who had a rather handsome face despite his uncharacteristic appearance, simply nodded his head in agreement.

Her guardian walked away from the window to open the door next to the torn green and yellow striped couch. He wore a black leather dog collar around his neck with silver spikes and a black t-shirt with an image of a band on the front.

She glanced quickly away when he caught her looking. She couldn't explain it, but she knew he was no threat, and not because of his effort to alleviate the uncomfortable stench.

Unlike the glares of Peter and Unibrow, this stranger merely gazed at her as if she were another stupid adult not capable of understanding who he was. He crushed his cigarette butt out on the cement floor. He didn't reach for another one in the pack in his back pocket.

"Who are you?" she asked. "Did you get kidnapped also?"

He didn't say a word. He pointed both index fingers to either side of his head.

His thoughts immediately intruded into hers. *You consider me to be rather unorthodox, but a true enigma is someone who can terrify the most talented dark arts magician known throughout the Southwest.* He grinned at her mischievously. *His wife is the only one, besides me, who is aware of how much you threaten him.*

Lorelei spoke out loud, forgetting his method of communication. "Did Emily tell…"

He merely stared at her.

Did Emily tell you this?

He continued to observe her as he spoke to her with his mind. *Hell no. That woman, like her husband, has no idea what you're truly capable of.*

Her mouth dropped. *So you're telling me you're able to read Peter's mind.*

His grin became much broader.

Lorelei spat out loud. "No more games. If you know so much, then what the hell is he planning on doing with me?"

His smile quickly faded. And he no longer spoke to her— telepathically or otherwise.

"Damn, you!" she yelled, throwing her head back against the wall.

Suddenly, tenderness and passion flowed through every fiber

of her being; like an angel had enclosed Lorelei in its arms.

"Don't give up," came Ian's voice. "I'm holding your necklace tightly in my hands. I hope this means I can hold you, at least in my thoughts. I had planned on asking you to marry me before..." There were a few seconds of silence. "But I figured if you can hear me, and if this keeps you going, that I should give it a try. I love you, baby. I know you're coming back to me. Because I don't think the ancient ones would have it any other way."

Lorelei pulled her knees up to her chest and closed her eyes to absorb the sensation as long as possible. The ephemeral feeling had subsided within seconds. The pain of being away from him was almost too much to handle.

"Shit. This is another mind trick. Peter's playing with my emotions."

Lorelei stared intently at the gothic man. For the first time, he spoke out loud.

His brown eyes focused intently on Lorelei's. His facial expression changed to one of concern. "No. It's really Ian."

"Who are you and why are you here? You aren't like Peter or anyone else he hangs out with."

He didn't respond. A single phrase echoed strongly in her mind. Dagon. My name is Dagon and you're no longer in Arizona.

She gasped aloud. "Where am I?" she yelled. "What the hell is going on?"

Dagon stood up and walked by her into the hallway without saying a word. Her headache vanished the second he passed by.

Her wrist and ankle cuffs unlocked themselves and fell to the floor.

She pulled them off hurriedly and ran after Dagon, down an empty hallway with yellowed, dusty walls and into the living room.

He was nowhere to be found.

"Dagon," she yelled. She looked out the large bay window at the front of the house.

Stunning, towering, reddish pinnacles rose into the sky. A dry wash led further into the canyon with its steep sandstone walls topped by more breathtaking formations.

"I'm in Utah," she whispered. "How did they get me here?"

She stepped cautiously out onto the partially collapsed wraparound porch. A barely discernable dirt road led to a stand of cottonwood trees. An old burgundy horse barn was surrounded by five acres of bright green grass.

She wandered down the makeshift dirt road overlooked by sandstone spires hundreds of feet tall. Lorelei listened but could hear no sounds of civilization. No cars, no cattle, and no people. Only the trickle of a nearby stream.

Completely alone. Yet somehow, not alone.

Chapter 30

Lifeless. The detailed, painted eyes that held such mysticism, color and vibrancy two days before held no emotion. Ian wondered if it was because of what happened to Lorelei.

"The Caves of the Watchers," Joe whispered.

Ian glanced at Joe. "Yes. That's the name Mattie called this place in her journal."

Joe paced slowly back and forth, staring at the painting. He glanced at Ian and then Brandon. "Did you notice anything unorthodox about this drawing when you were down here before?"

"Not at first," Ian said. "When Lore was trapped in one of the other chambers, she noticed them following her movements. They did seem more animated when we first came down here. Almost as if I were staring into actual human eyes that were telling a mystery."

Joe took his cowboy hat off and wiped his brow. "I had heard rumors this place was in Arizona." He looked over at Ian and Brandon. "I've also heard these caves were associated with other sacred sites in Utah, New Mexico and Colorado."

"There are four chambers," Brandon said. "Maybe they tie to each of the Four Corner states."

"Good thought," Ian said. "Though we haven't come across any clues to verify that. But we already know what sort of power this underground realm holds. Lore, Shannon and I were all caught up in what seemed to be a near death experience the next level down. The passage started spinning and brilliant light emanated from the direction of the cave."

Ian placed both hands on Joe's shoulders. "Peter and Emily are probably searching for these caves and maybe for other sites in the Four Corners. Peter knows of Lore's connection to the ancient ones, so they might think she knows much more than she does."

"The FBI couldn't find any evidence of Peter or Emily being down here," Joe said. "I believe they are aware of such a remarkable cave system, but I'm sure they're searching for the same answers as us. If they had discovered this site, I'm not sure they'd need Lore."

"Hey, man," Ian's voice choked. "I have to find something out." He sat on a large boulder and slumped over. "I'm probably going back to Phoenix tomorrow without her. I need to know there's hope."

Joe put his arm around Ian's shoulder, then quickly pulled out his cell phone from his pocket and dialed a number while watching the pictograph above him.

Ian gazed up at the light filtering through the hole in the cave's roof while Joe talked to one of his contacts. Please God, let her be all right. This may be happening for a reason, but take care of her for me.

Joe disconnected from his phone call. "I left a message for an FBI agent from Utah. He's the one that helped me infiltrate Vincent's cult. He has connections with the National Park Service and is familiar with many bizarre subterranean locations and ritualistic sites. Perhaps he can provide the tie-in between these series of caves and any other sacred places in the Four Corners."

Brandon handed a bottle of water to Ian. "What does the National Park Service have to do with any of this?"

"Because another rumor is that some of these sites may be located in national parks due to the beauty and spiritual surroundings. Consider Sunset Crater Wupatki National Monument where Peter and Emily were operating their pottery theft ring. However, the ancients had these places chosen long before the parks were created. "

Ian took in a deep breath, his eyes wide. "What if they've taken Lore out of Arizona? There are so many parks in the Four Corners region." He placed the palm of his hand on his forehead. "Bryce, Zion and Canyonlands are three in Utah alone."

"That is part of the reason I'm trying to talk to Alan. He might have an idea of how this place relates to the Four Corners. And what all this," Joe motioned his hand toward the ceiling and the cave, "really means."

Ian stood up and the underground chamber began to spin. The ray of light peeking into the cavern seemed to circle the room repeatedly.

Joe grabbed Ian's right arm and Brandon supported him on the left.

"We need to get you out of here," Joe said.

"No," Ian yelled. "We have to check the caves out again. Maybe Peter's hiding her here."

Joe sighed. He reached into his backpack, pulled out a sandwich and handed it to Ian. "First, you need to eat something. You're dizzy because you haven't taken care of yourself. Second, Shannon mentioned a team of agents were already here checking out the two caves you were in Saturday. I told you before, they didn't find proof Peter had been here."

Ian took a bite of the food Joe had given him, but he almost threw up smelling the potent tuna. He knew he needed to take care of himself for Paul, so he forced himself to take another bite. "What about the second level under this with the east and west caves?" Ian glanced around the chamber. "Lore found another passage with strange openings lining the walls, which could have been chambers where the ancients performed their astral feats."

"Ian, Shannon knows," Joe said. "She was with you, remember? She and another agent tried to enter the east/west tunnels. However, Shannon couldn't access that section of the cave system by standing on the symbol of the triangle within the circle. Those boulders were back and weren't budging. She's hired a helicopter with thermal imaging technology to scan a twenty square mile radius of Vulture Mine. If there's any sort of activity going on underground, or in the middle of the desert, Shannon will send a team to check it out."

"This has to be revenge," Ian said. "Peter found out we were here. Lore walked right into his trap by going back out to the ghost town. Have the caretakers confessed to entrapment?"

"No. It's a matter of waiting for the prints and hair samples from your car. But Shannon's hired me as a consultant to head to the Phoenix office and interrogate them."

Ian finished the sandwich and stood up slowly. "You definitely have a way of getting information out of people. When are you going to Phoenix?"

Joe hesitated, staring at Ian. "Today. I need to find out if Ronnie or John have any details on where Peter might be hiding her, and what he is up to. I think you and Brandon should go back to town as well. You know Shannon and I will contact you as soon as we hear anything."

Ian nodded and then started to climb up the boulders to exit the cave. Towering ochre-colored buttes with sandstone fingers carved into them dominated his vision. Tight knit formations of glowing red pinnacles rose hundreds of feet into the air. He waited, frozen on the last boulder, as the last of the images faded.

"Ian, are you all right?" Brandon asked.

He turned to face Joe and Brandon. "Bryce Canyon."

"What?" Joe climbed up on the rock next to Ian.

Ian gazed back down at the floor of the cave. "I never get visions that intense. Guys, I think Lore's trying to communicate with me," Ian said excitedly. "You mentioned sacred sites in the Four Corners and possibly within the National Park Service. Bryce is in Utah and it's a national park."

Joe and Brandon followed Ian out of the cave.

"Are you sure it was Bryce?" Joe scooted on his stomach out of the cave.

"Yes. I took Paul there a few years ago. That's not all. I saw a run down ranch at the end of a box canyon."

Joe and Brandon walked on either side of Ian, heading down the hill toward the narrow footpath.

"I'll find out from Alan if Bryce is one of the sites," Joe said. "I would think the park rangers there would know the location of the old house. Alan's also a pilot, so he could check out the area by plane."

"I can go back to town and get Paul, then head to Utah. Give me Alan's information and we can meet him."

"Whoa," Joe said. He grabbed Ian's arm and stopped him. "You don't need to be including your son in what could turn out to be a wild goose chase. I understand you feel like you need to be doing something to find her, but you could end up hindering the investigation and endangering yourself and Paul."

Ian looked up at the sky in frustration. "I know. I feel so fucking helpless."

"Of course, and that's normal. But Lorelei wouldn't want you to risk your own life to save hers."

Is Lore trying to communicate? Ian held the emerald charm tightly. Or is her necklace allowing me to see what she is?

Chapter 31

Ronnie shifted her weight in the chair, observing the two-way glass in anxiety. With her wrists handcuffed, she lifted her fingers to her mouth and bit her fingernails. Her heels tapped nervously on the ground.

"Are you ready?" Shannon asked Joe.

He nodded and walked inside the interrogation room.

The minute he sat down across from Ronnie, she relaxed, sitting back in her chair. She placed her arms calmly on the table and her legs ceased their restless movement.

Joe leaned forward and gazed into Ronnie's eyes. She sat up and leaned in closer to Joe while he started to question her.

"Your prints have been found on the car Lorelei Lanier was driving. This includes the outside drivers door and on the passenger seat where you rifled through her belongings. Your husband's fingerprints were discovered on the passenger side, so we know you both attempted to get rid of the evidence."

Shannon thought Joe would push Ronnie into asking for legal representation. If that occurred, they would have to discontinue questioning until an attorney arrived. That would take valuable time they didn't have.

"You and John had no idea who Richard Warburton really was?" Joe leaned back in his chair. "Did you?"

Ronnie didn't say a word. She shook her head slowly back and forth.

"What does Peter Taylor, or Richard as you know him, want with Lorelei?"

"I, I don't' know," Ronnie stuttered. "He told us to make sure we got Lorelei back to Vulture Mine on Sunday. But we didn't have to do a thing. She ended up contacting us about the original caretaker of the property."

Ronnie started wringing her hands.

"So you called Peter right away and let him know the trap set itself."

Ronnie stared at her lap. Then a tear rolled down her cheek. "I told her to give us an hour or so before she came. When I called Richard, or Peter, he was already on his way. Said he knew exactly when she would be there."

Ronnie wouldn't look back up at Joe. "Peter arrived as soon as Lorelei pulled into the parking lot. I think he somehow encouraged your friend to come back to Vulture City through mind control."

Shannon entered the room with the stark white walls, her fists clenched. "You stood there in front of the gift shop and watched while she was pulled from her car."

Ronnie glanced up at Shannon in surprise. "What? How could you know that?"

Shannon slammed her fist on the table. "Where did he take Lorelei? And what the hell was Peter doing in Wickenburg?"

The pounding of her fist startled Ronnie so much she glanced at them both. "I'm done talking."

Joe shot Shannon a dirty look. He had warned her to keep quiet no matter what. Now she understood why. He had somehow managed to get her to confess, but they still needed to know what Peter had planned. She had inadvertently ruined Joe's attempt to get further information.

She motioned for Joe to leave the room with her.

Shannon observed Ronnie through the glass. "Let's leave her in there for a few hours and try again. At least you got her to admit she was involved in the abduction. She also confessed to watching while Lore was taken."

"How did you know Ronnie and John were standing there watching while Lorelei was abducted?" Harris asked. "We don't have any witnesses."

Shannon glanced at Joe.

Agent Harris' eyes opened in shock and his jaw dropped. "Lorelei's astral abilities. I should have known when you told me about the barn." He looked at Joe, then Shannon. "She escaped there for a brief period to connect with you."

Shannon let out a deep sigh. "Astral projection, or out of body travel, isn't exactly considered a true science. Just like the paranormal or supernatural, it's not taken seriously, especially by law enforcement. So I wanted to keep that fact to as few people as possible."

"Since I was assigned to this case, I should have been informed," Harris said. "I may have been somewhat of a skeptic, but seeing what I did at that ghost town, and hearing experiences from the evidence response team and other agents working out there." He shook his head and threw his hands up. "She sounds like a pretty amazing person."

Joe tossed his long dark hair behind him. "Yes, she is. And the man that has her is more dangerous than most criminals you may have encountered. He's capable of torturing you in ways you never thought possible, and we're not talking only the physical level."

"Lorelei confronted him with the powers of the ancients a few months ago, stripping him of his astral abilities," Shannon said. "We don't know if Peter's taken this opportunity for revenge, or to find out more information about the ancient ones—an amazing race of people that took astral travel to a whole new level."

Shannon turned to Joe. "Were you able to find out anything from Alan about those supposed sacred sites in the Four Corners? You mentioned Ian was all excited about a vision he had of Bryce Canyon because he thought her necklace provided a possible connection to Lore."

"There are four sites, the Caves of the Watchers here in Wickenburg, maybe Bryce Canyon in Utah, an unknown site in Colorado, and a mystical location in New Mexico. The latter could be Shiprock due to the image on the petroglyph Lore identified at Vulture Mine."

Harris watched an attractive blonde staff member walk by. "What is so special about these places?"

"We're not entirely sure yet," Joe said. "This race of people Lore has bonded with are tied to the universe in ways most can't imagine. For them, a true journey meant travel to the stars, not to earthly destinations. Based on the evidence found in the Caves of the Watchers, the ancients used every ounce of their willpower to connect with the solar system."

Shannon glanced around to see if anyone was listening. "For some reason, this astral race also created a near death tunnel leading to one of the four caves. Perhaps Lore's own brief astral trip to reveal the east/west passage triggered something. Lore, Ian and I witnessed the blinding light, angels in the distance and experienced a spinning sensation as the tunnel walls moved. We thought we were meeting our makers." Shannon thought back to the unusual encounter and to the unidentified figures waiting in the radiance. "No wonder those particular caves were further underground."

Joe nodded for Shannon and Harris to follow him outside. "To die is to cease connection with one's silver cord, so maybe a near death experience helped them identify with relatives who have passed on, or NDE might increase their focus during astral travel. Alan is very excited about the Caves of the Watchers because of the stuff he's heard. He wants me take him out there."

Shannon threw her hands up. "Lorelei is supposed to be the focus here. Her life could be at stake and you're talking about going on an adventure with an old buddy."

"You didn't give me a chance to explain. Each of the chambers in the Caves of the Watchers supposedly has a clue representing the Four Corners locales. Alan thinks that's what Peter and Emily are here for since they also have a fascination with astral travel. They are probably seeking those sacred places for power, treasures or both."

"Are you confirming Lorelei's experience in that bed-like chamber?"

"Yes. It's believed the insets in the tunnel walls were used for out of body journeys. But Alan's never heard of anyone being able to access those portions of the cave system, let alone experience what Lore did."

"Lore said something touched her, activating her pendant. She thought it might have been one of the ancient ones." Shannon touched Joe on the arm. "Wait, how does Alan know about those passages?"

Joe took a drink from the water cooler. "Alan's gone undercover with some of the most elusive underground cults dealing with mind control, toxic herbal potions, demonic evocation, sexual rites, shapeshifting, hypnosis, casting curses and astral projection. Some people specialize in more than one of these, including Vincent Joiner who attempted to kill Lorelei in Dragoon. I watched as Vincent performed a ceremony combining astral projection and mind control to make his victim commit suicide, though I had no idea of his intentions at the time."

"Does Alan know Peter?"

"He's never met him, but others who practice the dark arts have mentioned Peter is one of the most dangerous—another Tony Slaughter."

"Who is Tony Slaughter?" Agent Harris asked.

"Another darks arts master from the 1930's," Joe said. "Melissa Harlow saw Tony's lifelike spirit on her ranch, which initiated the whole murder mystery in southeast, Arizona. Melissa's ex-husband, who was Vincent Joiner, tried to draw on the power of the area and the ancients to rule the very beasts Tony created so long ago, but Lorelei managed to stop the destruction."

Shannon rolled her eyes and groaned. "If Peter can really read Lore's mind, then she might have revealed the location of the Caves of the Watchers."

"I'm guessing the ancients are ensuring he can't achieve that feat, at least not as far as the caves are concerned. Alan thinks Peter and Emily knew about the cave system and its capabilities. They just didn't know where to look."

"If Peter and Emily think Lore knows something about the caves here, why would they have taken her out of Arizona?" Shannon asked.

"Not sure. Lore might still be in Arizona. Peter could be trying to throw us off through Ian's vision. Though you'd think Ian would have seen Lore. Or..."

"Or what?" Shannon asked.

"Maybe Lore's necklace picked up on where she really is."

"What about the black Mercedes?" Harris asked.

"Hasn't been seen since it vanished on the highway in front of the Hummer," Shannon said. "But that makes sense if Peter and Emily aren't in the area anymore."

Joe placed his arm around Shannon's waist. "Since we aren't getting a whole lot to go on, I'll have Alan fly us over Bryce Canyon and the abandoned ranch after Alan and I go on a tour of the Caves of the Watchers."

"Who named those caves?" Shannon walked down the long hall lined with cramped interrogation rooms with Joe and Agent Harris. "Or did Mattie Olson, the original caretaker of Vulture Mine, name them that in her journal because of the art?"

"Alan said they were called that way before Mattie mentioned it in her diary. And Mattie probably had some assistance finding that place."

"You mean someone else in the area knew about them?" Harris asked.

"No," Joe said. "She might have discovered them through an out of body journey."

"That entrance is still rather difficult to see, even for someone doing astral travel. But what if Mattie was guided there physically?" Shannon stared at Joe in astonishment. "Consider how this ancient race guided Lorelei back to the Indian ruins in Dragoon after the mystery had been solved."

Joe nodded. "Let's just say those four chambers work together and exude a power none of us can completely understand. Alan referred to them as if they were a living entity, using the words "they" and "it." He thinks Mattie was called to the caves in Wickenburg and given that talent because she was pure of heart and mind — like Lore."

"So Mattie definitely had a connection with the ancient ones?" Shannon asked.

"Yes. And that must be why she left her journal with Lorelei. Mattie knew Lore was like her."

Chapter 32

Dramatic orange skies dominated the darkening sky with pink and purple streaks, creating a dramatic backdrop for Mother Nature's arrangement of time-weathered cliffs.

After Dagon disappeared, Lorelei considered trying to escape. With no food or water, it would be futile. Or was Peter's intent to let her suffer out here in the middle of nowhere? If so, why did he assign Dagon to watch over her?

The brilliant colors of sunset faded from view and whispers began to emanate throughout the house, along with voices speaking in the dialect of the ancients. One of those voices sounded familiar.

She quickly got up from the built-in wooden corner kitchen table and looked around.

"Dagon, is that you?" Lorelei cautiously approached the hallway and stared toward the spare room where she had first seen him.

"Did you miss me?"

She spun around to see Dagon standing behind her.

"Why would you leave?" she asked. "Aren't you here to make sure I don't escape? Peter would kill you if he knew."

Lorelei's eyes widened in shock. She took two steps toward Dagon. after releasing her from the chains, hearing the language of the ancient race right before he reappeared, and his attempts to make her feel comfortable and safe. Had the astral beings assigned Dagon to her as a guardian angel?

A smirk slowly crept into the corner of his mouth. He stood within a foot of her, and something made her reach out to him. Dagon didn't move as she touched his arm. Her hand went right through.

She gazed into his eyes in astonishment. "Who, or what, are you?"

He answered her with his lips. "You already know. My name, rather my new identity, is Dagon. I died tragically three years ago.

But the heavenly masters have transformed me into something I could never have imagined."

"Peter," Lorelei whispered. "He's a master at telepathy. How can he not know?"

"He's powerful in his own right, I suppose, but not enough. We aren't only experts at universal travel. We can use a magician's own talents against them."

"If you have such powers of coercion, why are you letting this happen to me?"

"It has to be. The Caves of the Watchers demands it."

She shook her head in confusion. "Wait, those are the chambers near Vulture Mine. The place Mattie referred to in her journal."

"They are so much more than mere stone. They are our lifeblood. The soul of those caves is the soul of our being."

An angelic iridescence surrounded Dagon and lit up the small farmhouse, rescuing Lorelei from the recent darkness.

"What do you mean by "'lifeblood?'" Lorelei remembered the high readings in the exact center of the tunnels, and the paintings of the mysterious orbs that had hypnotized her, causing her to be held captive after the cave-in.

She gasped. "The sets of eyes work together as one entity."

Dagon started to fade away.

"No! Don't go yet."

She had so many questions she wanted to ask, but didn't know where to start. She began with the one person that was always on her mind. "Am I going to see Ian again?"

"Of course. Sooner than you realize."

"When is this nightmare going to end?" She gazed into his dark eyes imploringly. They changed ever so slightly, just like the pictographs in the Caves of the Watchers.

Dagon touched her face gently. She closed her eyes in response to the tremendous reassurance she felt. Sudden exhaustion overcame her. Lorelei could no longer keep her eyes open. She collapsed into arms she thought were Dagon's.

She awoke on the couch in the spare bedroom a few hours later. She wasn't alone. Someone lay next to her, arms wrapped tightly around her. She quickly sat up.

I'm dreaming. This can't be.

She remained motionless, staring down at the man beside her with wavy, messed up locks of blond hair, dressed only in boxer shorts with that sexy morning look.

"Ian." Lorelei touched his face with the back of her hand to make sure he was real.

He awoke with a start. "Lore? Baby, is that you?" Ian sat up and glanced around the room.

"This can't be." She became wracked with sobs.

Ian pulled her toward him, kissing her on her lips, face and neck. "If this is a dream, I hope I never wake up." He pulled her away for a few seconds. "Are you okay? Did he hurt you?"

Lorelei couldn't tell him what she had been through. She knew he wouldn't be able to leave her when the time came.

"Dagon, he told me I would see you sooner than I realized. This must be what talked about." She pulled away for a few seconds, wiping her tears. "I've missed you so much."

Ian didn't ask who Dagon was, or where they were. He kissed her with a passion that made her tremble with desire. She ran her hand down his chest, holding firmly onto the curly hairs. The salt from his tears mingled with her own as they kissed. He began to shake, holding her head in his hands.

She gasped as he placed his hand in the small of her back. Then she grabbed his hair, entwining it between her fingers. She knew this wouldn't last and she wanted to feel alive.

He stopped kissing her and gazed into her eyes. "I don't know why or how I'm here. I just want to be so close to you until they decide it needs to end."

He stepped back and slipped his boxers to the floor.

"Where are you taking me this time?" She whispered breathlessly.

"Baby, we're already there." He picked her up and carried her out into the cool grass with the moon shining down upon the mystical spires. She should have been freezing in the late February night air. But she wasn't. Neither was he.

His warm breath and the wetness of his tongue worked their magic from her chest to below her stomach. Then Ian placed his fingers inside her, and traced his way back up her body.

The pinnacles seemed to bend over in response to the intense heat going on far below as her head bent way back. Ian lifted her head off the ground and pulled her into a sitting position. Still crying, she placed her hands tightly on his shoulders, grinding against him.

"Yes," she whispered in his ear, pulling him down on top of

her. He teased her endlessly with his passion inside her, moving it in circles and able to take her to new heights. Their bodies rose gradually above the earth while they exploded inside each other.

Ian traced her lips with his fingers. "Your pendant showed me a vision of this place. I knew it had to be you."

"Honey, the caves Mattie found, they're a significant part of who the ancient ones are and where they're getting their energy. Dagon mentioned those chambers and passages were their lifeblood."

"Who is Dagon?" Ian stroked her hair.

He is responsible for us getting together. Dagon was human until he died, but now he's one of them. This astral race can change spirits into something as powerful as they are."

Ian carried her back into the house and they held each other close on the couch. "They brought me here to keep you going." Ian's voice broke. He held her so close she could feel his heart beating. "And I have to leave you, knowing Peter will be back."

About to fall asleep, Lorelei knew it was now or never. "Yes," she said softly, taking the pewter pendant hanging from his neck in her hand. "I'll marry you."

He placed his leg over hers, pulling her closer. "I love you. And I'll be waiting."

Chapter 33

Shannon stared at the DNA analysis results on her laptop, wondering why Mattie Olson's bones were discovered in the same barn where Lorelei was held captive. Tooth remains indicated Mattie was seventy-two years old when she died. The forensic anthropologist also mentioned blunt force trauma to the skull. Did the original caretaker of Vulture Mine die in the old structure? Or was she murdered and carelessly dumped there? Shannon wondered if the answers could be in the diary Mattie gave Lorelei in the Caves of the Watchers.

"Mattie obviously had a connection with the ancient ones," Shannon muttered. "Was it to the same extent as Lore, or was Mattie even more powerful? Did she go to her grave because of it?"

Shannon glanced at her watch. It was 1:10 p.m. Her meeting with Ian was at 1:30 p.m.

She closed the lid on her laptop and placed it into her black bag, then ran out of the office to her car. Ian had sounded excited about something, but he wouldn't say what over the phone.

Thirty minutes later, she pulled into his driveway. Ian flung the front door open as she got out of her car. He seemed excited. His blue-grey eyes sparkled and he stood straight up, rather than hunched over and forlorn.

"You seem rather chipper," Shannon said. "What's going on? Did you find something out about Lore?"

Ian pulled her gently into his house, past the copper wall fountain with its steady trickle, and into the living area with its warm tones and western style theme.

"I saw her last night."

"You can't be talking about Lorelei."

He nodded. "I thought I dreamed it. I woke up this morning and found this."

Ian indicated a bite mark on his neck. "From when we..." He

cleared his throat and blushed, looking at an abstract painting of a Native American Indian on the wall.

Shannon walked up within inches of his face. "Ian, what the hell are you telling me?"

A single tear rolled down his face. "I was asleep. For some reason, I woke up with a start. Lorelei lay next to me."

Ian took Shannon's hand and pulled her next to him on his couch. "Shannon, I was transported to where she is being kept. The very same place I saw in my vision."

Shannon leaned forward and felt his face with the back of her hand. "Honey, it must have been a dream."

"I knew you'd say that." Ian got up and walked over to a built-in bookshelf. He slipped an object from one of the nooks and showed it to Shannon. She stared at the emerald ring Ian had given Lorelei at Sunset Crater Wupatki National Monument north of Flagstaff.

Shannon took the ring from Ian, turning it over and gazing at it in astonishment. "Where did you get that? I saw her with that on the day she was taken."

"That's what I'm trying to tell you. It was on my finger when I woke up. I think she wanted me to understand what happened. The ancient ones wanted me to be with her. I remember giving her the necklace back for the same reason."

Ian pulled his collar aside to show her he wasn't wearing the pendant.

"I thought this race only specialized in astral projection. Didn't Peter have an objection to you being there?"

"He was nowhere around. Lorelei was alone. This ranch is in the middle of nowhere. With no food and water, she wouldn't be able to make it out."

Shannon started to pull out her laptop to get information for Utah. "I need to contact the Utah division and get a helicopter. Or I can get Joe's friend to do a flyover of Bryce."

Ian stopped her by grabbing her hand. "No. Lore's going through this for a reason. I can't explain it, but this has to play out."

"Are you insane? This is someone you plan on proposing to. You want to take a gamble and leave her in his hands!"

"Lore heard my proposal somehow. She accepted before I left her." He placed his hands on her shoulders and gazed into her eyes. "While I was with her, a forceful, yet gentle voice told me I was there to give her strength. That she needed to go through this experience, but she wouldn't be alone."

"I don't get this." Shannon threw up her hands and ran her hand through her hair. "If the ancients can transport you from your house to where Lorelei is, then why the hell can't they get her out of there?"

"They can, but it would interfere with something much larger. She has to go through this. I couldn't accept it either, until I was in that room with her, making love to her. I have to admit, there's a part of me that thought if I held her tight enough, she would be transported back with me."

"Did these voices give you any indication of what she's supposed to do? Because I hope it has something to do with helping the FBI catch that son-of-a-bitch and rescue herself."

"I'm sure that's part of it. But intuition's telling me it's also about her abilities and tie to this race."

"Well I'm not going to stop this investigation. Whether," Shannon used her forefingers to form a quote, "they like or not. I'm going to hire Alan to fly me over that damn canyon and find my friend."

Shannon's BlackBerry buzzed and she glanced down to see Joe's name. She angrily slid the lid open and answered the phone. "How's the investigation at the Caves of the Watchers going?"

"It's not," Joe said breathlessly.

"What are you talking about? I thought you and Alan were headed up there."

"We were." He exhaled deeply. "I mean we're here now. But the two entrances are closed."

"What? Honey, you're in the wrong place."

"No. These chambers are sealing themselves off."

Shannon sighed. "The excitement never ends," she muttered. "By that statement, you're hinting the Caves of the Watchers are alive."

"It sure seems that way." Joe's voice became fainter. "The access point to the tunnel between the north and south chambers had a large black boulder over it. I slid the rock aside and saw the hole sealing itself. It looked like a layer of dirt was being spread over the opening by invisible hands."

"Okay, you've been out in the sun too long."

"Shannon." The tone in Joe's voice became serious, yet with an eerie calm. "Something is going on out here. We're standing by the top-most entrance under the butte and hearing movement beneath our feet. It's not like someone's down there moving a few rocks. The whole fucking place seems to be shifting. Here, listen."

Static blasted through as he moved his cell phone. Then she heard the noise clearly. It sounded like mammoth stones sliding across the ground, not the sudden and intense crashing of rocks falling in on each other as with a cave-in.

Panic set in when she realized Joe was at ground zero for whatever was occurring. "Get the hell out of there!" No response. "Joe!"

She jumped off of the couch and started pacing the floor with the phone in her hand. "Joe, are you there?" The sounds of shifting earth became louder.

Ian stood completely still staring at Shannon, his mouth slightly agape.

"Shit." Shannon couldn't breathe as she gazed back at Ian, her hand tightly gripping her cell. She said hurriedly, "Joe's out at the caves with Alan. Something big is going on."

"Joe," she yelled again.

Finally, she heard his voice, faint and fragmented. "Babe, I'm all right. We're running back to the trail now. I'll call you in a few."

Shannon looked at Ian. "Did Lore happen to mention anything about those caves near Vulture Mine when you were with her last night?"

"As a matter of fact, yes. Dagon told her the Caves of the Watchers were their lifeblood. And to save you from asking your next question, Dagon is her guardian, sent by the ancient ones. He died a few years ago, and they transformed him into a protective spirit of sorts. Maybe his was the presence I felt when I first awoke to see Lore."

"Are those caves really alive?" Shannon asked. "Because something's going on out there."

"That's what it sounds like. If that cave system drives who the ancients really are and what they are capable of, then maybe they have plans on showing Lore her future."

Chapter 34

Lorelei couldn't see who dragged her by her hair. She could only feel the violent pain as her captor gripped her blonde locks, sliding her across the cracked wooden floor. Tears of agony rolled from her eyes while she willed the torture to stop.

One minute she held her necklace tightly in her hand; a reminder of the night the ancient ones had given her with Ian. The next minute, she had been grabbed from behind while she stood in the living room, watching the towering sandstone formations and hoping her nightmare would end.

Peter hovered over her as she was ruthlessly deposited in front of him. She glowered at him. His icy gaze pierced her soul. Holding a book in his hand, he knelt down within inches of her face and traced his fingers down her neck and to the chain holding her emerald pendant. Then he yanked the necklace so forcefully it broke.

Lorelei attempted to snatch it out of his grasp, but Peter was too quick. A satisfied smirk crept across the corner of his mouth.

"So this is how you did it," he said, cooing at her. His warm breath smelled like garlic and onion. It made her want to vomit.

Peter toyed with the pewter charm, though he stared at her the whole time. "Guess this prize is an added bonus, considering you used this to strip away my astral abilities."

She screamed as the person behind her rolled a huge chunk of her hair into their hands and yanked so hard her head snapped back. Lorelei saw Mr. Unibrow directly behind her.

"You have no idea how much power I still hold," Peter said.

"Power through violence?" Lorelei asked angrily as she tried to pull her hair from her captor's grip. "

Where is Dagon? Why isn't he here to help me?

Dagon's intermittent presence and her discovery of his powers, and the hard reality that his help, or the assistance of the ancients, was nowhere in sight. Lorelei suddenly realized her enigmatic guardian hadn't been there to help her escape or avoid harm. She would have to figure that out herself.

Peter held up the book that had been tucked under his right arm. Mattie's journal.

"Is that what you've been after?" Lorelei yelled. "Mattie's spirit gave the diary to me. What the hell do you want with it?"

Peter nodded to Unibrow to let Lorelei go. He walked slowly around her in a circle. "Like you, I want to know the secret to their power. But unlike you, I know what the astral masters are truly capable of." He lifted her chin so she looked into his eyes. "You're going to help us by deciphering this journal."

"You're a professor. Can't you read? Or was your profession a lie also?"

"You haven't noticed?" Peter opened the diary to the last third of the book and held it in front of her.

Her eyes widened in surprise. Mattie's handwriting lay sprawled across the yellowed pages in an unfamiliar dialect.

"I'm giving you one chance only," Peter said. "I want you to read the last part of this diary."

"If you're so good at reading minds, then you'd know I can't understand what she's written."

"Can't understand, or refuse to comprehend what you've been given? You've communicated with this race many times. Though it's been verbal, you already know their language, written or otherwise."

She took a second glance at the writing, but nothing came to her.

"Maybe this will serve as a reminder."

Lorelei felt herself lifting off of the floor, floating to within a foot of the ceiling. Her body hovered helplessly for a few seconds then slammed into the dining room wall behind her.

As she slumped to the ground, she tried to focus on her surroundings, but the drab room, Peter, the junipers outside the window and sunset-colored pinnacles became a blur.

"Why did the old caretaker choose you?" Peter stroked her face gently. "Mattie must have known you both had something in common." He whispered in her ear. "You speak their language and they communicate with you, though I have no idea why when you don't even have the will to escape. I left you alone to see what you could do, but you proved yourself a worthless adversary."

"Not alone," she said weakly. "Dagon's here."

Peter glanced at Unibrow. "Leave her. She's delirious."

Chapter 35

Shannon sat next to Joe and across from Alan in the Gold Nugget Restaurant in Wickenburg, Arizona. Her eyes roamed from the stained-glass windows etched with a vine of roses, to the brightly flowered wallpaper, wooden banisters enclosed in slate blue curtains, oak wooden-beam ceiling and the elegant antique chandeliers.

Her attention snapped back to Alan when he unfolded a map of the Four Corners on the royal blue table cloth. He indicated the area where Arizona, Colorado, New Mexico and Utah came together; the area said to be somehow related to the Caves of the Watchers.

"Ian mentioned the Caves of the Watchers were the lifeblood of the ancient ones," Shannon said. "So what does the Four Corners have to do with this extinct race? And with the strange occurrence you and Joe experienced at those caves?"

Alan blew on his coffee and took a sip. "I believe those chambers sealed themselves off because they sensed Peter's curiosity and evil intent. They didn't want anyone to figure out the relationship between the Caves of the Watchers and the four locations connected to each chamber. However, no one knows for sure the sacred sites associated with the Four Corners. Shiprock near Farmington, New Mexico is said to be one of the places due to the myths and spiritualism surrounding the pinnacle."

"Why were Ian, Lore, Brandon, Dale and I allowed down into their cave system?" Shannon asked.

Alan leaned back in his chair. The whitish, uneven patches of burn scars covering his left cheek, neck and arm only served to enhance Alan's slightly spiky pitch black hair with a hint at sideburns.

"Possibly because of your friend, Lorelei. She obviously has one hell of a bond with the ancient ones. She was the one that discovered the next level of passages—the very tunnels said to enhance their abilities," Alan said.

Joe yawned and rubbed his eyes. "Each of the sets of painted eyes is tied to one of the four sacred places." He took Shannon's hand and held it. As usual, her heart jumped a beat. "Babe, they're called the Caves of the Watchers because those amazingly detailed pictographs keep track of what's going on at the remote locations in Arizona, New Mexico, Colorado and Utah."

"How can anyone possibly know that for sure?" Shannon glanced from Joe to Alan. "Unless you know someone capable of seeing through eyes drawn onto rock. If that were the case, then that individual could possibly identify the other Southwest locations."

"I've met such a person." Alan leaned in closer to Shannon. "With eyes as dark as those on the cave walls, which can transform from one color to another in seconds."

"So you have been down there," Shannon whispered.

Alan shook his head. "But I've heard stories, including what happened to your group."

Shannon took a sip from her soda. "So how do we find this person or spirit who might know about the Caves of the Watchers?"

"You don't," Joe said. "They find you. And they're not so much spirits as ex-humans transitioned into powerful beings."

"No wonder you and Joe are such good friends. You're both so good at taking people in circles." She threw her hands up. "I've got an alert out to agents in Utah to scour Bryce Canyon. See if anyone recognizes Peter, Emily or Lorelei. Unfortunately, the park rangers claim to know nothing of the dilapidated ranch where Lore's being kept."

Shannon stared at Alan. "Wait, Joe said that they find you. What made you so special?"

Alan's voice lowered and he gazed beyond Shannon's shoulder at a picture of Monument Valley. "Not just me. I was in Farmington, New Mexico to interview witnesses for an investigation. It was late at night and my partner and I decided to check out this myth of glowing red eyes that are seen at night in the vicinity of Shiprock. We drove down a jeep trail toward the main spire, stopping at the bottom of the formation. Eddie, my partner, decided to get out and take a pee directly on the sacred Tsé Bit' A'í, or what the Navajos call the Rock with Wings."

Joe took a large gulp of his iced tea then shook his head in disgust.

"Words can't even describe the sensation of that place when he urinated. The very air around Shiprock seemed alive. I didn't know what Eddie had done until we started to hear a woman's voice singing, though we couldn't understand the words. It sounded like it came from all around us."

"You didn't see any other cars around?" Shannon asked.

Alan shook his head vehemently and pushed his empty plate back. "But Eddie claimed to have seen those red glowing eyes right after he peed. The atmosphere changed, from merely electric to evil. We didn't say a word. Both of us jumped back in the car and peeled out of there, but that wasn't the end of the adventure. We heard two loud popping sounds in succession and Eddie lost control of his vehicle. Turns out our vehicle got two flat tires on the way out. The drivers side front and back."

"Revenge," Shannon whispered. "For his disrespect. But where does this supposed deceased human-turned-ancient come in?"

Eddie put his hand up. "I'm getting to that. So we're out in the middle of nowhere and our car isn't moving. We both got out of the car to replace a tire and attempt to make it back to civilization with only one flat. While Eddie was getting the spare out of the trunk, the temperature dropped by twenty degrees. We both looked at each other and knew we were in trouble because my partner disrespected the land. I've never seen Eddie move that quick. He yanked the tire out of the trunk and pulled the blown-out tire off the rim."

Alan shuddered and stared out the door of the restaurant as if reliving the incident.

"That's when we both saw them. At first, I thought I was hallucinating. Then I saw Eddie glancing around as we worked hurriedly to get the new tire on. He kept saying, "They're here.""

"Were these Native American spirits?" Shannon asked.

"Not sure. We kept seeing those glowing red eyes in the distance as pinpricks of light. They kept getting closer. And fast. I stood up and noticed we were surrounded."

"All you both saw were red lights?" Shannon asked. "No mists or shadows?"

"No, more like floating lights. As these things got within twenty feet of us, Eddie and I suddenly found ourselves by the main highway, staring out at Shiprock. Both of us were still in the same standing position with Eddie by the back tire and me next to him."

Shannon glanced at Joe and back to Eddie. "You were teleported, or instantly moved from one physical location to another. Ian mentioned that's how he ended up with Lorelei at the ranch house."

"What happened next was just as strange," Eddie said. "A man stood in front of our car, staring at us. I thought maybe he had seen what happened, but the look on his face didn't reflect shock or surprise. He seemed to expect us to appear out of nowhere. This stranger was also by the freeway with no vehicle in sight. He walked closer to us, but for some reason, neither of us felt threatened. He stood within a foot of both of us and said, "Be careful what you wish for." Then his eyes transformed from black to dark blue to the brightest green I've seen. I turned toward Eddie, and when I looked back, the stranger had vanished. Both of us had a very bizarre dream that night connecting the dark-haired person who we believed saved us, to the Caves of the Watchers. Distinct visions of Shiprock, a set of dark eyes, and the four underground chambers near Wickenburg invaded our sleep the whole night.

Shannon took a bite of her burger and watched as the bleach blonde waitress seated a young family. "And Bryce Canyon wasn't in your vision?"

"No. But your friend Ian obviously had a similar experience regarding teleportation. I mean, he somehow ended up in Utah with Lorelei in the middle of the night."

Joe placed his arm around Shannon's waist. "I don't think those supposed sacred sites represent where they lived, more like special places that might have something to do with their abilities and connection with the universe."

Shannon pounded her fist on the table, shaking the filled water and soda glasses, rattling the silverware and dirty dishes, and catching the attention of patrons sitting nearby. "I'm trying to find Lore, but none of this is getting me anywhere. Joe mentioned you were a pilot. I can hire you to fly us over Bryce to see if we can find that ranch. I can't sit idly by and wait for Peter Taylor to harm her."

Alan leaned across the table, whispering to Shannon. "There's a reason the park rangers told you they didn't know about that old ranch house. It's because they really aren't aware of such a place. I've flown over many of those parks in the Four Corners and have traveled extensively through there. I also know a park ranger who worked in Bryce Canyon and happens to be a sorcerer in a very exclusive cult. She mentioned there was no such landmark." He glanced around the room. "At least normally."

Shannon could barely breathe.

"Would you like more water?" The waitress asked.

Shannon shook her head emphatically and waved her off abruptly. "We're talking teleportation of the ranch, or maybe someone wants us to think it's there."

Alan stared at her in response.

Was the ranch teleported before Lore arrived, or with her inside?

"Is Peter capable of such a feat? The driver of the Hummer saw the black Mercedes vanish before his eyes."

"He doesn't have that much power." Joe mopped up the remainder of his turkey gravy with a roll. "But Lorelei does. Somehow, he knows it."

"For some reason, the astral masters didn't want you to find Peter and Lore, which is why their vehicle disappeared," Alan said. "This ancient race must have also placed that old ranch where it is. And Emily and Peter must have had help finding it."

Chapter 36

Lorelei stood at the top of Tsé Bit' A'í, a dormant volcanic pinnacle 7,000 feet above sea level, gazing down upon the stark New Mexico desert landscape. A herd of wild horses grazed upon the tufts of grass far in the distance. Winged dark walls of lava rose 1,700 feet into the bright blue sky south of her vantage point.

She shivered as a strong gust of wind blew by, carrying with it the sounds of ceremonial chants and singing. Only no one else was around.

The bruises Peter had inflicted were forgotten temporarily as she closed her eyes and imagined gentle kisses from Ian in the midst of a dream she hoped would never end.

She was alone, yet not alone.

A powerful aura emanated from the sacred peak. The soles of her feet vibrated slightly and a peculiar warmth overcame her. Shiprock was alive with energy, carrying a force that produced the strongest vision she ever had.

She saw the Caves of the Watchers retreat further into the depths of the earth, sealing itself off from the outside world. The trembling of the effort seemed to affect the clipper ship-like rock she stood on, for it also began to quake. The massive eyes painted onto the cave walls briefly illuminated in her mind, gazing back at her with a plea in their reflection.

Balanced precariously on top of the tallest spire, she spread her arms out wide.

Then jumped off, descending in rhythm with the Caves of the Watchers.

* * *

Lorelei sat up quickly, looking around in the dimly lit room. A tall shadow observed her from a chair in the corner.

Peter's voice shattered the silence. "I didn't think you would go very far, at least not without this." He slowly stood up and walked toward Lorelei with her necklace in his hand.

"What are you talking about?" Lorelei scooted away from him. "I've been here the whole time."

"Are you sure about that?" Peter leaned down and picked up a few objects by her feet.

She couldn't believe what he held.

Three chunks of lava rock lay in his palm. He stared intently into her eyes. "You've been to Shiprock," he whispered.

How can I have visited a place without knowing it? But then, I didn't think I was capable of astral projection.

She screamed in agony and squeezed both sides of her head. A dagger pierced the inside of her skull. "What do you want from me?"

He yanked both her arms and pulled her to her feet. "I want to know their secrets, just like you. And I want my astral abilities back."

She felt him tremble, though she couldn't tell if it was from anger, excitement, or both.

"And be able to teleport anywhere I want." Peter put an emphasis on each of the next three words. "Just like you."

"You don't deserve such power. You can use all the damn mind control you want." Lorelei glared at him and tried to pull away from his vise grip. "But you can't find out information from someone who isn't aware of what's going on."

The sound of footsteps echoed toward her and Peter from the hallway. A woman's sultry voice said excitedly, "Peter, honey. I don't know how, but he was here. I recognize his cologne."

Peter glanced up briefly to look over Lorelei's shoulder at the newcomer. "Who was here?"

"Ian. My ex-husband. Her future husband."

Lorelei turned her head to see Emily. Her prominent cheekbones, soft olive skin and catlike eyes gave her a more striking appearance than Lorelei remembered. And she had changed her hair color to auburn, and wore high-heeled black boots, tight black jeans and a fur-lined jacket that emphasized her petite, lithe frame.

How does she know about Ian's proposal?

"You bitch!" Lorelei yelled, managing to free one of her arms to get a better look at Emily. "You abandoned your own son. Paul's been having nightmares for months. And he's terrified me and Ian will leave him." Lorelei glanced up at Peter with hatred. "What kind of hold does this man have over you?"

Peter slapped Lorelei on the face. Emily walked over and placed her arm around his waist as if to calm him. Peter's eyes softened, becoming tender and concerned. His body relaxed as he looked at Emily. He kissed his wife so gently Lorelei couldn't believe it was the same man who had been torturing her.

Emily whispered something in Peter's ear and then he closed his eyes and stroked her neck. Emily wasn't under Peter's spell. He was completely under hers.

Peter opened his hand and showed Emily the dark rocks. "She isn't aware of what she's doing," he said. "She teleported without knowing it to Shiprock in New Mexico. It's possible Lorelei teleported Ian here by merely thinking of him."

"Either that, or she could have company here we don't know about."

Peter circled Lorelei like he was inspecting a piece of meat, with her pendant wrapped around his fingers. "Dagon," he whispered. "Before you passed out after my interrogation about the journal, you mentioned you weren't alone. Why haven't I been able to read your mind about this mystery person?"

"We can't leave her anymore. She's beginning to realize the powers she has, even if she doesn't have them under control yet," Emily said. "We need to find out how Shiprock ties into all this. Mattie's journal didn't mention that site, though it is highly sacred to the Navajo or Dine'."

"We've got to figure out the last section of Mattie's diary," Peter said.

He positioned himself so his face was within inches of Lorelei's. "But what can we do to make her remember?"

Lorelei felt relieved when Emily's phone rang.

Emily answered the call. Her face turned ashen after a few seconds.

Peter walked over and placed his hands on her shoulders. "What's going on?"

Emily gazed back at him, her eyes wide with shock. "Lexi says there is no ranch at the coordinates we gave her." She glanced at Lorelei. "There is no such place in Bryce Canyon."

Peter nervously looked around. "Then where the hell are we?"

"A more appropriate question might be why." Emily's hand trembled as she held the phone. "I'm starting to believe we're the ones being tortured."

Chapter 37

Ian observed the five-story tall, white-capped hoodoo formations of Bryce Canyon from Alan's Cessna plane. Similar in shape to a totem pole, the rocks had been carved by wind and rain over the last several million years. He realized Lorelei could still be down there among some of Nature's spectacular artwork. Shannon, Joe and Paul were with him in hopes of finding the ranch where Lorelei was being kept, but Ian knew they wouldn't find it, or Lorelei. They weren't meant to.

The last thing he wanted to do was leave her, knowing Peter would return. Ian stood there staring at her before he returned home and immediately understood he didn't have a choice. Someone, or something, had infiltrated his very being at that moment, creating a new reality that she would return to him, but only when the time was right.

He smiled, watching his son Paul stare out the other window. He didn't want to bring him along considering the circumstances, yet he didn't want to deny him the adventure. Ian hoped Paul's nightmares would soon be replaced by new memories.

"Having fun, buddy?" Ian placed his hand on Paul's shoulder.

Paul smiled, though briefly. His eyes looked into Ian's pleadingly. "Are we going to find Lore and bring her home? I really miss her."

Shannon glanced back at Paul and Ian for a second. Then she removed her sunglasses and wiped her eyes.

Ian pulled Paul close to him. "Remember what we talked about? She's fine and will come back to us. Lore loves us both very much."

Paul's eyes sparkled. "Yeah. I can't wait until you get married."

"You do know she didn't desert you." Ian kissed him on the top of his head. "This is an adventure of her own. We all believe she has to go through this to learn more about who she is."

"I know. I can't believe mom and Peter are trying to hurt her."

Paul stared back out the window of the plane. "Are they going to come after us too?"

"Oh, Paul no." Ian hugged his son. "I never mentioned that's who abducted her. How did you know?"

"In my dreams. I even saw you and Lore together the other night."

Ian blushed, wondering exactly what Paul had seen.

"I saw you appear next to her on an old, ugly couch. You woke up at the same time and you both were crying. That's when he came and told me I would be all right, and that you would be back real soon."

"Paul, who told you this?" Joe asked in a soft voice. "Who was in your home? Are you sure you didn't dream the whole thing?"

Paul shook his head emphatically. "He had a strange name. Dragon, I think."

Ian gasped and Joe's eyes flew open.

"You mean Dagon?" Ian asked.

"Yeah."

Ian turned to face him. "You saw him?"

"He was cool looking with long dark hair to the side, and the other side of his head was shaved. He stayed with me until you got back."

Were the ancient ones responsible for Paul's dreams? Or is he developing his own talents?

"What did the two of you talk about?" Joe asked.

"He said Lore loved me very much and wouldn't leave me like mom did, and that dad needed to be with her for a little while. He also said the three of us belonged together."

"Hey, sweetie." Shannon turned her head to look at Paul. "Did he tell you about himself?"

"Not really. But I had the best sleep I had in months while he was with me. And since Dagon visited me, I haven't had any nightmares."

"Ian, keep an eye out for the ranch," Alan said. "According to the description you provided of the property, there's only one place it could be and we're almost there."

Ian looked down to see the winding canyon of spires. He recognized the area because the canyon ended at a gradually sloping palette of earthen-colored, iron-rich sediment, which used to be the sides of a massive lake.

"This looks like the area," Ian said. "But I don't see the ranch."

"We've flown over the whole park," Shannon said. "There is no such place, like the rangers told us."

"Perhaps there is," Joe said. "Maybe the ancients teleported it back to its original property, wherever that is."

Ian wondered if Lorelei got transported with the ranch, or if it was still there, sight unseen.

Ian fiddled with Lorelei's ring she had given him as a memento of their brief time together. He knew they wouldn't find the ranch or Lorelei, but Shannon was insistent.

He had helped Shannon and Joe contact various archaeological societies and university professors throughout the Southwest, but none of the experts were familiar with the astral race.

The archaeologists insisted on going back to the history of the ancestral Puebloans, or Anasazi, who inhabited the Four Corners from 700 A.D. through 1300 A.D until they abruptly vanished. Current theories suggest the culture gradually migrated from their Four Corners strongholds to the Rio Grande valley and the Hopi mesas where they became today's Zuni, Pueblo and Hopi Indians. However, Joe's Hopi and Navajo friends verified the recordings of the ancient ones' are nothing they've heard.

"Alan, do you have any idea exactly what, or where, those sacred sites are?" Shannon asked. "You mentioned you knew someone in a very exclusive cult. Would they be able to help us find Lorelei?"

"No one seems to know the precise locations," Alan said. "Lela, the occult expert, mentioned she thought the hallowed sites were under the earth, as is the Caves of the Watchers. She also believes Peter and Emily are trying to find the sites through Lorelei, since she is innately tied to the ancient race."

"What would anyone gain by finding these consecrated places?" Shannon asked.

"Power. Or at least that's what many people think. It's rumored anyone who enters the shrine of the masters of the universe can gain their abilities."

"But in reality, they select who develops their talents," Ian said. "Lorelei and Mattie were two of the chosen ones." He turned to stare out the window. "Though sometimes, I wish…"

Ian watched in the area of the horseshoe-shaped amphitheatre where he thought the ranch had been. Resplendent flashes replaced the Claron limestone and sandstone thousands of feet below.

"Alan, make another pass," Ian said. "There's something

going on down there."

Alan slowly banked the plane to the left while Shannon and Joe stared at the open section of canyon.

Five stone pillars and a single ruin briefly flashed into view; the same massive monoliths they had all discovered in Dragoon.

Ian was about to ask if Shannon and Joe had witnessed the sight, but her gasp told him she had.

The plane was directly over the spot where the decrepit ranch had been. The engine started to sputter. Paul's eyes widened in fright and he looked over at Ian. He pulled Paul close.

"That's strange," Alan said. "This plane's only a year old and I did a thorough maintenance check before taking it up. And it has plenty of fuel."

Ian stared at the layers of brown, ochre, tan and white below. *It's them. Their energy is interfering with the plane.*

Paul trembled in his arms. Ian closed his eyes and preyed.

"Alan, what's going on?" Joe yelled.

The engine continued to sputter and cough. Then it went dead. Ian held his breath while Alan muttered cusswords under his breath, messing with the controls. After Alan had cleared the area where the ranch had once been, the Cessna's engine came back to life.

"Is everybody okay?" Shannon looked back at Ian and Paul.

They both nodded.

"That incident with the plane must have had something to do with what we saw," Joe said. "Those monoliths from Dragoon which vanished, I saw them appear right below us. We all know how much energy the tunnels and pueblo held."

"Traveling ruins," Shannon said. "I wonder how they connect with the Caves of the Watchers. If they do."

"They're called that because of the painted eyes," Paul quipped. "But the eyes, or the watchers, aren't just pictures. They're the ancient ones' themselves drawing on the powers of the universe."

Joe glanced at Paul, then Ian.

Ian looked at Paul. "I never told about that place. How did you know it existed? And how do you know about those pictographs?"

"I dreamed about the caves."

"When?"

"The night I met Dagon. The eyes in the four chambers looked exactly like his. Dark, yet full of color."

Chapter 38

The ranch house, along with Peter and Emily, started to fade from view. Once again, Lorelei's whole body was on an unfamiliar journey. She felt nothing during her teleportation experiences, merely disappearing and reappearing without knowing her destination.

Peter dangled her pewter pendant from his forefinger, grinning maliciously. "She'll be back," he said to Emily.

She gasped, rubbing her eyes. But when she opened them, the couple and Bryce Canyon had disappeared.

She materialized in tenebrous surroundings, rubbing her arms and patting her body in disbelief from the unorthodox journey. A damp chill seeped through her skin and infiltrated every part of her. It became more pervasive the longer she stood, until she was frigid and stiff.

Her heart pounded with fear. Her breath came in short spurts. And her mind went back to the time she fell into a mine and spent the night in a deep shaft in the middle of the desert. At least then she had the moon peeking in on her. Now she faced a solid wall of darkness.

Taking deep breaths, she extended both arms out to see if she could feel something, anything. Lorelei took small steps, unsure of what might be ahead. Her legs trembled as she walked. She slowly knelt down on her knees and her fingertips met cold stone.

"Am I back in the Caves of the Watchers?" she whispered.

She ran her fingers gracefully across the smooth surface. Then another vision slammed into her thoughts so zealously, she fell backwards and sat stunned, hands against rock and legs splayed out.

Massive stone monuments, like those discovered in Dragoon, tiled themselves into her mind. Only these weren't in a half circle.

She slowly stood up.

"Is anyone here?" she yelled. Her shaky voice echoed back.

If she stopped, the deafening silence would overtake her. She might be too afraid to go on.

"Come on, Lore," she muttered under her breath while she continued forward.

She lost her balance and instinctively reached out again. Her hand met something solid and she recoiled briefly from the surprise.

The slightly pitted, smooth surface felt familiar. She jumped as something grabbed her hand, running it toward the top. She felt something etched into the stone; a horizontal line that turned into a backslash.

She found herself speaking their dialect. "A travel rune. Are these the same monuments that disappeared from Dragoon? If so, where am I?"

A soft but deep male voice responded. "You're in the very heart of who we are. The Caves of the Watchers."

"Dagon, is that you?"

There was no answer.

"I was in the Caves of the Watchers before." Lorelei looked around, staring into the darkness to see if anyone appeared. "The team and I didn't come across these stones. Only four caves, a lower level lined with bed-like chambers, and that passage where we had a near death type of encounter."

"This is below the place you speak of. Underneath the very center of the caves. It gives life to the watchers. And to us."

The massive room suddenly illuminated with flickers of warm light that decorated the stone walls and bounced across the ceiling. Hundreds of unseen candles were everywhere.

Lorelei stood in front of a slightly curved line of seven twenty-foot tall pillars of rock five feet apart. She gradually turned in a 360-degree circle and noticed six more monuments. They seemed to be in the shape of an eye. Dagon stood directly in the center; a golden phosphorescence emanating from his body.

"How did I get here?" Lorelei walked toward Dagon. "Did you bring me here?"

Dagon didn't answer. His intense, dark gaze threatened to overtake her. For a split second, she saw a flash of brilliant green, then sky blue, radiate from his irises.

Multiple voices, male and female, whispered from all around her. Lorelei couldn't distinguish any words. The gradual, deliberate, back and forth movement of Dagon's head told her he had nothing to do with her being there.

"Great," she mumbled. "Getting used to my medium abilities,

discovering my astral talents and tie to an ancient race, and now teleportation." She gazed in wonder at the magnificent stone spires surrounding her. "Why would I transport myself here rather than home?"

"You can't go home." Dagon said. "Not yet. Ian knows this. So do you."

She began to yell. "Damn it, you all give me these powers, yet tell me nothing about why I have them or who the hell you are. I call you the ancient ones because of the psychic impressions I received in southeast Arizona. How ancient is your race? And why am I endowed with these supernatural powers? I don't want to be a heroine. I only want to live a normal, happy life with my future husband and his son."

A single tear started welled up in her right eye, tickling her as it gathered momentum and rolled down her cheek. She felt a hand on her shoulder, though Dagon stood a few feet away. Warmth and tenderness flooded through her in the dank, dimly lit environment.

This time she could feel breathing over her shoulder. "You are not the only one. There are others who have lived a highly spiritual past life. Others who have been dealt abilities beyond their comprehension."

A stark vision of the elderly caretaker of Vulture Mine intruded into her mind. "You mean Mattie," she whispered. "Peter and Emily have her diary. They want me to translate the last third of her writing, but I can't understand the words."

Gazing into Dagon's dark eyes, she started to realize she wasn't supposed to be able to interpret Mattie's words. At least not yet.

Dagon continued to stand in the center of the eye-shaped collection of monoliths. The iridescence surrounding him extended itself toward her. Soft tendrils caressed her arms. Invisible threads wrapped themselves around her fingers for a few seconds.

Then she understood. This whole nightmare wasn't just about Peter and his need for power.

Lorelei took a step toward Dagon. "I'm here to learn about the Caves of the Watchers, the entities who feed off of such a sacred place. And about myself."

Dagon didn't nod or shake his head.

"How is the Caves of the Watchers associated with the site in Dragoon and why did I somehow transport myself to a place as remote as Shiprock?"

"There is no sanctity amidst the boulders of what you call Dragoon anymore. Malevolence has entered our realm too many times. This drains our energy, preventing us from helping others and from being able to pass our abilities on to those few on Earth who are truly worthy."

Dagon smiled at Lorelei and made a sweeping motion with his arm to indicate the series of tall stones. "But we can restore the power of the obelisks, and our sanctum, within these very walls, then transfer them to other special sites."

"Where is the pueblo that looked down upon the five monuments?"

The warm candlelit glow gradually became a bright white light that made Lorelei shield her eyes for a few seconds. An intense orange-red hue exploded from the magical monoliths before her, making them appear as if they were on fire.

Inexplicably drawn toward one of the gigantic, primordial effigies, she reached up and placed her hand over the travel rune sign. Her whole body became bathed in the rock's luminosity. There was no burning sensation, only comfort and familiarity.

She had come home.

Images of Canyon De Chelly, Monument Valley and Mesa Verde flashed through her mind. Then the ruins and five pillars from Dragoon appeared in her thoughts. For some reason, they weren't in southeast Arizona. The pueblo where Vincent Joiner had attempted to transform a peaceful dimension into something evil had been teleported to the ranch in Bryce Canyon.

Lorelei began to realize she wasn't a prisoner of Peter and Emily's.

The visions abruptly ceased. She repeatedly repositioned her hand on the smooth surface of the stone.

"Come on, damn it. Don't stop now."

Then the sacred place of the Navajo, the Rock with Wings, came into view. Another eye-shaped group of obelisks were revealed under the surface of Shiprock. It hit her. The ancient race who had endowed her with her prodigious abilities revered Tsé Bit' A'í as much as the present day Dine'.

The monoliths below Shiprock were grouped the same as those where she now stood. But another presence waited inside the middle of this formation. Her vision honed in on a tall woman with wavy red hair.

Lorelei gasped. Shannon! How is she tied in to all of this?

She quickly removed her hand from the column and turned to look at Dagon. He had vanished.

The caves close to Vulture Mine weren't the only energy emitters. The watchers extended throughout the Four Corners; a series of passages, chambers and monuments that fed off each other. They all worked together. The ancients' existence as supernatural, powerful spirits with the ability to recruit others in the afterlife extended their reach not only into the universe, but other dimensions.

Lorelei stared at the source of her astonishing visions. The stone's radiance had dissipated. It's warmth gone, but not forgotten.

"The visions from the stone explain why you were all able to help the badly injured miner. And why the ghost of the little girl at the Vulture Mine playground knew about your race," she whispered."

The atmosphere changed. Lorelei was being watched. She glanced from one pillar to the next, and found herself standing in the center, where Dagon had been. A message implanted itself clearly into her thoughts.

"Use the abilities we've given you to the fullest to develop a stronger connection to the earthly entities. Help guide them to their destination. They will follow your astral form. Teleportation will provide energy and answers for those you seek to help and for yourself."

Lorelei threw up her hands in frustration, staring at the silent stones. "How am I to know which entities to help? Thousands of people pass over to the next life every day. And I can't even control when and where I teleport, so how can I help anyone else?"

There was no answer—from Dagon, the ancient ones, or the proud stones surrounding her.

A youthful, distant voice yelled her name. She turned to see a faint outline of Paul, his arm extended toward her in desperation.

Chapter 39

Paul gazed up in child-like wonder at the tall boulders surrounding him. He had seen them before.

He stared intently at Lorelei. The glow from the unearthly monuments invaded her, starting with her hand, flowing into her arm and then the remainder of her body. He knew it wasn't a bad energy, though he couldn't explain why. Paul touched her other arm gently, but she didn't seem to notice. She continued to concentrate on the live obelisk before her.

"Lore," he whispered.

Dagon placed a hand on Paul's shoulder, gently pulling him back.

"Am I dreaming again?" His eyes looked up imploringly at the dark-haired gothic type man standing next to him.

"You have placed yourself in the middle of Lorelei's lesson, my friend." Dagon's scary appearance belied his actions and tone. Paul had never felt so protected.

"You have the ability to not only dream of things as they occur, but place yourself where and when they happen."

"Can I bring her back home with me?" Paul glanced at Lorelei. "Dad and I really miss her." A single tear ran down his face.

Dagon leaned down, taking Paul's hands in his own. Peace and tenderness overcame him.

"Unfortunately, no. This is your dream and she isn't aware you're here. She has her own path to follow right now. When her journey is complete, she will come back to you and your father. You are also on a path to discovery about your own talents. Talents that will bring the two of you closer than you can imagine."

Paul wanted to ask Dagon what he was talking about. Before he could open his mouth, the massive cave he had been in began to fade out.

Lorelei turned toward Paul.

"Lore," he yelled again in desperation. He reached desperately out to her as he quickly withdrew into nothingness.

* * *

Paul awoke; wetness on his pillow where his face had been. He lifted his head and ran his finger down his cheek to discover tears from his recent endeavor to connect with Lorelei.

A deep moan startled him. He rolled over abruptly to see his dad lying next to him.

Should I tell him about my dream? But is it a dream if it's really happening?

Paul laid his head back on his pillow. He didn't understand what was going on. First, he can see the future in his dreams. Now he's able to appear in other places through his dreams and experience events as they happen.

Though his father is Pagan, Paul knew he didn't have the unique gifts that Lore and Paul did, but he wondered if his mom had the same talents. After all, she was also able to foresee certain events from time-to-time. Maybe she had passed these strange skills on to Paul, like Lorelei's mother.

His dad stirred slightly in his sleep and suddenly woke up, smiling tiredly at Paul. His wavy hair lay partly across his face.

"Can't sleep?" Ian asked.

Paul didn't know how to respond. He knew his father would believe him, yet he didn't want to torture him with thoughts of Lorelei.

Ian leaned up on his elbow. "You had another vision, didn't you?"

Paul sat up in bed. "Dad, no. I was there with Lorelei, though she didn't know it. Dagon was there also."

Ian sighed, got out of bed and put on his robe. It only upset his father to hear about her knowing he couldn't do anything to help her on her journey.

Ian stopped in the doorway for a second. "I'm going to get some hot cocoa and fix us something to eat. How about you join me?"

"Okay." Paul jumped out of bed, ran over to Ian and hugged him. "I'm sorry."

"You have nothing to apologize for. Lore has these amazing abilities and seeing what she's going through is hard enough. So thinking about the talents you're obviously developing..." He pulled away from Paul. "How can you be sure you weren't only dreaming?"

"Because Dagon was there. He told me I was in the middle of Lorelei's lesson."

Ian stroked Paul's brown hair. "I always knew you were capable of anything. Though this scenario is a little beyond what I had imagined."

His father walked out of Paul's bedroom and a startling vision came to him. An image so vivid, Paul had to stop and grab onto the wall.

His mom and Peter were in some dark, remote place with the silhouette of an extremely tall, craggy pinnacle in the background, and a solid barricade of stone extending from it. They looked terrified. Peter stood in front of his mother trying to protect her from something.

Red pinpoints of light appeared out of nowhere. His mom and Peter were soon besieged by a crowd of bizarre, rapidly approaching orbs.

Paul remained frozen, hand flat against the hallway wall, mouth agape and unable to breathe. He wasn't seeing his father's house; only the wide open landscape and what looked like hundreds of pairs of creepy eyes floating freely among the blackness.

He wanted to scream, but couldn't. He wanted to run, but his legs wouldn't move. Though he was wrapped in nothing but total silence, Paul could still sense the malevolence hanging in the cool night air.

Is this a future vision or current reality?

The scarlet objects loomed ever closer. Emily and Peter tried to back away but the entities were everywhere.

A piercing scream cut through the heaviness. Paul realized it was his mother's.

"No!" Peter yelled.

Paul gasped, taking in a harsh breath of air while he held onto the beige wall. His sweaty hand trembled along with the rest of his body. He heard his father yelling his name from the kitchen, but he couldn't take a step.

"Paul!" His father's voice got closer. Within a few seconds he stood in front of Paul, his slate blue eyes reflecting worry and confusion, but Paul couldn't say a word. All he could think about was his mother and Peter, and the agonizing death awaiting them in the midst of the fiery, floating spheres.

* * *

Paul's pale face and quaking limbs made Ian wonder what had happened in the thirty seconds since Ian had walked into the kitchen to make cocoa. He quickly swept Paul into his arms and into his bedroom.

You can't have him. You have Lorelei. Isn't that enough?

Ian grabbed a washcloth and ran it under cold water. He wiped Paul's forehead, and he began to stir.

"Hey, buddy."

"Dad, I was awake this time, and right there with them, like with Lorelei, but..."

"Whoa." Ian held Paul's hand. "Who were you with?"

"Mom and Peter and they were in trouble."

"Is this something happening right now?"

Paul became frustrated and tried to sit up. "I can't explain it, but what I saw is something occurring in the future. This wasn't like the thing with Lore."

Ian wondered if Paul really dreamed himself into Lore's actual experience. If so, was it a one time thing? And what the hell did he see with Emily and Peter to make him so damn scared?

"How about that cocoa?" Ian started to get up from Paul's bed. "Then we can talk about what you saw."

"No! Don't leave me alone. I'm fine now. I want to go with you." Paul leapt up and ran over to Ian.

He placed his arm around Paul's shoulder, curious about what his son had seen involving his mother; the first vision while he was awake.

Could it be possible that Emily and Peter will get payback for all the suffering they had caused to himself, Paul, Lorelei, Alicia Atwell and everyone else who wasn't in alignment with their plans?

Paul still trembled slightly from whatever vision he had experienced.

Ian and Paul sat down at the dining room table and Paul placed both hands around his favorite mug with a color photo of an orca whale leaping from a deep blue ocean. Paul stared intently into the chocolate liquid with miniature marshmallows, perhaps reliving his recent vision involving Emily.

"Dad, they were everywhere."

Ian reached across the table and held his hand.

"Red eyes floated in the darkness. They were after Mom and Peter. These things," Paul shivered, "were getting closer and closer."

"Do you know where this was at?"

Paul looked from his cup to Ian. "Not sure. But there was a tall rock with a weird wall of rock extending from one side."

Ian reached across the table, taking both of Paul's hands into his own. "Sounds like a formation called Shiprock in New Mexico." They had never been to Shiprock. And he didn't remember mentioning it to Paul.

Joe had mentioned his friend Alan had a very similar incident with his partner during an investigation.

"Son, listen to me. I know these visions can be rather strong at times. And now you've developed a new talent, which involves dreaming your way into what others are experiencing. Not to mention you're also seeing possible future events while awake. But you don't need to be scared because Lorelei, Dagon and I will be there to help you."

Paul's face transformed in a split second into the mature Paul. It was as if his son had grown up twenty years before Ian's eyes.

"You're avoiding what I saw about mom and Peter." Paul took a sip of hot chocolate. "They're trying to find out what Lore knows regarding the ancient ones. But the minions of Tsé Bit' A'í aren't going to let them get close. Not again."

Chapter 40

Hundreds of stacks of brochures lined the walls of the Wickenburg Chamber of Commerce. Colorful photos of Vulture Peak, Vulture Mine, the Nature Conservancy's Hassayampa River Preserve and historic downtown decorated the wall behind the front desk.

Glancing at her watch, Shannon noticed it was 2:10 p.m. Tim Jensen was supposed to meet with her at 2:00 p.m. She heard a male voice come from a room toward the back of the building.

"Hello!" she yelled.

The voice lowered to a whisper and stopped. Soft footsteps sounded on the hardwood floor.

Shannon was shocked to see a stout, burly man approach her from the hallway. He had light brown hair that looked unnatural with his darker eyebrows.

"I'm Shannon Flynn with the FBI." She pulled out her badge. "I had an appointment with Tim."

"I'm Tim Jensen." He extended a meaty, sweaty palm in her direction. "It's nice to meet you."

Something about him put her on edge.

"As I mentioned on the phone yesterday, I'm trying to find out about Mattie Olson, the original caretaker of Vulture Mine."

"Of course. Let's head back to the conference room." Tim turned quickly and walked ahead of her. A slight tremble interrupted his gait and his dress shirt was slightly wet with arm pit stains.

He showed her into a cramped room with an oval table surrounded by six brown leather chairs. A forced smile crossed his lips.

Tim entwined his fingers and placed them on the laminate surface. "Mattie was a widow when she obtained the property in 1965. Her husband died in the Vietnam War, though the date is unknown, and she decided to come to Arizona from Michigan to be closer to her son and daughter, both of whom lived in Phoenix."

Shannon knew something was off. Mattie mentioned in her journal she had discovered the Caves of the Watchers in 1955, when she was already established in Wickenburg.

Is this guy merely ignorant of the true facts?

Shannon leaned forward, listening intently and staring into his eyes, thinking he might divert his gaze. He watched her with indifference and audacity.

Most people would be intimidated by someone like the bulky historian sitting before her. During her many years in law enforcement, Shannon had come across the nastiest and most aggressive individuals she had known. There wasn't anyone that could make her feel uncomfortable.

"Interesting." Shannon took out a bottle of water from her bag and took a drink. "I heard Mattie moved to old Vulture City in 1952. I assume you have a property deed to show when she moved here."

"I was trying to locate the paperwork when you arrived, which is why I was a little late." He released a smile, the right corner of his mouth quivered slightly. "She died at the age of seventy-two and had lived on the property for eight years. She died of natural causes — possibly heart attack or stroke."

Not quite.

Shannon pulled out the coroner's report, slamming it on the table in front of him. "Not only are you wrong about the length of time she lived at Vulture Mine, but Mattie died from blunt-force trauma to the skull. Her bones were discovered in an old barn near Vulture Mine. Why are you lying to me?"

A petite, elderly woman stood in the doorway, glancing nervously from Tim to Shannon. "Don't forget about your 3:00 p.m. appointment in Phoenix." She gave an overly friendly smile to Shannon and walked away.

He glanced at his watch. "I have to go. I'll send over those papers pertaining to Mattie Olson."

Shannon knew she would never see them. There weren't any such papers.

Tim maneuvered his way around the room and she pulled out the sketch of the man described by Ronnie and John as Peter's right-hand man; the one who had helped abduct Lorelei.

The round face, bushy eyebrows, and massive body in the picture matched to the historian's features. Only the man before her had trimmed the unibrow and added an unconvincing hairpiece.

He attempted to escape, but Shannon slid her chair a few feet, slamming the door before he could get out of the conference room. She quickly stood up and placed herself in front of the door.

She wanted to scream at him and wear him down until he told her details about Lorelei's kidnapping. But this wasn't the place.

A deep, intimidating voice spoke to her, but his mouth didn't move.

"Why can't you accept it? You aren't meant to find her."

Shannon gaped at him in surprise. A loud noise on the other side of the door startled her. She glanced over her shoulder.

When she looked back again, Lorelei's abductor had vanished. What the hell!

Her phone rang. It was Agent Harris.

"Hey, I found the bastard who kidnapped Lore. Turned out he was the historian I was referred to, though I wonder if he's really employed at the chamber. With the powers these people have, it's hard to tell what's going on." She let out a deep sigh. "Anyway, I looked away for a split second and he disappeared."

"What? Are you telling me he's a ghost?"

"I don't know what to believe anymore when it comes to the paranormal. All I know is he was here one second and gone the next."

"You mean like the black Mercedes that Emily was seen getting into?"

She let out a heavy sigh. "Yeah, exactly like that. If his trick involved teleportation, Peter and Emily don't seem to have those abilities. Do they have any idea their sidekick has such talents? For that matter, do the ancient ones realize someone so malevolent is utilizing their skills?"

A car horn blared over the phone, followed by a few seconds of silence.

Shannon walked out into the hall. The place was empty. She glanced up to see a photo of a tall, handsome, athletic man with dark brown hair. The small gold plaque underneath read TIM JENSEN – HISTORIAN.

"Makes me wonder exactly what other kinds of powers these people have," Harris said. "Even worse, what they intend to do with them."

Shannon observed the picture intently. "You mean like trying to mind trick the FBI and convincing everyone in the chamber office that they are someone totally different?"

* * *

Ian understood Paul was developing an unbelievable connection to Lorelei. He also knew Paul had been selected, along with his future wife, to somehow help the extinct race. But how and why?

He was about go for a walk with Paul when his phone rang. His heart stopped when he saw SHANNON in the display. He wondered what news she might have, if any.

"Ian, something bizarre just happened. I found the guy that helped kidnap Lore."

"What? Where did you find him? Did he tell you if she's safe?"

"Whoa, slow down. I figured it out when I was interviewing him about Mattie. He's supposedly a historian. I recognized him from a forensic artist's drawing described by the caretakers."

"What do you mean "supposedly," and what happened that's so strange?"

"He was in the room with me behind a closed door. I looked away for a sec when a loud noise distracted me. He had disappeared when I looked back."

Ian had a horrible feeling. Could this man be responsible for the black car Emily had gotten into vanishing? "I didn't think they had such powers."

"Peter and Emily might not," Shannon said.

Ian walked out of the house with Paul. The gloomy overcast sky made him feel hopeless. If this guy did teleport before your eyes, though you didn't see him actually disappear, how did he obtain those powers? I thought only the ancient ones could do that."

"Except for the chosen ones, like Lorelei and Mattie. That's not all. I believe Lore's abductor made everyone in the chamber think he was someone else. Ian, I saw a picture of the real historian. Name's Tim Jensen and he looks nothing like the man I met. He might have been trying to throw us off the track."

"Why would the ancients give such powers to someone that would kidnap Lorelei, the very person they've chosen to help them?" Ian stopped suddenly. "Unless this man is one of the ancient ones."

Paul stared up at Ian. His big brown eyes revealed an awareness and confidence Ian didn't know existed. Then they turned dark with alternating flashes of green, blue and grey.

"Shannon, hold on a sec."

Ian kneeled down. "Paul, is there something you need to tell me?"

"They don't know," Paul said.

Ian looked back into Paul's mysterious eyes and knew something, or someone, had taken over his son. "You mean Peter and your mom don't know about Scott's powers?"

"That's right." Paul's voice deepened considerably. He stood completely still, staring intently at Ian.

Then it hit Ian. Why wasn't Shannon fooled by Scott's shapeshifting disguise?

Chapter 41

Lorelei stood in the darkness of the caverns with the monoliths surrounding her. There were no more voices. No whispers. No candlelit glow. And no Dagon. She was alone, yet unafraid in the atmosphere of the ancients.

She didn't want to go back to the ranch, but she had to. The sooner she dealt with Peter and Emily, the quicker she would be able to return to her family. She hoped. She closed her eyes and smiled. Part of her was worried Ian might not want to marry her, especially since her discovery of her teleportation abilities. It might be too much.

Lorelei got what she wanted; finding out about the covert, yet peaceful race of people so connected to the universe; at least details about where their powers and energy were focused. She still didn't understand how the sacred Four Corners sites and the Caves of the Watchers would help her through this harsh journey. Every time she considered teleporting home, Dagon's voice echoed throughout her mind.

It's not time.

She knew she didn't have the strength to fight Emily or Peter. So how could she single-handedly stop them from finding out what they wanted? If Lorelei discovered how to read Mattie's diary, Peter would know.

If I have these powers, then why can't I prevent him from reading my mind?

Taking a deep breath, she envisioned Emily, Peter's smug face, the dilapidated ranch and her pentagram emerald amulet in his sinister hands.

Instead of returning to the ranch, Lorelei found herself staring up at the silhouette of Shiprock in the darkness from the base of the massive volcanic rock. Vibrations emanated from the brittle ground. The atmosphere felt charged like right before a thunderstorm, and a low steady buzz came from everywhere, yet nowhere.

"The energy's coming from the obelisks underground," she whispered to herself.

She jumped when a dark, long slender snake with yellow lines along the length of its body slithered rapidly between her feet. The four foot desert-striped whipsnake hesitated for a few seconds, looking up at her, then shot off into the night.

A man and a woman whispered somewhere nearby. She squinted into the blackness, but could see nothing.

She felt a presence behind her and whipped her head around to see a man standing so close she could feel his breath on her face.

Though he looked slightly different with the trimmed brows, Lorelei couldn't forget Mr. Unibrow's face. She stared into eyes that were the same shade of the surrounding darkness. Then he disappeared right before her.

Is he associated with the ancient ones? Do Peter and Emily know what he's capable of? And do they have the same talents?

She realized if they did, they wouldn't need to kidnap her. Peter had watched her with jealousy when she teleported to the Caves of the Watchers, holding her necklace in his hand. So how did his nasty counterpart obtain such a gift?

A woman's shrill scream carried through the shadows. The sound sent a shiver down Lorelei's spine and the hairs on her arms stood up. It sounded close.

She walked slowly in the direction of the noise. Dry grass and earth crunched under her feet.

Small pinpricks of fiery red light sprouted among the landscape. They were everywhere. She peered closer and noticed they weren't merely floating lights. They were orbs that seemed to be paired together in the shape of eyes.

Another shriek pierced the night air. The reddish creatures traveled away from Shiprock and toward the voices. They were moving quicker than before.

Lorelei gasped as the orbs glided by, hovering for a few seconds next to her. There were no bodies or mists associated with the baffling spheres. Yet they seemed to stare right through her. Then they continued onward, gathering together twenty feet in front of her, guiding her to the confrontation.

Two humans attempted to back away from the onslaught. They were completely surrounded. A taller silhouette appeared to be protecting the shorter one. Lorelei stepped closer, not afraid of the outlandish entities all around her. Rather, she felt as if she were a part of them somehow. They moved aside as she approached.

The green glow of an object in the hand of the taller figure caught her attention. My pendant!

"Call them away," Peter yelled, looking straight at her. He tried to protect Emily, but there was no escape for either of them.

"What do you mean? I don't even know what these things are."

"Yes you do! We started seeing them the second I could read your mind, right after you got here. You were confused about why you ended up here instead of the ranch."

Peter no longer sounded threatening or intimidating. The creatures scared him out of his wits.

Lorelei glanced back at the proud volcanic rock that had generated so many myths. More glowing eye-shaped beings flooded from the base of Shiprock.

The orbs moved aside to let Lorelei pass. She walked up to Peter and grabbed her pendant out of his hand.

"What are you both doing here?" The words came out in a different dialect. As she spoke, her florid allies gathered in closer to the couple.

Emily and Peter stared at her in amazement, then nervously at the threat looming ever closer.

Lorelei glanced down at the pendant. The brilliance of the emerald illuminated the night sky, nearly blinding her. The scarlet eyes increased in luminosity while completely enclosing Emily and Peter.

"You can stop this," Emily yelled in desperation. Peter held her close, trying to protect her.

That's when Lorelei saw the outline of a building twenty feet away. It was the same size, and had the same wrap-around porch with decrepit stairs and partially collapsed roof.

She stared from the ranch house to Peter and Emily, wondering if the monoliths and the Caves of the Watchers were somehow involved with her return to Shiprock. And with Peter and Emily's journey here.

She noticed a bulkier shadow looming in front of the old house. Unmoving. His eyes weren't distinguishable, yet his glare cut through her core. The fiery orbs didn't seem to notice him.

Mr. Unibrow.

Lorelei suddenly realized why he was unnoticeable to the mysterious creatures. Mr. Unibrow had been chosen by the ancient ones.

An eerie silence overcame the desert. The pendants brilliant glow had dissipated. When Lorelei looked back, Emily and Peter had vanished, along with the vivid, inexplicable protectors of Tsé Bit' A'í.

Chapter 42

Joe could tell Ian's son was developing his own powers, though they weren't the same as Lorelei's. Paul's aura was gradually changing from an orange-yellow to reflect creativity and intelligence, to a light yellow for emerging spiritual awareness.

Lavender also continued to emanate and strengthen, representing ethereal and visionary qualities. That could explain Paul's strong dreams and ability to tie-in to Lorelei. Two new colors were the most vivid; clairvoyant, highly spiritual royal blue, and violet, the most sensitive, intuitive, artistic and magical hue, revealing psychic power and attunement with self.

Based on Paul's aura transformation, Joe knew the ancient ones were going to change Paul's life like they had Lorelei's. Joe's own recent visions taught him Lorelei and Paul would become bonded in ways most people couldn't imagine.

Joe wanted to tell Ian what he had seen in his vision. He knew it could hinder their plans and reflect on the outcome of what was to be. Like it or not, Ian would not be able to protect Paul. Just as he couldn't protect Lorelei.

Joe also knew something big had gone down at Tsé Bit' A'í last night. His potent dream of the forty-million year old volcanic pinnacle flashed through his mind, slamming into his thoughts so forcefully that he sat straight up in bed, scaring Shannon out of her sleep. The vision had to do with Lorelei.

His phone rang and he glanced down to see Shannon's number in the display.

"Hey," she said breathlessly. "A group of geocachers, those treasure hunters who go around with their GPS devices or smart phones searching for clues to hidden items, found something interesting in the vicinity of Shiprock near Farmington, New Mexico. The same place where Alan and his partner had their bizarre experience with those red floating eyes."

"I know," he blurted quickly before she continued on.

"Anyway, they came across something unusual leading to Peter and Emily." She paused for a few seconds. "What did you just say?"

He sighed. "I said I know about Lorelei and Shiprock. Well, not about the geocachers, but that Emily, Peter and Lore were there. I had a very strong vision last night and saw her arrive near the pinnacle out of nowhere. I also noticed two other shadows in the distance, which I sensed were Emily and Peter. Something very big was going down."

"There has to be some evidence they were all there. Maybe we can find Lorelei."

A heavy sigh burst from his lungs. "No, you're not going to find her. Listen, you have to promise me you'll give this search up. We all know she's coming back, and we all know how. You're the only one that won't come to terms with it."

He didn't hear anything on the other end of the line.

"Shannon. I know you heard me. I understand it's your job and she's your best friend, but as well all know the supernatural doesn't play by FBI rules."

Joe heard her muttering softly to herself.

"Okay, okay. I'll let it go. But what about Emily and Peter? Did you see anything else in your dream? And why the hell didn't you tell me about this considering I was with you last night?"

"First, no. I didn't see anything other than Lorelei, Emily and Peter in the darkness. I can't explain how I knew it was them. I could definitely feel their fear. They were holding onto each other for dear life and I heard Emily whimpering. Regarding your last question, you left this morning while I was in the shower, so I didn't get the chance."

"Sorry, honey," Shannon said. "I didn't mean to run out on you." Her tone became deeper and more sensual. "Especially after your amazing performance. But I received a call from Agent Harris about the treasure hunters."

"What was it they found?"

"A hat with Emily's name on the inside. They claimed to have found it near an old ranch."

Joe sat down on the couch. "There are no homes close to Shiprock. Are you sure that's where these people were?"

"Yes. The geocachers sent pics of the landscape and the ranch. The funny thing is that the house they described seeing isn't in any of the photos the group took. They described it the same way Ian did after his teleportation to Lore. Joe, this has to be the same structure where she was, or is, being kept. I mean, considering what we witnessed in Bryce Canyon during the plane ride. It was as if the house just vanished, or attempted to reappear."

Joe stared at a photo of himself, Shannon, Lore and Ian next to an extremely twisted Juniper tree off of the Vista trail in Boynton Canyon, red rock country in Sedona, Arizona. "Yeah, I recall seeing brief flashes of the place looking down from the Cessna. But if we couldn't see the place, why would the group of geocachers be able to?"

"Not sure yet. Perhaps someone in their group is connected to the ancient race."

"I'll call Alan," Joe said. "We need to head up to Shiprock to see if there's any clue about the ranch having been there. What time did they see it?"

"Five o'clock in the morning. It was supposedly their first stop of twenty geocache locations in the Four Corners area. They were making a long weekend of it."

"I'm coming to get you at the office and we'll head to the airport."

As he hung up, Joe realized the ranch could be another type of portal connected to the enigmatic race of astral travelers. Hard to believe the ancients would let such strangers see their sacred sites. Could the treasure hunters be associated with the ancient ones? Or were they simply in the right place at the right time?

* * *

Wild horses running gracefully with manes flying, the majestic peak of Shiprock, and high, solidified lava walls running north from Utah and south from the main spire; Shannon could pick up on the spirituality of the place from the plane, and understood why the mysterious ancient race would choose it as one of their sites.

The Shiprock Police Department had assured her no such ranch existed near the formation. Yet the geocacher, John Silvers, had insisted an old building sat within a half mile of the massive peak. Shannon had a forensic artist sketch John and Ian's perspective on the ranch. Both were very similar.

Twenty minutes later, Alan landed the Cessna on the dirt trail running parallel to Shiprock. Shannon, Agent Harris, Joe and Alan walked to the coordinates John, the lead geocacher, had provided.

Alan's eyes darted nervously from the wide open landscape to the massive volcanic formation.

Shannon wondered if he was remembering the incident that occurred after his partner urinated on Shiprock.

Alan closely inspected the hard ground, ant mounds and wildflowers. "There's no debris or outline of any kind to indicate the structure was here."

Shannon slowly walked around the section where the house had been seen. "If the ranch was really here, and if it's really a portal like the Stonehenge-like rocks and ruins in Dragoon, then I'm not sure there will be any indication."

"John stated nobody went into the house," Harris said. "Then why would this be inside the coordinates?" He pointed to an antique silver bracelet that had fallen into a baseball sized hole. He picked the piece of jewelry up with a glove and dropped it into an evidence bag.

Shannon leaned down to take a closer look at the ground. "There are four separate sets of tennis shoe prints leading to the boundary of where the front of the house has been sighted, but only three heading in the opposite direction. John said there were four people in his group."

Joe stared at the impressions in the ground. "Maybe four people walked in to investigate the house, but one didn't make it out in time."

Shannon shivered thinking what might have happened to the fourth person. Then she dialed John's number. He answered on the third ring.

"John, Agent Flynn."

He didn't respond.

"Are you sure you didn't see anyone else out here?" Shannon watched a group of turkey vultures circle above them. "We found a silver bracelet in the middle of where you saw the house."

"None of us know what happened!" John yelled so loudly that Alan and Harris could hear. "We went in to check out the old place. We thought she had followed us out, but we turned to look back and the damn house was gone. So was she."

"Who are you talking about?"

"Susan Olson. She was the newest member of our group."

Olson...could she be any relation to Mattie?

"You told me you didn't go into the home."

"You have to find her. I haven't been able to sleep."

"Sure. Change the subject, then act like you give a damn," she muttered. "Do you know anything else about her?"

"She was," he cleared his throat. "She's from Tucson. Lived there alone which is why she was trying to make friends. She was in her late thirties and her grandmother lives in Tennessee. That's the only family she talked about."

"Did you hear anything before the house vanished?"

"No. One minute it was there." John hesitated. "The next, gone."

Shannon sighed. "If I discover you're holding out on me again."

"I'm not," John pleaded. "I've been afraid to tell you about Susan because I didn't want you to think I had something to do with her disappearance."

"Hiding important facts doesn't exactly make you look innocent. Let me know if you think of anything else."

Shannon walked over to where Joe and Agent Harris stood. Two other pair of shoe tracks near the first prints also led away from where the house had been seen. These looked like boots compared to the sneakers of the geocachers.

"John, are you sure you didn't notice anyone else out here other than your fellow treasure hunters?"

"Positive. Unless there was a vehicle parked on the other side of Shiprock."

"Thanks. Tell the rest of your group I'll be in touch." She disconnected the call.

"So where is Susan, and what the hell happened to Peter and Emily?" Shannon gazed in awe at the wide expanse of grassy flatland, the 7,000 foot tall craggy spire rising dramatically from the desert, and the line of dikes extending from the main formation, formed as magma filled cracks in the ground during a period of eruption.

"Was Lore responsible for the ranch, along with Emily and Peter, covertly appearing at Shiprock? Or could it have been the man that helped abduct her? It seems he has the same teleportation abilities."

"Whatever occurred here happened hours before John and his friends arrived," Joe said. "The treasure hunters and this evidence back up what I saw in my dream. I just don't get why the damn house was still here when they arrived. Why would the ancients leave evidence of a portal, and their power?"

Shannon realized how good he looked. She checked out his long braid, firm butt in his form fitting jeans and slight bit of chest hair revealed at the top of his button down shirt.

Joe looked over at her and gave her a smirk. She blushed and glanced away for a second.

"Unless they meant to." She looked from Harris to Joe. "The girl's last name who vanished with that house was Olson, as in Mattie Olson, the original caretaker of Vulture Mine. It's a very common name, but something to start with. John mentioned her grandmother lived in Tennessee. We need to find Susan's grandmother and see if there's any blood relation with Mattie."

"While you were on the phone, I contacted evidence response," Harris said. "They're coming out to see what else they can find regarding Emily, Peter and Susan." He lowered his voice. "If there is any other proof."

Joe left the boundary of where the old ranch home had been sitting earlier in the morning. He headed toward Shiprock. He seemed to be in a trance.

"Joe," Shannon and Alan yelled at the same time.

He didn't acknowledge them or turn around.

She continued to watch Joe while her BlackBerry buzzed an incoming text message from the forensic artist at FBI headquarters. DOES THIS PICTURE REMIND YOU OF ANYTHING???

Shannon scrolled down to see the full image. She looked at the familiar picture. Her jaw dropped.

Glancing up briefly, she noticed Joe had stopped, standing on the trail near the Cessna, staring at the peak.

Her hand trembled as she read the last part of the text message. THE RANCH IAN AND JOHN DESCR'D IS WHERE MATTIE LIVED.

She scrolled down some more to see the rest of the message. AT VULTURE MINE.

"I thought Mattie lived in the old caretaker's house on the hill," she whispered.

Handing Harris her phone, she started to shout for Joe, who was chanting words she couldn't make out. A bald eagle flew gracefully with wings outstretched toward him. The beautiful bird circled Joe three times, only five feet above his head.

Only Shannon and Agent Harris looked surprised. Alan watched Joe with nonchalance.

The air currents lifted the eagle higher and it let out a shrill scream.

Shannon jumped. Then the giant bird flew toward the massive volcanic pinnacle.

Joe turned to face Shannon, Alan and Agent Harris as if nothing unusual had occurred.

"You can call your actual power animal?" Shannon asked. "I knew shamans could draw on the energy of their animal guide but..."

"It was sent as a messenger." Joe stood within inches of Shannon. He placed his hand on her face, tracing his thumb sensuously across her lips.

Shannon inhaled sharply in response to a subtle jolt of electricity. She closed her eyes, forgetting where, and who, she was. For a split second she hovered on the air currents, surrounded by blue sky, lost in her own freedom.

"Lorelei's still here," Joe said. "But not for long."

Chapter 43

Millions of stars sparkled down upon Lorelei's backyard. The stately big dipper watched over all of Phoenix. Ian's gaze wandered to the North Star. He thought he caught a glimmer of green.

Not green, emerald.

He took a deep breath, gazing hopefully into the sky.

"Seeing what I want to see," he whispered. "Looking for a sign Lore will be back."

Standing in the middle of the cedar bark path lined with brick, he watched the distant twinkling lights of Sedona. The view was the reason she had bought the house. Ian wanted to be in her modest Mediterranean style home to feel a part of her somehow, even if he couldn't be with her.

Paul and his friend played kickball, laughing and yelling happily, occasionally drowning out the sound of their feet colliding with the football. He inhaled the scent of steaks on the grill. Without thinking, Ian had placed three on; one for him, one for Paul, and one for Lorelei.

Ian walked back into the home. He opened the cupboard and removed three plates and sets of silverware.

Damn it, Ian. She's not here.

He heard the sliding glass door open but didn't look.

He put the third plate back in the cupboard, and the extra set of silverware into the drawer. "Hey Paul, dinner's ready. Pick out which steak you want."

Ian grabbed the dishes and turned quickly to walk back outside. They slipped through his hands and crashed to the ceramic tile floor. He could hear blood pumping through his ears. His heart skipped a beat. He no longer saw the warm tones, soft lighting, or tapestries of winding sidewalks and spectacular Greek homes lining the Aegean Sea.

He could only see Lorelei. She looked more stunning, more

magical and more content than he remembered. Her long silky blonde hair had a soft glow.

It's not just her hair. Her whole body is radiating light.

"Just in time," she said softly. "I'm starving."

"Is this really happening?" he whispered. A tear rolled down his right cheek. But Ian didn't wait for an answer. He ran to her and placed his strong hands on either side of her face. She closed her eyes and their tears melded together as they kissed.

Then he pulled her to him and held her head against his chest. "I know this was all supposed to happen, but it didn't make it any easier to leave you at the ranch like that."

"You didn't have a choice." Lorelei kissed him lightly on the lips. "I had to do it, honey. I had to send you back."

Ian pulled her chin up. "What? I thought Dagon was responsible for that?"

"So did I. At first."

"Paul told me you would come back this way, through teleportation. He dreamed it. But I had no idea. I mean, you were so surprised when I showed up at Bryce Canyon."

"Of course. Because I had no clue of my new ability at the time. I couldn't control it. I started thinking about how much I wanted you, and you were there."

"Paul said Dagon was here watching over him."

"Yes. He knew the bond you and I had and that I would end up calling you to me."

"Lore, why would an ancient one personally protect my son?"

She put her arms around him with her head against his chest. "You know the answer to that already."

Ian pulled her to him so fiercely. He didn't want her to go again. "The day the three of us were at Sunset Crater and he fell from the ladder. He saved himself, didn't he?"

She only nodded, tears welling in her eyes. "I'm sorry. I know this is all so overwhelming. I didn't want to bring this up. It's bad enough you have to handle this stuff with me, but now your son."

He took her hands in his and placed his forehead against hers. "It's not your fault Paul's been chosen."

Lorelei grazed his cheek with her lips. "Paul and I aren't the only ones." Her hazel eyes stared into his. Her sensuous lips curled up gradually.

Ian glanced up to see Paul staring into the house in disbelief.

He came running in and threw himself into Lorelei's arms. "We missed you. I knew you would come back. I saw you when you were with Dagon at the monuments underground. You had teleported there, but I couldn't talk to you because…"

"You came to me in your dreams," Lorelei said. "You noticed me first. Then I heard your voice and turned to see you fading away."

She gave Paul a big hug. "You have a talent the ancients call "dream realism," or the ability to dream your way into peoples' reality. I believe those you connect with in this manner will be other chosen ones."

"Maybe Paul just has a connection to your reality." Ian held Lorelei by her waist, pulling Paul close with his other arm. The wisdom in her eyes told him she had learned more than he could imagine in the past few days. She was telling Paul what he needed to know.

Lorelei glanced at the floor and up at Ian. Her eyes reflected sorrow.

"Okay, I'm sorry," Ian said. He kissed her on the top of her head and then looked at Paul. "With everything you've been through this past week, you should know exactly what's going on."

Ian smiled at Paul. "Looks like the ancients have as much in store for you as they did Lore."

"What do they need me to do?" Paul looked at Lorelei.

"Sweetie, I'm not sure. Dagon said you'll know when the time comes." She bent down and took his hands in hers. "But your dad and I will be here to help you through this."

"That's a hell of a responsibility." Ian started picking up the broken plates. "What is he supposed to be doing with this dream realism?"

Lorelei looked at Ian then Paul. "Not sure yet. That's going to be his challenge."

Ian threw the ceramic pieces into the garbage, shaking his head in frustration. "I know there's a reason for all this, but I can't bear to think of what he's going to go through."

"Paul will have his own challenges and scars in all this." She cupped Ian's face in her hands. "But he's more prepared than you realize. Think about the incident at Sunset Crater, the change in his demeanor and voice at times. It's like he matures instantly."

Her gentle touch brought him to the edge. He wanted nothing more than to hold her in his arms and never let go.

"There's one thing that will make it so much easier for Paul to deal with."

Ian stared into her eyes. "What's that?"

"He's going to have me and you to show him the way."

* * *

Shannon watched as Lorelei poured glasses of red wine for herself, Ian and Joe.

The same long blonde hair. The same fair features. The same confident gait. Yet something seemed different.

"Lore has an inner light now," Joe whispered, as if reading her mind. "She comprehends her path better and where she stands in the universe. Astral projection, teleportation and connecting directly with Dagon have answered many of her questions and made her feel more secure."

Shannon stared at Joe. "How do you get into my head like that?"

"I didn't have to. I saw the way you looked at her."

"Is Lore the one who sent you the eagle messenger at Shiprock?"

Startled, Shannon turned her head to see Lorelei standing in front of her, waiting to hand Shannon her glass of red wine.

Lorelei's smiling eyes gazed into hers. "I was the messenger." Then she winked and gave Joe his wine. Rather than let go right away, Lorelei held onto the glass, staring intently into Joe's eyes.

Shannon understood everyone in the room had developed such a strong spiritual bond to each other. Lorelei and Ian, Ian and Joe, now Lorelei and Joe.

Once an outcast, always an outcast.

Joe picked up on her brief thought. He pulled her closer.

Shannon took a sip of wine. "So you're telling me you can shapeshift?"

"No, more like the ability to communicate with nature through astral projection."

"Makes sense considering your unusual bond with animals," Ian said.

"That means you were there, watching while we were looking around out at Shiprock?" Shannon asked.

"Yes, though not for long. I sensed what was happening above ground with you and Joe. I also spent time underneath Shiprock with the obelisks, trying to understand my part in all this."

Shannon and Joe followed Lorelei and Ian out onto her patio.

"Lore, those bones you discovered in the barn are Mattie's," Shannon said. "The lab results showed blunt force trauma to her skull from what looked to be a large round rock. Though there weren't any rocks large enough to be a murder weapon inside the structure."

Lorelei observed Shannon with a kind yet bored, "I already know everything you're telling me," stare.

Shannon sighed and sat down heavily on the couch. "I think we should start with what you found out on your," Shannon used her two forefingers to emphasize a quote, "journey." Then I can go back and fill in any details."

Ian and Joe passed a nervous glance. Shannon caught a brief look of hurt cross Lore's face. A second later, it transformed into what she could only describe as forgiveness.

Lorelei placed her own glass on the tiled mosaic patio table and approached Shannon. "I'm sorry this was so hard on you, from a friendship standpoint and because you feel you haven't been able to help solve this case. So far. But this isn't over, Shannon. Yes, Mattie was brutally murdered and I picked up on that because I was being held inside her home, which used to be located at Vulture Mine. However, there are still other things left unanswered."

"Like what, Lore? Mattie gave you her diary and you were inside her home obviously to find out more about yourself and her. I'm sure you can tell everyone about Susan Olson—an innocent victim who so happens to be a distant relative of Mattie's. Is Susan all right? And what about Peter and Emily? Did you single-handedly tackle them, sending them to your magic triangle of soul-splitting madness?"

"That's enough." Joe grabbed Shannon's arm gently. "I can't believe you're acting this way. Aren't you glad she's home?"

Shannon half expected Lorelei to walk away from her. Maybe that's what she really wanted in order to feel she had the upper hand.

Instead, Lorelei gazed back at Shannon in a way she had never seen, with experience, calmness and confidence. Then she pulled Shannon close and wouldn't let go. "I know this wasn't easy on you," Lore whispered in her ear. "You were tireless in your efforts to find me, yet everyone told you not to bother because I would return when the time was right. You never stopped, Shannon. I will never forget that."

Shannon started to quake in Lorelei's arms.

Damn it! I'm not going to do this. Not now.

She could no longer control it. The tears began to flow and she sobbed hysterically. "I'm so sorry."

Joe handed her some tissues. Shannon wiped her eyes and blew her nose. "This sounds so selfish, but I guess I'm partly jealous. Lore, you have this amazing connection to Ian, Paul and now Joe. Every one of you has these unique abilities to help others."

Joe turned Shannon to face him. "You're helping people also. Every day of your life. Just because you're not clairvoyant or a healer doesn't mean you're not special."

Lorelei took Shannon's hands in hers. "This isn't completely over. After all, the man that helped abduct me is still out there, and he has the same talents I do, though why the ancients would gift him is unknown. We don't know who killed Mattie either, or why. And I'm not entirely sure about Susan, or if she's related to Mattie."

"Where did Mattie's old ranch house go to?" Shannon asked.

"It's back home, at the ghost town," Lorelei said. "I envisioned the whole incident with Susan right before it happened, but I wasn't around when the geocachers were there. As I mentioned earlier, I was underground, underneath Shiprock."

"The only house at Vulture City is the one at the top of the hill, which you can see from the parking lot," Shannon said.

Lorelei shook her head adamantly. Mattie built the ranch near the old schoolhouse by that arrow-shaped rock. The formation was in her backyard. It's much more than a large boulder. That leaning rock was a gateway for all sorts of specters, both Vulture City inhabitants and non-residents. They all sensed something special about the old woman. Her home soon became home to hundreds of otherworldly visitors, some friendly and others not so much. Mattie occasionally stayed in the house on the hill to avoid some of the more threatening spirits, but she never considered it her true home."

"Did you find this all out from her journal?" Ian asked. "Or did she appear to you again?"

"Honey, I was in her dream home, where she died. The building itself eventually told her story. The diary was meant to be taken by Peter, Emily and Scott. I wasn't supposed to understand those words in the last third of the journal because they were a curse, though it doesn't appear to be one initially. Scott read it out loud in the ranch house, or portal to the other realm, and developed similar powers as the ancient ones. But those powers have a price only Scott knows." Lorelei sat on Ian's lap.

"Where is he now?" Shannon threw her hands up in the air. "I didn't see any sign of him at Shiprock."

"He did appear in front of me during the episode with Peter and Emily, although he didn't say anything. As for where is now, I'm not so sure."

"Are you ready to tell us what happened with Peter and Emily? They didn't end up in that same portal, Mattie's house, because their footprints led away from the boundary, but not back to it," Shannon said.

Ian and Lorelei glanced nervously over at Paul, who had run over to the edge of the property to play with the neighbors golden retriever.

"Paul had a rather startling vision of his mom's fate," Ian said. "It wasn't dream reality since he wasn't there when it occurred. But Lore's experience matched what Paul saw exactly."

Shannon looked at Lorelei. "Those floating eye-shaped things. Are they associated with the intricate paintings in the Caves of the Watchers? If so, what is their purpose? They sound malicious because Alan mentioned they threatened him and his friend, and because of what happened to Peter and Emily."

Lorelei smiled. "Though they seem intimidating at night, the guardians are aware of everything going on, and not only at Tsé Bit' A'í. Their presence extends to all of the ancients' sacred sites. If someone wanders their way, not respecting the land they inhabit, then the watchers can turn sinister."

"Alan's partner urinated on Shiprock, which was obviously disrespect," Shannon whispered. She looked at Joe and Lorelei. "Do you know about the man with the dark eyes who supposedly saved Alan and his friend from Shiprock's guardians? Alan mentioned they were outside their car changing a tire one second and by the side of the highway the next. This stranger told them 'be careful what you wish for.'"

Lorelei waved at Paul and smiled. "They encountered another earthly spirit who had been changed by the ancients, which explains the dark eyes. However, Alan and his friend weren't saved by the human entity. The guardians themselves teleported them away from their sacred ground. They were teaching the interlopers a lesson."

Shannon put her arm around Joe's waist. "You still haven't

answered the question of how Emily and Peter ended up in New Mexico and what these creatures did to her and Peter."

Lorelei stared at the small bright yellow and green tiles on the table, gripping her emerald charm tightly.

Shannon suddenly realized, whatever had occurred to Paul's mother and her husband, had been Lorelei's doing.

"I, I had no choice." Lorelei's voice broke. "I didn't know what I was doing. I thought I had teleported into the midst of the scene." A tear lingered in the corner of her eye for a few seconds, wandering aimlessly down the side of her face, finally dropping onto the back of the hand that held the pendant.

"Emily kept screaming at me to stop."

Ian kept his arms around her waist, holding her as tightly as he could.

"The watchers were everywhere. Right after I showed up, they descended upon Emily and Peter so quickly. They might have known about their malevolent intentions because of me."

"You communicated with these eye-like beings?" Shannon asked.

"Not intentionally. They were one entity and could read my thoughts. That's how they keep guard over Shiprock—as one."

"Ian mentioned Paul never saw how his vision ended, only the gathering of these things around them," Shannon said.

Lorelei's whole body shook.

"After I grabbed my necklace from Peter, the creatures seemed to eat them alive. Peter and Emily were there. Seconds later they had vanished." She shuddered, rubbing her arms with her hands.

Shannon got up from her chair and knelt in front of Lorelei, taking her hands and holding them. "Maybe we should wait."

"No. You need to know what happened to them."

Shannon couldn't breathe, waiting for Lore to continue.

"The pinnacle transformed within seconds after they disappeared. Thick black smoke billowed out along with splashes of lava. I couldn't see Emily and Peter, but I did see the red orbs hovering around the opening. The eye-shaped lights turned to a brilliant orange. The same color as the lava. Then I heard their ear-shattering screams. Those sounds were almost unbearable in their fear and agony."

Paul's laughter and the playful barks of the retriever emanated from the side yard. "I, I'm sorry. I can't do this." Lorelei ran inside the house.

"How awful. Ian, does Paul know all this?" Shannon asked.

Ian sighed. "Somehow, yes. It might not be at the surface yet."

"No wonder there wasn't any evidence of Peter and Emily." Shannon looked at Joe. "You're aware of all the myths of that place. Do any of them have to do with Shiprock becoming active?"

"There are many," Joe said. "One is that the Diné, or Navajo medicine men prayed for deliverance from their enemies, so the gods caused the ground to rise, moving it like a great wave into the east away from their enemies. It settled where Shiprock Peak now stands. These Navajos lived on the top of this new mountain until the trail up the rock was split off by lightning and only a sheer cliff was left. The women, children and old men on the top slowly starved to death, leaving their bodies to settle there. There are also ceremonies, including the Bead Chant, the Naayéé'ee Ceremony, and the Enemy Side ceremony. However, none of those have to do with an active volcano."

A minute later, Lorelei came back outside. "I'm all right. I don't know why my emotions got the better of me. Something told me their fate wouldn't be pleasant, but those screams." She turned away from them and stared up into the stars. "To think I was responsible is too much."

"The entities that destroyed Peter and Emily made that decision," Joe said. "Did you stop to think the eye-like guardians might have been trying to protect you? They must have known what Peter and Emily were putting you through. Based on what happened at Shiprock, Emily and Peter are now in the ancients' version of hell."

Shannon poured another glass of wine. "What is the difference between the physical red-eyed guardians at Shiprock and the painted eyes in the caves?"

"They are closely associated. The supernatural beings that punished Peter and Emily inhabit Shiprock, an extremely powerful site. The pictographs in the Caves of the Watchers are capable of guarding the whole cave and tunnel system throughout the Four Corners. Speaking of which, even I don't know the extent of their underground structures. And Paul picked up on this earlier, but those paintings are also the ancient ones' drawing on the powers of the universe, indicated by the white and yellow stars on the ceiling."

"So you were responsible for Peter and Emily arriving at Shiprock? In order to…" Shannon looked away, unable to finish the sentence that would cause Lorelei additional pain.

"I'm not sure. Peter and Emily thought so. It's possible, but I remember focusing on the old ranch, Peter and Bryce Canyon to return to that environment. Perhaps the Caves of the Watchers were encouraging their destruction through me. Part of me wonders if Scott had something to do with it considering his teleportation abilities. He wasn't afraid of the guardians and they weren't targeting him. I got the sense he enjoyed seeing Peter and Emily suffer."

Lore admitted teleporting Ian into her arms at Bryce without realizing it. Shannon didn't want to tell her friend, but perhaps she had done the same with Peter and Emily. After all, the couple was destroyed because the watchers were able to read Lore's thoughts.

She received a call on her cell phone. "Excuse me everyone." Shannon got up from the table and walked into the house. It was Agent Harris.

"Hey, I got in touch with Susan Olson's grandmother in Tennessee."

"What did she say? Has she heard from Susan recently? Have her neighbors seen her?"

"No, and I'm not sure they're going to."

"Harris, get to the point."

"The address her fellow geocachers gave us, and where they picked her up before leaving for their trip, is home to a family of five, last name of James. Apparently, Susan was waiting outside the James' house when they arrived."

"Does Susan live with this family?" Shannon asked.

"Not quite. Susan's dead. Died three years ago but has been hanging around what used to be her home. The James' family and their neighbors have seen her repeatedly."

"What? How did she die? How the hell could these guys not have known? There had to be some clue in that long trip from Tucson to New Mexico." Shannon spoke so loud, Lorelei, Ian and Joe glanced over at her.

"You should know about this. Ghosts can seem as alive as any of us at times," Harris said. "Susan must have appeared to the group of geocachers in solid form. Regarding her death, her grandmother mentioned Susan and her fiancé were killed in a car accident off of New Mexico State Highway 666, on a trip to the Four Corners."

"Wow. Highway 666. How ironic. But what does that have to do with John and his friends?" Shannon asked.

"I came across her obituary. John's friend Matt looks very

similar to her fiancé'. The day John, Matt and his other friends went on the trip was the three year anniversary of the death of Susan and her lover."

Shannon developed goose bumps all over her body. "Susan is searching for her love. She doesn't know he's dead. For that matter, does she realize she's passed on."

"That portal was no accident," Harris said. "Since that was Mattie's home and Susan's grandmother confirmed she was a distant relative of the old caretaker of Vulture Mine, perhaps Mattie felt an obligation to help her move on."

"What was her fiancés' name?" Shannon asked.

"Thomas Hanson. Good looking guy with long dark hair, but very different looking. I sent over a photo."

Shannon looked at the happy picture of the couple on her phone. Susan was very attractive with olive skin, medium length dark brown hair and matching eyes. Shannon's mouth dropped when she saw the image of the man standing next to Susan.

She ran over to Lorelei, showing her the picture. "Who does this look like?"

"Dagon," she whispered.

"This guardian of yours and Paul's was Susan Olson's fiancé'. They both died in a tragic car accident."

Chapter 44

In two days Scott had aged twenty years. He glanced at himself in the bathroom mirror, tracing his finger over the wrinkles on his forehead and cheeks. He shuddered. The day before, they were fine lines he contributed to tiredness, but the creases had deepened substantially.

He suddenly realized there was a cost for his newfound abilities.

"Still working your magic mother." He ran his hand over his graying hair. "Bitch!" Scott threw a bottle of mouthwash at the glass. It shattered the mirror, spraying minty green liquid and shards over his face, bare chest and blue boxer shorts. Another line began to form on his chin while he wiped the blood that trickled down his rapidly aging face.

He ran into his bedroom, unlocked his safe, and rustled among papers, jewelry boxes and a large stack of money to get to the diary.

Scott quickly read over the words again, silently. "She put a fucking curse on me. I didn't start aging again until I read this damn thing." He angrily ripped the pages out of the journal, two and three at a time. They fell at his feet in a crumpled pile.

It wasn't enough to assuage his anger. He stomped on the yellowed pieces of paper scattered around him.

How could I not have known? That woman's had it out for me my whole life! I thought I got rid of her, but she still finds a way to torture me.

He scooped some of the pages quickly off the floor, holding them high in the air with his fist. "You're not going to kill me, Mother. You hear me?"

Scott never understood why she wanted to move to that godforsaken place in the middle of the desert. What kind of living did she think she could at an old mining town? But then he and Mattie had never agreed on anything. He was always looking for a way to make a buck, whereas his mother only wanted to live a private and peaceful existence. He was into the dark arts, and she had focused on herbal remedies and healing others, including the local spirits.

"I suppose you were worth something," he muttered. "After all, you did come up with the youth formula, which allowed me to stay young for so long."

He wasn't going to sit idly by and wait for death. He would fight. Peter and Emily weren't around any longer. Lorelei had seen to that at Shiprock; whether she realized it or not. He had hoped his teleportation abilities would take him to the Caves of the Watchers, but instead, Scott had somehow ended up at the solidified lava core along with Peter and Emily.

He saw the terrifying red-eyed creatures pour from the base of Shiprock and head toward Peter and Emily. That's when Lorelei arrived. Within minutes, the fiery beacons surrounded the couple, rising from the earth with Peter and Emily. They both vanished, Emily's screams echoing into the night.

Scott heard Emily screaming at Lorelei in desperation. He knew he didn't have the skills to transport Emily, Peter and himself. It had to be Lorelei. Peter had been right all along. Lorelei was just as powerful as Mattie. That's why he couldn't stand her.

A sudden realization slammed into Scott's thoughts while he stood gazing onto his unkempt backyard with overgrown weeds a foot high, which were taking over the gravel and brick-curved grass area.

The enigmas had ignored him, not because he had teleported out of harms way, but because they knew his fate was already sealed.

Chapter 45

"Mattie, are you here with us now?" Lorelei glanced around the living room of the dilapidated ranch house, now back at Vulture Mine, for any sign of movement. She tried not to focus on the drag marks where Scott had violently pulled her by her hair.

Ian saw her hesitate, staring at the section of flooring. He walked over, placing his arm around her waist.

"If you're here, can you tell me if you're responsible for this house, or portal, ending up in New Mexico? We know about Dagon and Susan. Did you entice Susan into your home so they could be together again?"

She couldn't hear anything, but hoped her audio recorder would reveal additional evidence about the woman who had been so violently murdered.

"Can you tell us who killed you?" Shannon asked. "We found your bones in a barn near here. It was so long ago, but we'd like to know what happened."

Twilight delivered a brilliant orange sunset that contrasted with the darker clouds above. The glow reminded Lorelei of the first day she had awoken in the strange place, with the fiery spires of Bryce Canyon looking down upon her. She had never felt so alone.

Footsteps came from the room she had met Dagon in.

Lorelei followed Brandon to the back of the house. They didn't see anyone.

"Mattie, was that you?" Brandon asked.

The crunching of dirt and rocks made Lorelei, Ian, Brandon, Dale and Shannon rush outside.

Lorelei noticed someone hunched over, holding tightly onto the arrow-shaped rock; the portal that the spirits had used to reach Mattie. She knew this was no entity.

She cautiously approached the frail figure. "Are you all right?"

The person turned, causing a gasp from everyone. The elderly man before her was bent over so severely, he looked much shorter. His legs trembled from the effort of standing. His face shocked her the most. Harsh lines and creases had taken over, and tufts of white hair stuck out from his head.

There is something familiar about those eyes.

Lorelei dropped her voice recorder and camera. The thick eyebrows and malevolent stare gave him away.

"Help me." Scott spit out in a weak and wheezy voice. "She's killing me." He grabbed his heart and fell to his knees, holding a slip of paper in his hand.

She heard Shannon call the paramedics but Lorelei knew he wouldn't make it.

She walked right up to her abductor, knowing he was no longer a threat. "Who's killing you, Scott?" He didn't get a chance to respond. He fell to the desert ground, releasing the note he had grasped so securely. She could shed no tears for such a violent and heartless person.

Lorelei knelt next to the body and checked Scott's pulse. He had passed away. She could see the writing without touching the 8 ½ by 11 piece of paper. It was a recipe, and though she couldn't read most of the ingredients, the handwriting matched Mattie's. The top of the page was titled, MATTIE'S REVERSE AGING CONCOCTION.

"Looks like Mattie did much more than watch over this place," Lorelei said.

Shannon knelt on the other side of the man. "I can't believe this is the same guy. Scott couldn't have been any older than forty when I talked to him."

Lorelei showed the note to Shannon.

"How long did he stay fortyish?" Lorelei asked. "Judging by this recipe', he could be much older. Maybe the natural aging process caught up with him."

Shannon removed Scott's wallet. She opened it and looked through his identification and other papers. "His ID says Scott Reid and shows the same man I interviewed, the supposed historian and your kidnapper. He's obviously tied in to Mattie. Did she give him this youth formula?" Shannon looked up at Lorelei and the rest of the team. "Or did he murder her in order to get it?" She stood up and pulled out her BlackBerry. "Excuse me, but I need to follow up on that hair sample I was able to get from this guy before he vanished."

"Whoa!" Dale yelled from inside the house.

Lorelei, Shannon and Ian ran back into Mattie's old home.

Dale did a 360-degree turn. "Something walked right through me."

"Probably a breeze," Brandon said.

"This was not wind," Dale said excitedly. "Legs stepped from my back into the front of my body. And I felt the rest of the spirit pass through."

"Ian, did you catch anything on thermal?" Brandon asked.

"Unfortunately not. I was focused on Shannon, Lorelei and the deceased. But we did have a static camera focused in Dale's direction." He motioned his hand toward the tripod in the corner of the back bedroom.

Lorelei heard a scuffle and stepped into the hallway to see two shadows running through the closed front door. She glanced around and noticed no one else had reacted. "Follow me and have your equipment ready."

There were no other people at Vulture Mine except for the Arizona-Irish Paranormal Research Society. Since Scott had passed away, Lorelei sensed quite a bit of tension in the air.

"Holy shit!" Brandon said. "The energy level is off the charts. The needle's over fifty milliGauss."

"I have a hit on the thermal," Ian said. "Two shapes that seem to be struggling. One has longer hair, looks like it could be Mattie, and the other figure is male."

Dale and Brandon took pictures where Ian had the IR camera pointed.

Lorelei heard the entities arguing. Then Mattie and Scott appeared in almost solid form.

"Why did you do this?" Scott's ghost yelled. "You tricked me! That damn entry in your journal was a curse to reverse your youth formula."

"I could never have imagined my own son would be so greedy, wanting more money, more power. You thought you had it all when you got my formula. The pain you felt right before your death was nothing," Mattie said.

Lorelei gasped. She couldn't believe Mattie and Scott were related. She realized Scott had to have been fortyish for sixty years.

Mattie turned to face Lorelei and smiled. The old woman spoke no words, but Lorelei understood they needed to quickly leave the house. Scott murdered Mattie here, and his slow, agonizing death was just beginning.

Scott's eyes were fixated on Mattie. Lorelei sensed terror and confusion.

Lorelei pushed Shannon and Ian in front of her and motioned to Dale and Brandon. "We need to get out of here. Now!"

Dale started to grab the camera and tripod, but the foundation began to quake. Wood planks cracked and splintered, then fell beneath the house. Chunks of the peeling walls dropped onto the rapidly vanishing floor.

"No," Lorelei yelled. "Dale, leave it!"

A huge gap in the floor of the house revealed a fiery flash of molten lava. Dale was stuck on the other side. Scott's spirit desperately grabbed onto Dale, whether to prevent his own eternal damnation or perhaps a last ditch effort to bring an innocent person down with him.

"Dale, you have to jump!"

"I can't! Something's got me."

Mattie's son suddenly disappeared, sucked into the ground with his hands high in the air, his screams so loud the team had to place their hands over their ears. Dale struggled to maintain his balance.

Lorelei stepped to the edge of the precipice, closed her eyes and concentrated. Within seconds, Dale had vanished and reappeared on the opposite side of the chasm.

Dale glanced from the spot he had been standing on the opposite side of the crack to where he now stood. He stared at her in astonishment, his mouth wide open.

"Let's go," Lorelei yelled.

Ian had a tight grip on Lorelei's hand. They ran behind Dale and Brandon to safety.

Shannon remained in shock in the front room. Lorelei wasn't sure if she had observed Dale's teleportation, Scott's nasty demise, or both.

Ian grabbed Shannon with his other hand, dragging her and Lorelei out of the house.

Horrible shrieks, trembling ground and searing heat kept them all running.

Lorelei glanced back to see a fiery plume erupt from the earth, overtaking Mattie's home. It reminded her of the viscous, glowing lava that took Emily and Peter at Shiprock.

"Lore, please." Ian's sweaty hand yanked her onward. "It's too dangerous. We need to keep going!"

Lorelei, Ian, Shannon, Dale and Brandon stopped at the end of the Jeep trail near the parking lot.

Lorelei bent over to catch her breath. When she looked up again, she saw Mattie watching the decrepit structure mollify and bubble, spitting out the last few droplets of lava as the home she once lived in slowly descended into the earth.

Mattie wasn't alone. The children she had seen playing Ring-Around-the Rosy with Dale during their investigation only a week earlier stood on either side of Mattie. The little girl... with the braids and blue hair ribbons held her right hand and a young boy stood on her other side, holding on to the waist of her long white dress.

Everything seemed back to normal. The desert floor held no scorch marks, and nothing remained of the home Mattie once lived in. Or Scott.

Ian focused the thermal device in the direction Lorelei stared. Then Brandon lifted his camcorder to film.

Entities started appearing where the portal had been. A cowboy in a long coat sitting on a horse, a young couple dressed in fifties clothing holding hands, and the miner the ancient ones transformed from a tortured residual soul to a man who never seemed to have suffered.

Surrounding the twenty or so spirits was a ten foot by ten foot circle of various sized stones with a triangle of stones in the center.

Ian observed the heat signatures of the spirits with the thermal imaging camera.

"Honey, is this a ceremony?" Ian glanced up from the viewfinder, staring into the darkness.

"Not sure."

Mattie stepped into the triangle of stones.

"I am seeing a medicine wheel, which is a place dedicated to the invitation of the divine powers," Ian whispered. "Stepping into one means honoring, healing and transformation of lives, communities and the planet."

Shannon leaned over to look at the moving images on the thermal screen. "Joe has one of those in his back yard for drumming ceremonies."

Ian nodded. "This woman had to have been a shaman. She developed that youth formula. And now we're seeing first-hand her capabilities at gathering the expired inhabitants of Vulture City. I have a feeling she had a rather strong connection with these spirits in life."

"Lore, are you hearing anything?" Brandon asked.

"Low murmuring."

"Why would ghosts be concerned with life changes and healing?" Dale asked.

Mattie suddenly glanced in their direction and intense flames emanated from the center of the circle.

"Because Eric Olson, Mattie's son, is where he belongs," Lorelei whispered. "Mattie became their friend, and a very powerful one. This sounds strange, but when she was killed, they died all over again. That's why the ghosts have been so restless lately. They expected something like this to happen."

"Damn, the thermal stopped working." Ian turned the equipment off, then back on. It still wouldn't record.

"So did my camcorder," Brandon said.

"Mattie doesn't want evidence of what's about to happen." Lorelei put her arm around Ian's waist, realizing Scott's demise wasn't the only reason for celebration.

"What's going on?" Dale asked.

Lorelei watched as a striking dark-haired couple appeared next to Mattie, facing each other and holding hands.

"Susan and Dagon, or her fiancé Thomas, are back together."

Dagon turned to Lorelei and winked. He held out his hand to her and she walked slowly toward the group of entities. Dagon nodded toward Ian.

Lorelei reached back and grabbed Ian's hand. "They want you to come into the medicine wheel with me."

Shannon, Brandon and Dale remained completely still, gawking at each other.

"Uh, are you and Ian going to be safe?" Shannon asked.

Lorelei smiled at her and she led him into the circle.

The blaze suddenly erupted again and a flash of fiery light exploded skyward. Lorelei didn't feel the overwhelming heat, rather a warmth that made her completely at ease. She glanced over at Ian, who stared directly into Mattie's eyes. He could now see everything that was happening.

Mattie spoke loudly. "This sacred circle is now complete. Heaven and Earth have been reunited. The living and the ancients gather together to welcome a new dawn."

Facing Lorelei and Ian, Mattie gently placed her hands on their shoulders. Lorelei glanced quickly around as whispers from the crowd of entities surrounded them. She looked up as familiar, ancient echoes descended from above. When she glanced down in response to a kiss on the cheek from Ian, Mattie, the spirits of Vulture City, Dagon and Susan had vanished.

* * *

Ian watched Lorelei as she slept, her silky blonde hair cascading over the pillow, her eyes twitching slightly while she slept. Was she reliving their recent experience at the ghost town? Or something much worse?

He gently stroked her face with the back of his hand. She instantly relaxed.

Ian didn't understand what Mattie meant during the ritual when she spoke about Heaven and Earth being reunited, or the living and the ancients gathering together to welcome a new dawn. It was as if the ancients and spirits all knew Lorelei would be at Vulture Mine and had planned for Scott's death at that very moment. Peter and Emily had also died violently and in a similar manner to Mattie's son; through burning subterranean annihilation. Had Lorelei been responsible for his ex-wife's death, or had Mattie somehow influenced their destruction?

Lorelei had told him when she first returned that Paul would be learning how to deal with his dream reality, and that Ian was somehow supposed to help. But how was that possible if he didn't understand his son's tie to the astral race?

Lorelei had always been fairly confident. But after everything that happened during her abduction, she seemed even more self-assured. A continuous glow emanated from her. Ian supposed it was her growing bond with the ancients' and the universe. Astral projection was one thing; there are many capable of such a feat, with or without assistance. But teleportation is unheard of, even for scientists and the most extreme magicians.

He wondered if her newfound ability was due to the ancients,' or if it was another skill she already had, but hadn't tapped into.

Ian kissed her lightly on the cheek and whispered in her ear, "I love you." He got out of bed and went into her office to check his email. Brandon sent a communication with the subject 'EVIDENCE

REVEAL.'

Ian, I wanted to send this video to both of you. Unfortunately, I didn't catch too much evidence, even before the camcorder stopped running. There was this weird whitish blob over all of the film. Except for this bit of tape I've attached that occurred at the very end. Listen for the audio that goes with it and let me know if either of you understand what the voice is saying.

Ian opened the file. When the video uploaded, he noticed thick opaque tendrils cloaking the lens; gradually massing thicker together.

Ten seconds later, a child's face appeared briefly through the strange fog. She had brown hair, big brown eyes and fair skin.

"Cara," Lorelei said in disbelief.

Ian turned around. She had come into the room without him hearing and was staring at the screen. "You mean your childhood playmate?"

She stepped closer. He rewound the video and paused it at the point Cara appeared.

Lorelei walked up to Ian and placed a hand on his shoulder. "Is that all you see of her?" she asked.

"Yes. There's also a brief period of some sort of fog covering the lens. See for yourself." Ian replayed the footage.

Lorelei sat on his lap and he placed his arm around her waist. "Are you sure it's her?"

"I could never forget her." Lorelei smiled, remembering fond memories. "But what would she be doing on this piece of tape?"

"I haven't heard any audio yet. Brandon did say there was something we needed to listen to. I think he wanted us to verify what he heard."

He continued to play the video. Thirty seconds later a distinct voice called out. "Cara! No, come here."

"That is Mattie speaking, right?" Ian asked.

Lorelei trembled in excitement. "Sounds like it, but how is she connected to Cara?"

"What if Cara's associated with the ancient ones? Maybe she's partly the reason for your powers." Ian closed his eyes while Lorelei stroked his hair. He took her other hand in his and kissed it.

"That could be. I thought some of my powers evolved from my reincarnation of Annie O'Shea. She must have had teleportation abilities also."

Paul charged into the den, breathless and excited. "Dad, Lore, you have to come see."

"See what?" Lorelei asked. "What's the matter?"

"She's in my room. Or was. Then she disappeared in front of me."

"Calm down." Ian got up and placed his hands on Paul's shoulders. He wondered if Paul had seen his mother. "Tell us who you're talking about."

"A little girl with brown hair. She wanted to play with me." Paul walked up to the computer screen and pointed. "That's her!"

"Wow." Ian remembered Mattie's features from when she faced him and Lorelei in the magic circle. He held Lorelei's hand tightly. "Think about it. Cara and Mattie have the same features, though Mattie's eyes aren't as distinct." He zoomed in on Cara's large eyes and round face. "Could Mattie be Cara's mother?"

Chapter 46

Shannon observed the picture of the good looking guy with long dark hair on one side and shaved head on the other. Thomas Hanson, or Dagon, had an image on the National Crime Information Center database. Above his picture, the word WANTED. The record was from seven years ago, when Thomas was twenty-seven. And alive.

Thomas had hacked into two major credit card company databases and sold credit card information, making millions on the sale of corporate and private cards. He had also sold counterfeit computer products online. Considering his criminal past, the next detail she saw on his profile really shocked her. He graduated from Harvard University.

The ancients only recruit the best. But why did he turn to crime when he could have any job he wanted?

As Shannon stared at Thomas's photo, Special Agent in Charge, Adam Frasier, ran into the room.

"The caretakers of Vulture Mine have vanished," he said breathlessly. "They were both in their cells and the two guards heard screaming. They ran to check it out, but Ronnie and John were gone."

"Did any of the other prisoners see or hear anything?" Shannon asked.

"Yes. Three of them stated they saw glowing orange-red lights right before the screams. This incident has all the prisoners pretty shaken up. Some of the religious fanatics in there believe the devil is coming to get them all one by one."

"Sounds like the creatures Lore witnessed prior to Peter and Emily disappearing, and the same things that Alan saw years ago when he and his partner were driving out near Shiprock," Shannon said. "But the guardians of Shiprock are associated with the ancient ones. As far as anyone knows, they've only been seen at Shiprock. John and Ronnie are considered small potatoes in comparison to

Emily and Peter, so I never thought they'd be in danger."

"Maybe the ancients aren't so happy that the caretakers helped with Lorelei's abduction," Adam said.

Shannon quickly pulled out her BlackBerry and hit the speed dial for Lore and Ian. Ian answered on the first ring but didn't give Shannon a chance to mention what had occurred.

"We know already. Paul was taking a nap and saw the same thing happen in New Mexico with the caretakers of Vulture Mine. Like with Emily and Peter. He woke up a few minutes ago."

"So Paul dreamed his way into their demise? That would make sense with the timing, since Ronnie and John vanished about then."

"Yes. He's a bit shaken."

"I can imagine. Did Lore teleport anywhere right before his vision?"

"No. She was here with us. Shannon, I don't think she's responsible for the justice being dealt."

"Do you think Paul could somehow be involved?"

Absolutely not!" Ian yelled. "I realize he sees this stuff, but…"

Shannon heard him sigh. Then Lorelei muttered something in a reassuring tone.

"That's not all. Cara, Lore's childhood spirit friend, showed herself in the video Brandon took during that strange ceremony with Mattie. We have reason to believe she might be Mattie's daughter. And now Cara's appearing to Paul."

Shannon looked to see Adam staring at the piece of paper in front of her. Without realizing it, she had drawn a triangle within a perfect circle. And the initials P, L and I were placed in black ink on each corner.

Chapter 47

Waves pounded against the shore. The wind whistled fiercely outside the massive cave, and a solid downpour made the atmosphere heavy and damp. The high priestess' voice managed to resonate over all else. Tall and lithe with long, light brown hair, the woman speaking remained stately with a golden glow surrounding her. She began to sway slowly from side to side as she spoke.

"Awaken now all spirit beings. Dance nature's power dance. Dance the cycles of life and death, hope and fear, good and evil. Dance the cycles, now and again. Lower world, upper world, and all in between. Join us on our journey, our celebration. Dance the dances, again and again."

Anxious faces and frightful eyes roamed the wide-mouthed entrance to the cavern. The waves worked their way ever closer, crashing into the rocks and up against the sheer cliffs. Large droplets of rain blew in, hitting everyone's skin like bitter cold bullets. But the priestess continued to chant and sway, the ceremony at a feverish pitch. The stones making up the circle they all stood inside quaked. The torches and candles flickered and went out.

Gasps of surprise and fear echoed throughout the chamber.

Yet she kept the ritual going.

"Cliffs, sea and sand, elements of nature, come together as we have tonight. Awaken now, all spirit beings. Give us your power and strength so that we may carry you forward."

A crack of thunder split the air, the cavern shaking with its force. Bats dropped from above and flew haphazardly in every direction. Large rocks fell from the ceiling in retaliation.

Thunder, lightning and wind suddenly seemed to intensify ten-fold as the last verse was spoken. Their private retreat collapsed as the elements incessantly made themselves known. The high priestess watched as a large rock separated itself and fell onto a member of the coven.

"Get further back into the cave," she yelled. "It was too late. Utter chaos had taken over.

"Nooo!" the high priestess screamed as her best friend ran out into

Mother Nature's fury. Only to be struck by lightning.

Her blood-curdling screams of distress echoed throughout the chamber, though no one else could hear; except for the robed figures pulling the priestess away from the dead body outside.

"Lore, honey, wake up," Ian said.

She awoke to find Ian stroking her hair, staring into her eyes with concern.

"You were screaming." He pulled her close, the warmth of his body so reassuring in comparison to the chill of the pouring rain in her dream.

"Did you have another vision?"

"I don't think so." Lorelei snuggled closer and ran her hand down his chest. "It involved some sort of ritual in a cave. But this ceremony ended in a few deaths. Mother Nature herself seemed to object to what was happening."

"The last thing I heard you say was, 'What have we done? It wasn't supposed to be like this.'"

Lorelei leaned up on her elbow. "I believe I was Annie O'Shea in that dream. I don't feel it was a vision, rather something from the past. I couldn't tell who the woman performing the ritual was though. She was tall with long brown hair, but I stood behind her in the circle most of the time. Somehow, I think she was Annie's sister."

Ian pulled her back down into his arms. "I thought Annie was an only child."

"So did I — at least, that's the impression I received in Dragoon. I sensed a bond in the dream that could only be blood relation."

"Did you pickup on a name?"

She shook her head. "Nothing came through."

"You'll figure it out in time." Ian threw his leg over hers. His desire was a drug she could never deny. "You always do." He lightly brushed his lips against hers while tracing his fingers down her neck.

She placed her arms around his neck and arched her back. The rest of her body lifted slowly off the bed. Ian hovered above the bed and he had taken her with him. It wasn't the first time it happened and usually occurred after one of her strong dreams or visions.

He supported her head with his hand and wrapped his legs around her. Then his tongue flickered over her nipples and breasts. His manhood rested against her pubic area and he slid down to place it directly against her vagina. He didn't make love to her just yet, gasping aloud as her wetness surrounded him.

A foot above the bed, she rolled him over and threw her head back in ecstasy as she positioned him inside her. Ian sat up slowly, wrapping his legs around her, and Lorelei did the same. She closed her eyes and ground herself against him until she thought every muscle would burst.

When she opened her eyes, she and Ian were surrounded by stars. A warm glow emitted from her emerald pendant.

"You're imagining the heavens," Ian whispered, his hands running firmly down her back. He glanced around. "Or did you teleport us?"

She shuddered with desire as he drove himself deeper. A falling star whisked by. She hadn't even thought of making love in the heavens. Or were they really there at all?

They both yelled aloud as they became one. Tears rolled down her face while he told her he loved her.

Moments later, they were in Lorelei's home in Cottonwood again.

Lorelei stared into his eyes. "Heaven and Earth have been reunited. The living and the ancients gather together to welcome a new dawn."

"The ceremony with Mattie and Dagon," Ian whispered. "That was the earth portion of the ritual and our love making session happened in the stars. That must have been a continuation of the ceremony somehow."

Lorelei kissed him on the cheek and glanced at a picture of her, Paul and Ian together at the park. "Mattie must have planned this celestial journey. You, Paul and I all have an amazing role to play. Somehow our talents are feeding off of each other."

A pounding on her door made Lorelei jump.

"I'll get it." Ian ran down the hallway and into the living room where Paul groggily stood.

Ian peeked through the peephole. "It's Shannon and Joe."

When he opened the door, Shannon held an 8 ½ by 11 piece of notebook paper.

"I drew this while I had the conversation with you last night about John and Ronnie. I didn't even know I did it until Adam pointed to the image."

Lorelei gasped and placed her hand quickly over her mouth. Shannon had sketched a perfect circle with a triangle inside. The triangle had the letters 'P,' 'I,' and 'L' at each point.

"That's not all," Joe said, stepping inside and handing the paper to Lorelei.

In the middle of the triangle was a perfect replica of Shiprock and the volcanic wing.

"Adam watched her draw that." Joe pointed to the sketch. "She didn't trace any of it and she did that while talking with Ian. The most interesting part? Shannon drew it without even looking down."

"What's weird is I did that after I found out Dagon, or Thomas, was really a cyber criminal with an IQ of 172, meaning exceptionally gifted. The ancients' definitely pursue the very best."

Shannon glanced at Lorelei, then Ian.

Ian looked down at his feet. "I've been tested at 150 and Paul's IQ is 148."

Lorelei stared at him in disbelief. She knew he was intelligent, but she didn't know how much until now.

They all watched her — waiting anxiously.

She looked away and watched Paul get a bowl of cereal. "I, I'm not sure what my score is. I don't think I've ever been tested."

Ian gently turned her head with his hands so she stared him in the eyes. "Your IQ is higher than Dagon's, isn't it?"

She nodded.

Chapter 48

Lorelei rifled through Ian's top clothes drawer, though she didn't know why. She woke up from her nap with a sudden instinct to find something important, but she wasn't sure what until she felt a hard, unusual shaped object inside a felt bag. She pulled the small black bag from the very back of his sock drawer. The sharp edges of something poked through the material. Opening the drawstring, Lorelei saw a fist-sized lava rock and a partially melted red candle.

As soon as she picked up the lava rock, a vision slammed into her thoughts so forcefully, she had to sit down on the edge of the bed. Lorelei did more than see the young woman who interrupted her thoughts. She became her.

Abby's heart pounded. Her whole body trembled. She was too terrified to move.

Commanding and stern, the faceless figure remained perfectly still. The floor length black robe and hood hid all evidence of humanity. The voice abruptly and passionately erupted forth words she thought would turn her to stone.

"Before the mighty and ineffable Lord, and in the presence of all the dread demons of the pit, and this assembled company, I acknowledge and confess my past error. Renouncing all past allegiances, I proclaim that Satan-Lucifer rules the earth. I ratify and renew my promise to recognize and honor him in all things, without reservation, desiring in return his manifold assistance in the successful completion of my endeavors and the fulfillment of my desires. I call upon you, my brothers, to bear witness and do likewise." His robe shrouded arms reached out to his faithful audience, who bowed down on the cold cave floor.

Abby was sandwiched between two sets of brawny arms.

This can't be happening. What have I done to deserve this, she thought.

Her trembling became an earthquake. "Please, I'm freezing."

She tried to pull her arms away from her captors. The thin white robe that they forced her into earlier did nothing to protect her from the damp underground.

They did nothing, except bow down to their master on the altar above them. Then they forcibly pushed her down onto her knees. Abby gasped in terror when the thunderous voice continued.

"Come, O Mighty Lord of Darkness, and look favorably on this sacrifice which we have prepared in thy name."

They stood up, yanking her up with them and pushed her through the throng of sinister hooded figures.

She stumbled. Razor-edged rocks sliced her repeatedly, causing intense pain that radiated from her bare feet to her legs. She accidentally looked one of the worshippers in the face and was punished with a vicious slap. Her head reeled to the right. Since her hands were bound securely with rope, she nearly fell. "Stop it! Let me go," she cried. "Why are you doing this?"

Another slap in the face; much harder than the first. A coppery taste filled her mouth. One of her captors jerked her head from behind and gagged her with a cloth.

Tears ran down her cheeks. The man on her right lifted her up and placed her lengthwise on a long, fairly flat boulder, about ten feet off the ground. God, please help us both, she thought, as she glanced down at her protruding stomach.

The crying and terror led to choking. The choking made it harder to breath. Still, the nameless, uncompassionate voice continued the chant.

She could feel her baby kicking and knew it was close. When she started having contractions, they had ripped all her clothes off, threw a white gauze dress over her head, and dragged her here.

"Internal Majesty, condemn this young sacrifice to the pit. Welcome her to the doors of hell through the fire we strike. First we will bring her baby into this world. As the ultimate representation of Thy coming – the coming of Armageddon! Bring Thy wrath upon her, O Prince of Darkness, and tend her that she may know the extent of Thy anger. Call forth Thy legions that they may witness what we do in Thy name."

Occasional dripping echoed from the stalactites above. Her own muffled cries continued while another robed figure bound her ankles tightly together, threw her arms above her head and held them down with calloused hands.

All of Satans minions continued: "Let reason rule the Earth. Armageddon is at hand. But rather than God, it will be Thy Father, Satan, who takes over the world. Take this, our sacrifice in the flesh, for she offers Thy Father her unborn for the end of this world, and beginning of the next!"

A six-inch, solid black, double-edged blade slipped from the leaders robe. It twisted and turned carefully in his right hand, directly in front of her face. The engraved heart-shaped pit viper head stared at her with two red diamond eyes.

She screamed helplessly against the now blood-stained cloth in her mouth. Only muffled sounds emanated. The more she screamed, the more energized they all became. That's when the humming began.

This can't be happening, she thought. Wake up Abby, wake up!

The exotic, earthy, sweet aroma of black opium overwhelmed her.

The kicking intensified within her womb. Abby could have sworn she saw a sly smile cross his face right before the first slice above her pubic area on her left side. "Noooo!" she tried to yell.

A strong male voice echoed throughout the cave. A different voice than that of her attacker. Someone, somewhere played the tom-tom.

The knife stopped in mid-air as he was about to stab her in the stomach.

The drumming became louder.

The man performing the violent ritual and his audience became captive to something going on at the end of the altar.

Abby held her head up.

An eight foot rattlesnake emerged from the center of the basket at a beautiful Native American woman's feet. It was not alone. The wicker snake holder was bottomless. Five, ten, twenty, fifty, a hundred. The serpents continued to slither out.

The woman gently picked up one of the reptiles; the most colorful serpent with dark black, bright white and mocha markings. It wrapped itself around her firm stomach, then between her breasts. She threw her head back, gasping for air, groin gyrating slowly, methodically.

Two other venomous reptiles from the basket slithered out and up her long, endless bronze legs.

The serpents reached her waist and wound their way up and

between her breasts, facing each other on top. The snake she held worked its way down to meet the other pair on her chest. That is when the beguiling Indian woman changed. Bare feet and legs transformed into two more deadly serpents that dropped to the desert floor, while the three serpents at the top gyrated and slithered together, unabated.

The writhing, igneous mass soon disappeared.

All was quiet, but only temporarily.

Hundreds of Arizona rattlesnakes converged upon a circle of darkly robed figures. Western diamondbacks, Mohave, sidewinders, tigers, black-tailed, and Arizona black rattlesnakes. They were everywhere.

A single, powerful voice suddenly spoke. "Fitting isn't it? That Satan's followers should be brought to their knees by the devil's own cunning creature."

A striking man stood there in his dark purple robe with gold braiding. None of the evil-doers seemed capable of moving as the newcomer approached Abby, quickly cut her free, then picked her up. An almost angelic light emanated from his body. He grinned in satisfaction. Snakes were everywhere, yet made way for her handsome hero as he carried her through the throng.

He looked back one last time at the tall figure who had attempted to murder her. "Warning to all who attempt to harm another living thing. The venom of these serpents will pulse through your veins as a reminder of this lesson."

Lorelei sank to the floor, against the end of the bed, tears running down her face. She knew her future husband had powers, but she had no idea he was capable of such a feat. Ian had always made her feel she was the one responsible for their intense, vivid and surreal lovemaking.

Could he be partly responsible for the things that were occurring? How many others had he saved?

That must be why Dagon had me bring him into the circle with Mattie. And why Shannon saw him as part of the triangle.

She heard the front door shut, but thought Paul had come back inside from playing video games with the neighbor's kids.

"Lore?"

It was Ian. She quickly stood up and placed the rock inside the felt bag. She wanted to confront the issue, frustrated that he hadn't been completely honest with her. But the fact she had rifled through his own personal belongings didn't exactly make her innocent.

She had never felt so confrontational with Ian. Perhaps she wanted to know why he hid the fact that he was single-handedly able to call upon the forces of nature to bring down a group of Satanists. Or perhaps Lorelei wanted to know who the real power belonged to. Could she have been feeding off of him this whole time?

Ian walked in with a smile on his face. The smile that always took her breath away turned to surprise and astonishment when he saw what she held. Something much worse crossed his handsome face. Disappointment.

"Ian, I woke up and had this urge to find something." Lorelei looked down to see she still held the partially melted candle. "I knew as soon as I held this," she glanced at the lava rock, "what it was I needed to find."

Lorelei walked up to him and opened her other palm. "Why didn't you tell me what you were capable of? I knew you could cleanse a house of spirits, and perform certain rituals and spells."

Ian wouldn't look at her. Instead, he gazed up at the ceiling and closed his eyes. She couldn't tell if it were in anger, guilt or maybe both.

He sighed. "You envisioned the ceremony with that poor pregnant woman and the serpents?"

She didn't respond, waiting for him to continue. Tears fell helplessly down her face, remembering Abby's suffering.

"Lore, that happened before I met you. I was with a coven at the time. I had been for five years and had just been appointed the high priest." Ian's voice choked. "You probably didn't see what happened after that incident. It was only supposed to be a lesson to them. They were sacrificing animals and torturing innocent people."

He started to tremble.

Lorelei placed her hands on his face. He immediately stopped shaking. She desperately wanted comfort from the nightmarish scene she had relived, but she was too upset about Ian holding back.

"What you said at the end of that ritual, 'Warning to all who attempt to harm another living thing, the venom of these serpents will pulse through your veins as a reminder of this lesson.'"

"It wasn't supposed to be real venom, rather a serious burning sensation if they desired to hurt someone or something." Ian stared into her eyes. "There were two cult members that became deathly sick after sacrificing a stray dog. I heard about it and immediately reversed the spell. They were fine and it was enough to stop their cult from doing future harm. But I couldn't bring myself to practice serious spells or rituals after that."

"Ian, we agreed a long time ago to be honest with each other."

"If I had told you that, you wouldn't have had anything to do with me. Besides, I don't practice with a coven anymore. I only honor the eight major sabbats or festivals, and practice spells to keep you safe."

"The ancients obviously had a plan for you in all this." Lorelei lifted his hand and put the rock and candle into his palm. "What disappoints me is they know you better than I do."

She started to walk away, but Ian grabbed her arm, turning her to face him.

"Babe, I'm sorry. I didn't want you to be afraid, or think I was some sort of freak."

"Damn it Ian, look who you're talking to. I spent the whole investigation in Dragoon putting myself out there to help the FBI. The whole time you encouraged me to be proud of my abilities, teaching me to not be afraid. Yet you've hidden the one factor that could actually explain a lot of what's happening between us and the ancients. All because you were afraid yourself."

Ian kissed her on the top of her head and pulled her close. "I'm so sorry you had to witness what happened with Abby. I had forgotten what powers I held. Perhaps this is a sign from the ancients — to let me know they have more in store for me than I realized."

Chapter 49

Shannon noticed the raven-haired beauty staring at Ian as he concentrated on the book in front of him. Everywhere he went, he caused a stir with the opposite sex. But he didn't seem to notice. She wondered if that was part of the attraction.

Every man in the room watched as the 5'8, lanky stunner stood up and swayed toward Ian. When she sat down next to him, Shannon saw the jealousy in the other men's eyes, whether they were with another woman or not.

Ian only turned to look her way when she touched him on his arm in a deliberate and enticing manner. Leaning in, the stranger whispered something to Ian. Shannon didn't have to listen. She had always been good at reading lips.

"Hello, I'm Sasha. I noticed you sitting here by yourself, and thought I should introduce myself." She handed him a card. Shannon saw her staring at his engagement ring. Then she glanced up at Ian, flipped her long hair back, and gave him a sensuous smile.

Ian observed the mysterious beauty with an intensity Shannon had never seen. The woman who had been so confident and sexy before, nervously pushed her chair back and nearly tipped over to get away from him. She stepped three feet away, looked back, and then walked at a quicker pace.

A minute later, Ian smiled and waved at Shannon. Two other women crashed into each other while their eyes remained riveted on his face. They quickly glanced at Ian to see if he noticed. When they were satisfied he hadn't seen their minor misfortune, they walked away.

Shannon smiled and shook her head, amazed at how oblivious he was to the way women reacted to him.

They had come to the Wickenburg Historical Preservation Society to try and find information on Mattie O'Shea, and verify she had a daughter named Cara. So far, Shannon hadn't been able to locate any reference to the powerful shaman who had been murdered by her son. She also hoped she would discover why she was subconsciously drawing symbols pertaining to an ancient race and going into trances over their artwork.

Glancing up, she noticed Ian had stepped away from the table. Shannon jumped in response to a tap on her shoulder.

"Sorry," Ian said. "I didn't mean to scare you."

"You and Lore have a way of creeping up on people," she laughed.

Ian held an open book in both arms. "I found more answers than we were looking for."

She slid the large book out of his grasp and directed her gaze to where he pointed.

Shannon almost dropped the book. "Annie O'Shea and Mattie Olson were sisters."

"Yeah, that probably explains Lore's dream about the ritual by the sea. She sensed the woman performing the ceremony was close to her, or Annie."

"How sad," Shannon said. "This book mentions Mattie's daughter Cara died from a serious illness at the age of ten, though it doesn't say what." She looked up at Ian in surprise. "Cara wasn't just visiting Lorelei as a ghostly friend. Since Lore is Annie's reincarnation, Cara was visiting her young aunt, only Lorelei didn't know it at the time."

"The book briefly mentions that Mattie and Annie were both known for their expertise in the Wiccan and pagan religion," Ian said. "Which makes sense considering their past. However, Lore and I are very curious about the horrifying incident in Ireland. If that really occurred, did they both escape to Arizona in order to forget? Annie lived in Dragoon on the ranch and Mattie moved to Arizona after her husband died."

"Maybe they were trying to avoid the wrath of the loved ones whose family members were killed during the ritual." Shannon quickly perused the remainder of the page, but didn't find any reference to the accident. "I wonder how close they were. If they really were estranged, it's bizarre they both ended up in the same state."

Shannon's BlackBerry vibrated. She glanced down to see an image appear on her screen. A perfect circle appeared with the triangle inside. An image of Shiprock drew itself in the center. She scrolled down to see who sent it but there was no name or phone number.

"What the hell? Ian, take a look at this."

Shannon attempted to recapture the picture. It wiped itself away as she scrolled back through. One word appeared. GALIENA. Then her phone turned itself off.

* * *

Brandon couldn't believe what appeared on his laptop; a piece of video that hadn't been there previously. His camcorder had shut down right before Lore and Ian were called into the circle. Yet there it was. The mysterious bit of footage revealed Dagon motioning for Lore to bring Ian into the ring of stones. But right after they stepped into the mystical loop, something else began to happen.

Brandon leaned forward anxiously to catch what could not have been recorded. The camera had shut itself off. Yet the video revealed a dim, green glowing line forming next to Lorelei and Ian only. The color increased in intensity and then another line formed on the opposite side, but not in parallel. Brandon gasped, paused the video and reached for his phone. He was so excited he dropped the receiver. Yanking it off the pinewood desktop, he hit the quick dial for Ian and Lorelei.

"What's up, Brandon?" Ian asked.

"Hey, man. I found more startling evidence from our last excursion at Vulture Mine. It's about the ceremony and I caught film of everyone in the circle."

He could tell Ian had put the phone on speaker because he could hear Lorelei and Paul in the background.

"Honey, come here," Ian said. "Brandon, your equipment wasn't even working at the time. No one's was. How could you have video of that ritual with Maggie?"

"I don't know. It wasn't there before. I did find something else. Something that I would think you and Lore would have seen during the ceremony."

"What do you mean?" Lore asked. "

"A greenish, glowing, perfect triangle surrounded the both of you. And no one else."

Brandon could no longer hear anything on the other end of the line. Not even a single breath.

Chapter 50

Lorelei didn't understand what made her wake up at the exact second that she did. There were no visions or nightmares. Ian sat up at the same time. They looked at each other for a few seconds.

Paul burst into their bedroom, breathless. "I was there. It's all finished!" He ran over and jumped onto the end of their bed with his knees.

Lorelei took his hand. "You performed dream reality, didn't you? Tell us what happened."

He nodded excitedly. "Only I never know when it's going to happen. Sort of like your visions, I guess. I was back at those underground monuments where I saw you and Dagon. They were glowing an orange-red, like a volcano. They vanished while I watched."

Lorelei looked at Ian. "Those were the stone pillars from Dragoon. Dagon mentioned they were being re-energized since they had been transformed into those evil creatures and used for destruction."

She looked back at Paul. "Do you know what happened to them?"

"I heard a voice say, 'we're ready' before the monuments faded." Then I saw them positioned in that canyon we flew into to look for you. They were in the same spot where the ranch house was supposed to be."

"Bryce Canyon," she whispered, gazing at the wall-mounted waterfall with the scene of a mountain and lake at sunset. A small light at the top enhanced the realism of the setting. "I wondered why I ended up there and why Emily and Peter chose such a remote place."

"Were they underground?" Ian asked.

Paul shook his head. "I only saw them for a second before I woke up."

"I wonder if Dagon influenced Emily and Peter's decision to

bring you to Mattie's old place at Bryce Canyon?" Ian asked. "It's way too coincidental that the obelisks new home is the same place where you were being held."

Lorelei wondered if the very spot where Mattie's old ranch house had been at Bryce had tunnels underneath, like all of the other locations.

'We're ready.'

The alarm clock on the nightstand next to her said 5:30 a.m. Lorelei jumped out of bed and quickly slipped on a pair of jeans and a red sweater.

"Paul, go get dressed. Ian, you too." She threw his pants at him. "We're taking a little trip. The unconventional way."

Ian stared at her in disbelief. "You're not talking about teleportation?"

"Yes. It will be okay. You and Paul need to hold onto me the whole time."

"Where are we going?"

"Wherever they want us to." She walked into the living room where Paul waited. "All three of us are going."

"I know," Paul said. His voice transformed into the deeper, mature tone as it had a few times before. "You're going to transport us somewhere. But it will be okay."

Lorelei expected him to seem nervous and afraid. But he took her hand, then Ian's, and closed his eyes.

Ian yawned, then leaned over and whispered in her ear. "Don't worry, baby. I know you wouldn't be doing this unless you felt you had to."

Lorelei had no idea where they were going to end up. Since Paul had mentioned his brief encounter with the renewed obelisks, a strange feeling overwhelmed her. It was time to figure out her, Ian and Paul's exact tie to the ancient race and the symbol that keeps revealing itself. The triangle inside the circle.

Lorelei held on tightly to Ian and Paul's hands, then closed her eyes and imagined the three of them traveling through the universe. She expected the soft, familiar carpet beneath her feet to vanish. The floor in her living room remained firm, yet Ian and Paul's hands didn't. She opened her eyes to see she was still in her home in Cottonwood, Arizona. Ian and Paul had vanished.

She ran through the home but they weren't there.

Lorelei threw up her hands in frustration. Where did I send

them? And why didn't I go with them?

* * *

Seconds later, Ian opened his eyes. It was dark, but he could see the middle of two rows of grave markers with peeling white paint. All of the dirt mounds were only five feet in length, except for two bodies fenced in together with an elaborate iron enclosure five feet high and a single marble marker that read, MAGGIE AND ANNIE – ESTRANGED IN LIFE, BUT BONDED BY THE HEREAFTER.

Ian glanced around and panicked for a few seconds when he didn't see Paul or Lorelei among the desert scrub, prickly pear and mesquite, or within the small cemetery he recognized as the one he stumbled across during their investigation at Vulture Mine weeks earlier.

He started to yell for Paul, then a sudden, inexplicable warmth overtook him. He didn't know where his son or Lorelei were, but knew they were fine.

Walking closer to the graves of Maggie and Annie, he noticed a symbol at the bottom of the gravestone; a triangle within a circle. The cemetery was in a triangular shape. The outer rows of markers reached farther into the desert and the graves at end formed a perfect base.

He turned back around to see Maggie and Annie's graves placed at the very top of the triangle. "Why didn't I see this the first time? Is there some sort of circle surrounding this place?" Ian watched a few dark shadows dart back and forth across a dry stream bed within five feet of him. The taller shape became a lighter colored mist that rolled slowly toward him and stopped. The other figure remained cautiously behind. An arm-like protrusion reached out from the opaque haziness, beckoning him.

Ian followed the spirit for ten minutes until he reached the closed gates of old Vulture City. The mysterious figure crossed the rusting iron gates and vanished.

"The ancient ones' cemetery must be in the center of the Vulture Mine property." He thought back to Shannon's drawing and each of their initials in the three corners. "But I didn't see Paul or Lore at the other two corners of the triangle in the graveyard."

Ian slid under the gate and walked down the dirt road and past the row of old saloons and hotels. He was being guided.

Remembering he had placed his cell phone in his back pocket, Ian slid it out and called Lorelei.

"Ian, I'm so glad you're okay. Where are you and Paul?"

"It's good to hear your voice too," he whispered. "I ended up at the cemetery across from Vulture Mine. But I don't see you or Paul."

"Honey, I'm still at home. For some reason, you both teleported without me."

"What? I thought the ancients wanted us to figure out our connection to them. Speaking of that, I noticed the graves are in a triangular pattern. Mattie and Annie share a grave at the very tip of it."

"I don't get this," Lorelei said in frustration. "I'm sure Paul's okay, but why didn't I end up traveling with both of you? I thought we would be able to figure out the concept of the triangle."

"Since you and Paul aren't here, I don't think we're looking at a tie-in to a physical triangle. I did see the same symbol, a triangle inside a circle on Mattie and Annie's grave, and I'm being guided toward something in Vulture City. Maybe I'm being led to a circle surrounding this cemetery."

"Ian, I've tried transporting several times since you left, but I can't. I don't think they want me to." She sighed. "I hope Paul's not too frightened, wherever he is."

Loud crackling static came over the line, interrupting her next sentence. It was so loud he had to pull the phone away from his ear.

"Damn!" He snapped the phone shut and placed it back in his pocket. Breathing came from directly behind him.

Ian whipped his head around. "Who's here with me? Mattie, Annie, is that you?"

An unexpected breeze blew by. The hair on his arms stood on end. He squinted to see two dark figures walking together ten feet ahead. They stopped where the ritual with Mattie and Dagon had taken place.

"Why isn't Lore here?" Ian continued cautiously toward the shadows, which turned and stared at him. They were waiting.

The entities had long straight hair, though one was a few inches taller than the other. Both were women.

The spirits stood within a few feet of the arroyo where his car had ended up after Lorelei was taken. But they were ten feet apart. He knew where he was supposed to be.

Ian walked over and stood in front of the arrow-shaped rock near the old schoolhouse. He and the two entities formed a triangle.

While he remained in the exact spot, distinct images of Paul and Lorelei crashed in on him. Lorelei sat in her favorite bench in the back of her yard, watching the lights of Sedona. He watched her in longing. She swiftly turned to her side and looked directly at him.

"Ian," she said excitedly.

"I can't believe this. Can you also hear me?"

Lorelei leaned forward in anticipation. "Yes. Though I can only see you as I see certain spirits — in an opaque form."

"I'm standing at the point of this triangle with Mattie and Annie. They're both somehow helping us communicate with each other."

"The triangular doorway in the ruins and on top of the pueblo we discovered in Dragoon, the markings on the stones, and now all the symbols we're seeing are surrounded by circles. It must represent a continuation of the ancients' powers. Maybe the circle surrounding the triangle represents much stronger talents such as teleportation," Lorelei said. "Not to mention Dagon was able to move objects without touching them."

Ian tried to focus in on Paul, but there was only darkness. "Paul, can you hear me? Are you okay?"

"Please be all right," Lorelei whispered.

He waited anxiously for thirty seconds, wishing he could be with Paul.

"Dad!" A faint voice echoed in his mind. Ian glanced up. Mattie and Annie had vanished.

Lorelei jumped off the bench when she heard Paul.

"Lore and I are both here with you. Somehow." Ian closed his eyes to envision Paul, but he still couldn't see him. "How are you? Do you know where you are?"

"I, I'm fine. Not sure where I am."

"Lore and I can see each other through whatever type of communication is happening, but I can't see you."

"Dad, it's strange here. Everything seems warped and filmy."

Ian gasped. His son just described the dimension where the victims of Vincent Joiner's demonic creatures ended up.

* * *

Paul glanced around inside his watery-looking destination. A red sandstone pueblo wavered in the distance. The shimmering effect reminded him of the movies where an oasis with palms, waterfalls and lakes would appear out of nowhere for those who had just reached the top of a high sand dune, struggling from starvation and thirst.

He barely heard his dad and Lore talking to him. He could hear their voices, but not what they were saying.

"I'm still here," Paul said. "I'm walking toward a small ruin."

As soon as he finished his sentence, it became very quiet again. His father and Lorelei's voices had disappeared; if they were really there to begin with. He didn't understand how they could all be communicating, or how he had gotten here.

Paul slowly approached the ochre structure which seemed to spring from the earth itself. He stepped up onto a round, smooth, disc-shaped rock and into a large room with a rectangular stone altar. To his left was a triangular doorway where a soot-covered, overhanging canyon wall met the construction of the pueblo. He passed the remains of a fire pit and glanced twice at the two foot wide circle of stones. Intense heat emitted from within its confines and he could feel the warmth on his arms and legs. He quickly swiped his hand five feet above the ground where ash remains were, then pulled it back. A reddish splotch appeared on his palm.

Paul glanced around nervously. He wasn't alone.

Have I walked back in time with the ancient ones? Are these spirits aware of my presence?

Lore had told Paul of her experience at the ruins in Dragoon. She had come in from a downpour and an unseen fire and blankets had been waiting. Would he be as welcome?

Incomprehensible whispers and other sounds began to emanate from inside the ancient structure.

Feet scuffled behind him in the altar room. Paul turned to see three objects on the rectangular stone table; items that hadn't been there when he arrived minutes before.

A black lava rock, an emerald, and a dreamcatcher made of twigs and feathers were meticulously placed within inches of each other in a triad pattern.

Somewhere outside the pueblo, drumming began.

Paul's gaze diverted to the ground. A circle had been drawn around the altar, where none had been seconds before. A small flame burst from the center of the three items, floating inches above the altar.

"Why am I here?" he yelled.

The tempo from the unseen spirit drummers increased,

matching the pounding of Paul's heart.

He hadn't realized it when all the activity started, but Paul was standing under the triangular doorway. The temperature dropped twenty degrees. Brief breezes blew by, and mysterious, invisible tendrils wound themselves around his arms and legs.

He tried to step forward but couldn't. He was helplessly frozen.

Paul stared up at the point where the cave wall met the manmade structure. This is more than a doorway — this is a portal.

The dreamcatcher lifted off the stone surface and slowly moved to the southern edge of the dirt circle. The inside design involved a series of triangles made from sticks.

The lava rock hovered in thin air and positioned itself on the opposite side of the circle from the dreamcatcher.

The emerald reflected brilliantly, though there was no sun or light source. The last to exit the altar, it hovered at the westernmost part of the circle, or the tip of the triangle.

Paul realized he was watching a ceremony involving himself, his father and Lore by the artifacts being manipulated, but he didn't understand the purpose.

He tried to move again, but his legs felt like they were glued to the ground. His heartbeat intensified as unseen forces continued to move around him more fervently. His hair blew frantically from the spirit winds.

Dad, Lore, can you hear me?

He could no longer hear his dad or Lorelei. He was on his own.

Paul gazed out into the valley where the massive, undulating field surrounding the ruins revealed brief images of what looked to be a hundred people gathered. A line of ten Native Americans dressed in elaborate headdress and garb were at the front, drumming and sing-song chanting in a language he couldn't understand.

The audience didn't face the pueblo. They stared toward the bottom of the hill.

Suddenly, Paul was released from his grip under the mystical doorway.

The lava rock, emerald and dreamcatcher still floated in mid-air. Paul felt inexplicably drawn into the circle around the altar. He stepped within its perimeter and knew what he was about to witness.

He waited, staring into the valley below.

* * *

Shannon woke up and looked at the combination wall clock and picture of the Sonoran Desert. She knew she wouldn't be able to get back to sleep. She glanced at Joe while he slept. His long dark hair and naked body almost enticed her to stay in bed.

Deciding to make him breakfast, she quietly slipped out of bed and into the kitchen. Shannon prepared coffee then got out the eggs, bacon and pancake mix.

A half hour later, Joe snuck up behind her as she was piling the pancakes onto a plate. He placed his hands on her waist and kissed her neck. She could feel his passion.

"Smells amazing, babe. But I think breakfast can wait a little."

He loosened his grip on her. Shannon followed his gaze to the granite island next to the coffee pot. Then she dropped the plate of pancakes onto the floor.

She saw a brown ring of coffee grounds a foot wide. The granular substance had been used to make a flawless triangle within the circle. The mysterious symbol looked like a painting.

She started to tremble and felt light-headed.

"Go sit down," Joe said. He guided her to his couch.

"What's going on? Am I being taken over by something?" She stared into his dark eyes hoping to find an answer.

"If so, it's only for a very short period. I don't think that's the case. Perhaps your relationship with me is opening you up to spirituality."

Shannon ran to get her BlackBerry and hit the quick dial for Lorelei and Ian.

"Lore, what's going on over there?"

* * *

The first Stonehenge-like monument appeared in the valley, only twenty feet from the audience. The other columns came into view through the shimmering heaviness—one by one. They surrounded the pueblo so quickly Paul wondered if they had been there the whole time, merely coming out of hiding.

The huge crowd stared up into the sky in unison. A glowing emerald triangle formed over their heads and just above the monoliths.

The point extended into the ruins and the base into the valley.

The majority of the people walked out from under the perimeter of the magical shape above them; all except a small group of twenty. Each of them positioned themselves in front of one of the pillars and then held hands. Paul shielded his eyes as the luminous triangle suddenly intensified ten-fold.

The twenty individuals walked slowly toward each of their respective stones, and right into them, human and mystical artifact becoming one.

Then all monoliths vanished into the atmosphere, except for five lined together in a half circle facing the pueblo.

Paul turned to see the lava rock, emerald and dreamcatcher hovering in the same positions around the altar.

He knew the objects had somehow created the mystical triangle that combined people with monolith; items representative of himself, his father and Lore. He also realized he had witnessed a ceremony from the past since the massive stones that remained numbered five. They were in the same position as when discovered by his father, Lore and the rest of the Arizona-Irish.

The heat from the fire in the room behind him had dissipated and the candleless flame on the altar had vanished, along with the audience. The three objects were back on the primitive stone table.

The lava rock was larger than his father's and the rectangular chunk of emerald was in its natural, unprocessed state. Running his hand over the top of the emerald gemstone, Paul instantly received a sharp vision of Egyptian pyramids and pharaohs. He saw an underground mine busy with dust-covered workers extracting objects from the hard-packed walls. Excited shouting emanated from the deepest recesses of their dark, dangerous prison. A brilliant, greenish glow raced through the tunnels and toward the exit to freedom in the hands of one of the miners.

Paul quickly released his grip from the magnificent stone. The date of 1520 B.C. popped into his mind. The triangular shape, as discovered by Lore in Dragoon, was inspired by the southern triangle, a small constellation in the southern sky. But the dazzling emerald stone in Lore's necklace originated from the Emerald Mines, Marsa Alam, in Egypt along the Red Sea; a gemstone that represented eternity and power.

Chapter 51

The emerald pendant had showed the outline of a triangle; the southern triangle where Lorelei's astral form had journeyed to in Southeast, Arizona. A few minutes later, the image began to wane and the gem returned to its sparkling state.

Holding the necklace tightly in her hand, she suddenly realized Paul had somehow been teleported to the ruins at Dragoon, though they were no longer there. The ancients wanted to teach him something. They were the ones responsible for his journey. Not her.

She wondered why Ian ended up at Vulture Mine. He obviously had a tie to the cemetery of the ancient race. But what was the story between Vulture City and Paul's destination?

Closing her eyes and inhaling the relaxing lavender scent from the candles in her living room, Lorelei began to feel a sense of weightlessness. The solidness beneath her vanished, along with her sense of self. When she opened her eyes, she lay in one of the horizontal stone beds she had discovered in the caves in Wickenburg.

The chambers had long been abandoned, yet a single green tapered candle was lit in the sconce above her. She shivered slightly as a damp chill passed through her. She tried to move her legs but couldn't. Her arms and head also refused to move. Panic started to set in until a reassuring presence placed its hand on her frozen shoulder. Instant relief flooded through her. She closed her eyes and relaxed. Clear visions of the Dragoon monoliths, the ruins and the valley in between rushed through her mind.

* * *

Holding hands with two strangers on either side of her, Lorelei observed the massive monument within five feet of her. They all waited patiently to cross over.

No hesitation. No fear. Only anticipation of the long-awaited moment.

Utter silence filled the valley, though a hundred people waited behind the circle of the chosen. The shrill shriek of a hawk from somewhere nearby made her smile. It was a congratulatory cry coming from a friend. She couldn't glance up to show her appreciation or to recognize him, but he knew she was aware of his presence.

The beautiful bird of prey released another long screech. The ritual had begun.

She felt drawn toward the obelisk. Whispers and voices from previously chosen ones emanated excitedly from the towers of quartz and rock.

Each of those in the circle stepped toward their monument at the same time. Right foot, left foot. Lorelei walked in unison, feeling yearning and promise of those on the other side.

She thought she would feel the roughness, the coolness of the stone as she passed through. There was nothing. The primordial gateways allowed each of them to cross uninhibited.

Pinpricks of light dashed by so quickly that it was all a blur. Nothingness threatened to envelop her. She was changing, evolving — molecules transforming while racing through space.

Lorelei sat up quickly from the hard, uncomfortable stone bed, gasping in shock. The candle above her still lit. The presence she had felt earlier was gone.

Her last thought while she journeyed through space was of Annie's dark-haired husband, Jeff O'Shea.

"Annie," Lorelei whispered. "You walked through the gates to become one with the love of your life again.

"To somehow start over."

* * *

The screech of a hawk startled Ian out of his reverie. Annie and Mattie had disappeared. He wondered why he was still at Vulture Mine and what he needed to learn.

He observed the red-tailed hawk circling the currents high above. The bird started to descend slowly toward him.

It's headed right for me!

He stared, mesmerized, as the stocky, white-breasted bird dove at him. It's piercing dark eyes focused intently on Ian.

Ian's own gaze caught the fierce round orbs of the hawk. This was no ordinary bird. Fierce and threatening, something completely different lay under the surface.

Drumbeats began from somewhere nearby. The bird flew within five feet of Ian, wings outstretched, when a strong breeze swept by. Ian shivered, his eyes following the direction of the hawk.

He gasped. Ian nearly lost his balance when he saw where it had perched.

How can this be? I didn't call upon her powers.

Standing where Mattie had stood minutes before, was the stunning, enigmatic woman he had summoned as high priest of his coven a few years ago; the ritual where he attempted to keep the dangerous cult from killing. Unfortunately, that lesson had nearly turned deadly for a few of the members who sacrificed a dog.

Seeing the beguiling Native American beauty with flowing dark hair, endless bronze legs, curvaceous body with a five foot boa constrictor around her neck, struck a chord of longing. Not for the mysterious woman herself, but for the power and pagan talents he had hidden away.

The reptile didn't seem to notice the bird of prey, nor did the hawk have fear of the large boa. Rather, the seductive woman and her two guardians observed him with patience.

She walked toward Ian, slowly and sensuously. The reptile's tongue darted in and out repeatedly while it slithered from around her neck to her arm. The hawk stretched its wings. And his goddess of Mother Nature transformed. Not into the writhing mass of venomous reptiles from his ritual, but into the stately, grey-haired caretaker, Mattie Olson.

"How did you know?" Ian whispered. Mattie stopped within two feet of him, the hawk on the same shoulder.

"As a powerful shaman, I have learned my own lessons. You cannot give up on talents you were born for."

This time, Ian began to vanish. The familiar desert became a slow blur. Mattie's lips spilled forth one last sentence before he left her.

"Love her, trust in her, and never betray her."

Chapter 52

A slight breeze tracked the sweet scent of Jasmine through the air. The late morning sun began to warm the valley below. Lorelei turned to look at Ian. He had never looked so handsome. His wavy blond hair was set against his royal purple robe lined with gold braid. Striking was an understatement. Her heart pounded, knees trembled and she almost collapsed. Ian grabbed her and stared into her eyes. The specks in his own concerned eyes transformed to the color of his robe. They began to dance and swarm together.

"By air, by fire, by water, and by earth do I bless and consecrate these rings." Joe held up Ian's gold band with a pentagram in the center, holding a small emerald, and Lorelei's stunning gold emerald ring with ½ carat diamonds inset at the points of the pentagram.

"These rings, a token of your love for one another, serve as a reminder that all in life is a cycle; all comes to pass, passes away and comes to pass again. May the element of air bless these rings. Air is at the beginning of all things, the direction of east, and the dawning of a new day. May your lives through the reminder of this ring be blessed with continuing renewal of love."

Joe's hands disappeared briefly as he waved both rings through the thick cloud of flowery incense.

"May the element of fire bless these rings. Fire is the passion within your love, the spark of love itself, the heat of anger, and the warmth of compassion. It is the direction of south, the heat of midday. May your lives through the reminder of this ring be blessed with continual warmth."

Joe passed the rings through a flame from a red pillar candle.

"May the element of water bless these rings. Water nourishes and replenishes us. The waters of emotion and harmony pour vitality into our lives. It is the direction of west, the afternoon and evening. May your lives through the reminder of this ring be blessed with fulfillment and contentment."

Joe submerged her and Ian's rings in a silver goblet of water.

"May the element of earth bless these rings. All life springs from the earth and returns to the earth, the direction of north, the nighttime. May your lives through the reminder of this ring be blessed with strength and solidity." The shaman gently waved their rings over an assortment of colorful river stones, and a hand-sized stone similar to the appearance of the monoliths.

"May the lord and lady bless these rings, the symbol of union, with happiness, wholeness and love. Air for hopes and dreams. Fire for the spark of love. Water for harmony and healing. And earth for strength. May these rings be so blessed."

Joe placed one hand on Ian's shoulder and the other on Lorelei's. "By the exchange of these tokens of your love for one another, so are your lives interlaced. What one experiences, so shall the other. As honesty and love build, so will your bond strengthen and grow."

Ian held out the ring he had given her a year ago. The five points were the same and the ½ caret diamonds at each point, but the emerald was much bigger. "The circle is a perfect figure, without beginning, without end, with no area of weakness. It is a symbol of the cycle of life, of birth, death, and rebirth. This shall serve as a physical reminder of your vow, and that all things begin and end, and begin again, as the gods so decree. This ring I give to you is a symbol of our love, and of the promises I have spoken to you on this day. I shall wear this ring as a symbol of our love, being always mindful of the vows we have spoken."

Ian placed the ring on her finger.

Lorelei picked up the tapered red candle. "Let the fires of our love and the fire of our spirits mingle here and create a singular flame. By the bringing and sharing of light, our two fires shall merge as one."

Ian picked up the other candle and they united the two small flames.

"As the ring symbolizes the cycle, so does the hand symbolize the power of actualization and creation," Lorelei said. "Let this ring remind you of the many turns of the wheel through which our love shall pass. So mote it be."

Lorelei slowly slid the ring on Ian's finger. As they kissed, a shrill cry echoed somewhere high above.

* * *

Shannon watched, tears in her eyes, while Ian and Lorelei exchanged rings. Though she was happy for them, she wondered why she continued to unknowingly draw the triangle inside the circle. Each of the three points indicated Ian, Lorelei and Paul. At least that's what they confirmed upon return from their respective journeys. The triangle represented the power of the three.

Paul and Lore felt the circle meant the power and protection of the magical monoliths and ancient ones, since they had both teleported into a ceremony with the massive stones surrounding the pueblo.

Shannon hoped her recent talents would cease. Being an FBI agent, she needed to feel in control, and using coffee grounds subconsciously as art didn't classify as such. The dried grounds were so tightly packed together that the pattern looked like a painting.

Are the ancients trying to tell me I'm equally important even though I don't have any supernatural skills?

Shannon strolled into the valley while watching Ian and Lore exchange rings. Joe kept glancing up at her in confusion. She smiled, but he returned the gesture with a look of surprise as the wedding ritual came to an end.

Five minutes later, she wandered up to where the Lorelei and Ian were taking their final vows. Paul's big brown eyes were wide with shock. Ian and Lore followed his gaze, staring at Shannon's hands.

Terrified to look down, but knowing she couldn't ignore the truth forever, she diverted her eyes to her own arms.

A large chuck of unprocessed emerald with gold flecks, a small dreamcatcher and a lava rock rested in both hands. She delivered them as a waitress would a tray of drinks, or a servant a valuable item.

"I, I don't remember picking these up."

Shannon trembled. She heard nothing, yet the need to turn and look back was unbearable.

Joe stared at her in concern, placing his arm around her.

A circle of granite obelisks started to form at the bottom of the hill. Within seconds, they had surrounded Shannon, Lore, Ian, Paul, and Joe, circling the area where the ruins used to be.

The obelisks started to glow a reddish-orange. Human forms

took shape and climbed out through the stones.

Mattie was the first to appear from the monument directly across from where the pueblo used to be. Her daughter Cara and Annie stepped out on either side of her. Then Dagon and Susan appeared from two megaliths next to Annie.

She didn't know how, but Shannon suddenly realized those five people from the past represented the five monuments that herself, Ian and Lore had discovered in their attempt to solve the mystery in Dragoon.

Where are they coming from?

The remaining pillars were silent and still. No aura and no forthcoming spirits.

Shannon walked slowly toward the middle of the valley. She heard Joe calling her, but was drawn by a force she couldn't explain.

Dagon, Susan, Mattie, Cara and Annie watched her intently.

Joe walked next to her, saying something in an urgent tone. Shannon was focused on the stone pillars and familiar specters who were so closely tied to the ancients.

They smiled at her. She understood they weren't here for Lorelei and Ian. They were here for her.

Joe grabbed her arm, attempting to drag her away.

"No!" he yelled to the group of apparitions. "Please don't do this. I need her!"

Shannon turned to him, then saw Ian and Lorelei standing behind him, their faces pale and in shock.

Lorelei looked at Dagon who had stepped forward from the others. Tears started to roll down her cheeks.

"How come I never knew? She's my best friend." Lorelei dropped to the ground on her knees. Ian placed his hand on her shoulder. Then he looked up at Shannon in disbelief.

"You've been one of them all along. Lorelei's journey through the stone in her latest dream. It was you she played out, not Annie." Ian's voice choked.

This explains the shapes you've been drawing without knowing it." Joe trembled holding her hand. "I had my own vision only last night. I didn't want to believe."

"She's been here so long. She simply forgot," Dagon said. "Shannon, Galiena as we know her, is the real reason you all found each other." He glanced at Ian and then Lorelei.

Shannon stared into Joe's eyes. He pulled her so close she

could barely breathe.

"I don't care who, what you are. I love you. Don't let them take you from me."

Galiena took his face in her hands and kissed Joe lightly on the lips. "I'm sorry. I have to return home." She looked over at Lorelei and Ian. "I'm not needed here any longer."

Lorelei sobbed, enfolded in Ian's arms. Tears escaped his eyes.

Lorelei turned away from Ian. She threw herself into Galiena's arms. "I can't believe this is happening. We're going to miss you so much."

"I'll be watching over you all."

Galiena turned to face Joe. "You'll never be alone." She stared up into the afternoon sky and smiled. A red-tailed hawk swooped down out of the sun's rays and onto her shoulder, nudging its beak and dark brown head against her neck.

"I missed you too, my friend." She left Ian, Lorelei and Joe and took Dagon's hand. Dagon led Galiena to another Stonehenge-like monument.

"I don't believe this," Ian said. "The only one who didn't have any abilities. And it turns out you're an important part of the very people we've all been so connected to."

"Wait!" Lorelei yelled.

Galiena turned to look back.

"So you're like Dagon? I mean, they created a new identity for you?"

"No," she said. "I created his." She winked, then turned and walked into the massive boulder. The orange-red glow transformed her body and she experienced a warmth she hadn't experienced for over thirty-eight earth years—a warmth and peace unlike anything humans could possibly imagine.

Her friends hadn't known who she really was. She had almost forgotten herself. As the peacemaker of a race who had existed way before the earliest Native Americans, Galiena came to earth to help unite more earthbound souls, including Paul, Lorelei and Ian, who were still learning their purpose.

She turned one last time to look at Joe, Lorelei and Ian. Dale and Cindy stood behind them along with Brandon and his new love, Jacenda. Though Brandon might not be aware, Jacenda had her own hidden talents.

"By the way, the arrow-shaped rock at Vulture City can show

you your worst fears. But only for those incapable of evil. For those who are truly malevolent and unkind, its energy will call upon the underworld for vengeance."

Right before she blended with the aura of her gatekeeper, Galiena closed her eyes and thought back to that day at Vulture Mine only weeks before; the day when she unknowingly guided the miner to a better place. No more roaming the earth trapped in an endless loop of time, aimlessly seeking answers that will never come.

Humans, her friends, they weren't aware. Perhaps it was for the best. Astral projection and teleportation were merely tools for her race, passed on for those with responsibility.

Though her earthly friends were going to miss her, Galiena planned on keeping in touch with them in ways they couldn't imagine. For they were as important to her and the universe as she had been to them.

- THE END -

44886494R00152

Made in the USA
Middletown, DE
20 June 2017